NORA FUSSNER

THE INVISIBLE WORLD

Nora Fussner has a BA from Sarah Lawrence College and an MFA from CUNY Brooklyn College. Her work has appeared in *Longleaf Review*, *The Brooklyn Review*, and *Electric Literature*. She lives in Pittsburgh.

THE

INVISIBLE

WORLD

THE

INVISIBLE

WORLD

NORA FUSSNER

VINTAGE BOOKS
A Division of Penguin Random House LLC
New York

A VINTAGE BOOKS ORIGINAL 2023

The epigraph for this book comes from Caws, Mary Ann, ed., *Surrealist
Painters and Poets*, pages 461–62, © 2001 Massachusetts Institute of
Technology, by permission of The MIT Press.

Library of Congress Cataloging-in-Publication Data
Names: Fussner, Nora, author.
Title: The invisible world / Nora Fussner.
Description: New York : Vintage Books, [2023]
Identifiers: LCCN 2022060222 (print) | LCCN 2022060223 (ebook) |
ISBN 9780593684832 (trade paperback) | ISBN 9780593684849 (ebook)
Subjects: LCGFT: Gothic fiction. | Paranormal fiction. | Novels.
Classification: LCC PS3606.U87 I58 2023 (print) |
LCC PS3606.U87 (ebook) | DDC 813/.6—dc23/eng/20230113
LC record available at https://lccn.loc.gov/2022060222
LC ebook record available at https://lccn.loc.gov/2022060223

Book design by Steve Walker

vintagebooks.com

Printed in the United States of America

10 9 8 7 6 5 4 3 2 1

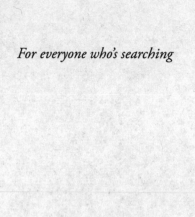

For everyone who's searching

Question: What is the night?
Answer: It's breaking the same heart eternally . . .
Q: What is death?
A: Traveling throughout the world with your eyes closed.
Q: What is dreaming?
A: A great burst of light right in the heart.
Q: What is desire?
A: A wonderful catastrophe . . .
Q: What's life?
A: It's desire eating the world.

—Anonymous, from a Surrealist game

DAY 1

There came a moment in every ride when the crew fell silent, the name-calling and conspiracy-theorizing tapering off as the van's occupants turned to the windows and the undistinguished beauty of the towns they were passing through. As a group they had been as far north as Maine and as far south as the Carolinas. While the more unusual scenery—the Connecticut coastline, for instance, surprising first for its existence, then for its interminableness—might have inspired contemplation among the crew, it was the small towns that most often urged silence, those little hamlets and villages that looked the same in each state. Just a mile or two from the van's destination, marked by white signs, these were towns of clapboard houses close to the road, worn libraries, accountants and orthodontists, parking lots just four cars wide. Small parks with World War II memorials, hair salons with posters fading to blue in the windows, that one spot on the corner perpetually available to rent. Sure, some had a preponderance of seafood restaurants, others antiques stores—no one in the car, not even the most city-boosterish among them, would claim that all of small-town America was exactly the same—but overall these towns had more in common with one another than they did with the major cities of their own states.

What quieted the TV crew was not the towns' paucity of services, but their sense of contentment in the face of such deprivation. The van typically held five to seven men, Brooklyn and Queens dwellers all, who were accustomed to Thai delivery until eleven thirty p.m., dropping their laundry off and picking it up in order to spend their free time discussing Korean films over hops-heavy microbrews in clean but divey bars in which any patron sitting nearby might overhear and understand their references.

The towns the show landed in existed without hybrid pastries and taxis summoned via smartphone; they were practically the wilderness for their lack of convenience, and yet they had enough for the people who resided in them, and cars pulled away from the grocery store onto the road with no air of resignation about the lives they had chosen. Were they really so bored, these men in the car, that anything less than "secret, pop-up" could no longer move them, when the people in these towns had probably eaten at the same diner every Friday for the last thirty-eight years, and loved it?

But these people weren't happy, the crew managed to remind themselves before resuming their banter, before easing to a stop in front of the house the GPS had been steering them toward. They wanted a change, and that's why they had called a reality show. They had no idea, without the guidance of producers and directors and marketing people from New York, how the hell to make that change happen.

———·—

Sandra needed only the last few minutes of the four-and-a-half-hour ride from New York to Ninebark to review the episode file. The old white farmhouse that Patrick, her director, pulled up in front of, though not without its charms, was merely this week's set of tasks. She scanned the couple's profile and keywords jumped out at her: "shadow figures," "objects moving," "noises." Enough to put the Hawthornes through the motions.

"What did Research find on the house?" Sandra asked Patrick, looking through the dossier again.

"What does it say?" Patrick clearly hadn't read it.

"It doesn't."

Patrick shrugged. "I guess they didn't find anything."

Sandra exhaled, in a controlled way. A haunted house without a ghost story was just an assortment of random occurrences, cabinet doors banging shut for replicable reasons, temperature fluctuations due solely to drafts. No one would watch a show about that. There had to be something.

"Ready?" Patrick asked, professionally whitened teeth agleam.

"Let's do this." Sandra got out of the car and walked up to the house. The front door was unlocked, as Sandra so often found them. "Hello? Mrs. Hawthorne?"

A slim woman, dark hair pulled back into a ponytail, bangs faintly sticking to her forehead with sweat, came bouncing down the stairs. "It was open," Sandra half apologized.

"No, no, we were expecting you!" She stuck out her hand. "Eve. Hawthorne." Eve looked a bit younger than Sandra, which was not the only surprising thing about her. Instead of the frumpy, pleated-front pants and kitten sweatshirts Sandra had come to expect from these shoots, Eve wore an oversized, slightly asymmetrical T-shirt over expensive leggings, a luxury athletic brand Sandra herself had coveted. Eve looked like she might have even worked out in them.

"Sandra," Sandra said. "We spoke on the phone. Meet *Searching for . . . the Invisible World*." Sandra stepped aside for her crew, a stream of men bearing equipment, muttering among themselves as they set up tripods and lights, scanned for outlets. Eve watched them with a sort of detached fascination, not wincing as many homeowners did when they began taping cords to the floor or roughly handling end tables.

Sandra handed Eve a printed copy of the agenda for the week, though she'd emailed it ahead of time, and an FAQ for participants: "What to Expect When You're Expecting a Reality Show to Descend on Your Home." The show's title was emblazoned across the top of the packet in a ghostly font. Eve gave it a tight smile, then folded it in half.

"Would you like the tour?" she asked. "Or should we wait until all this is ready?"

Sandra pushed herself to smile. "I'd love it if you could show me around."

"The first place we noticed activity was the dining room." Eve held out a hand for Sandra to go in first.

Production assistants trooped through the door, carrying blackout drapes to hang over the windows, a curtain against which interviews would be shot. Setup halted upon discovery of the spread that awaited them: coffee not in boxes from a franchise, but brewed from beans with provenance; bagels—real ones, not from the grocery store; pastries dusted with sugar. Rarely was the crew offered more than coffee. Someone had gone out of their way in a town with one grocery store to come up with whitefish spread and bialys.

Beyond the table, though, was what interested Sandra. A rumpled drop cloth lay on the floor, a ladder leaned near the window. They'd had months to prepare for the show's arrival, but this room was half painted, baseboards unsanded, old carpeting torn up and wood floor beneath left splintery. Sandra, against her better judgment, bit.

"Do you two eat in here?"

"No." Eve tilted her head. "Ryan doesn't think it's safe."

"What does he think could happen?"

"He should probably be the one to tell you that, don't you think?"

Irritation flashed through Sandra, then cooled. She'd been

in television only a few years, but had known them all already: the subject-directors, the "reluctant" confessors, the girls who needed just a tiny bit of liquor to cry. She'd been an ersatz social worker, an emergency babysitter; she'd baked a wedding cake when a caterer got food poisoning. This—taking direction from Eve—was nothing.

"Do you agree with him?"

Eve screwed up her eyes. "I'm not afraid of what happened in here. Our experiences have been . . . different," she concluded diplomatically.

Sandra nodded. "We'll get set up and begin by interviewing you separately. We'll start with Ryan." She pointed to the agenda, folded up in Eve's armpit. "We will try to keep this as disruptive as possible," Sandra concluded, then corrected herself. "As little disruptive . . . keep this from being as disruptive as possible. I'm sorry. I haven't had my coffee yet." It was a lie; she'd had two cups on the road. But Eve gestured toward the table, and then, to Sandra's relief, melted away.

Sandra walked the first floor of the house with a cup of coffee in one hand and her phone in the other, scrolling through the script with her thumb. The living room contained a sprawling sectional and those floating shelves Sandra only ever saw in catalogs. Like In the catalogs, the Hawthornes' shelves held vases and art books. One room was ready for *Architectural Digest*, the other was a half-finished mess . . . Sandra sipped the coffee. It was good. She wasn't sure why this, too, bothered her, why she hadn't introduced herself to Ryan yet, why it was only Monday and she was already out of steam.

Have you tried turning it off and on again? she thought sardonically. She got into these moods sometimes. Behind her, a PA dropped something heavy, but she didn't flinch.

TRANSCRIPTS courtesy Roving Eye Productions

Transcript: SIW-221a-1/CAMERA A, 10:15:13

INTERVIEW—RYAN HAWTHORNE

RYAN: How's my hair?

*Perfect. So start by telling me your full name, where you're from,
and what you do for a living.*

RYAN: My name is Ryan Hawthorne, born and raised in
Ninebark, and I own and manage a car stereo store, Liquid
Sound.

Let's do that one more time because . . .

RYAN: I know, I already screwed up . . .

You're doing fine. Just take your time.

RYAN: Okay, thanks.

One more time, tell us who you are and what you do.

RYAN: My name is Ryan Hawthorne. I have lived in Ninebark,
Pennsylvania, all my life. I own Liquid Sound, a car stereo
store.

*Great. So Eve's not from the area. Why did you decide to settle in
Ninebark?*

RYAN: First of all, Ninebark's not settling. Let's get that
straight. I'm just joshing you. We moved to Ninebark
because I already owned my store, I was already pretty set
up when we met.

Try to say "my wife."

RYAN: Yeah, sorry, I forgot.

No worries!

RYAN: My wife, Eve, moved with me to Ninebark because I

was already settled in the area, my parents live here, and I
already had my store.

Would you say you're both happy in Ninebark?

RYAN: I can't say Eve is happy; like, she doesn't love it here. I'm
sure she'll tell you that. I'm sure you'll get an earful.

*But together, as a couple, I mean, your family is nearby, you
said—does that make life easier?*

RYAN: Does living near my parents make life easier . . . ?

Let's say "family."

RYAN: Don't say?

Let's say.

RYAN: Okay. We ultimately came to Ninebark to live near
family and make life easier.

*Okay, great. Let's talk about the house. When you first saw this
house, tell me, what were your thoughts?*

RYAN: I got a great loan, my buddy Mark down at the credit
union hooked us up with a low-interest mortgage. So, yeah,
I'd say I was pretty excited to buy this house.

*Walk me through what you were feeling when you first pulled up
to the house and saw it from the outside?*

RYAN: It's a house, I don't know, it's white. It looks like a good
house to raise a family in.

Are you and Eve planning on raising a family in this house?

RYAN: I think you should speak to my wife about that. I'm
not going to say anything on the record that will get me in
trouble later, you feel me?

*It would be great to get one sentence about what you said, though,
that this looks like a good house to raise a family in.*

RYAN: Just that part?

If you don't mind.

RYAN: When I first saw the house, I thought it looked like a
good house to raise a family in.

Transcript: SIW-221a-2/CAMERA A, 11:04:23

INTERVIEW—EVE HAWTHORNE

*Thanks for sitting down with me, Eve. Let's start by telling me
your full name, where you're from, and what you do for a
living.*
EVE: My name is Eve Hawthorne-Malone. I'm an artist and art
educator here in Ninebark.
And where are you from?
EVE: New York, actually. Same as all of you.
*We don't typically refer to production in these interviews. We're
here to tell your story and share your experiences, but we won't
be interacting with you on-screen. I know this sounds a little
silly, but try to pretend we're not here.*
EVE: An invisible crew.
*Exactly! Pun intended. So let's try that again, about where you're
from, then why you moved to Pennsylvania.*
EVE: Before moving to Pennsylvania, I lived in New York for
eight years. I moved there for college, to study art. I worked
for a couple years while I built up my portfolio, then went
back to school for my MFA. I met Ryan right around the
time I graduated.
Question
EVE: We got married and bought the house pretty quickly. Not
because—I wasn't pregnant. Just "crazy in love," I guess.
Question
EVE: I knew something was going on with the house before
we moved in. But I wasn't scared. I could tell that this
house had, for lack of a better expression, something to
tell me.

INTERVIEW—RYAN

About how long after you moved in did you start renovating?

RYAN: We didn't do anything too extensive, to be honest with you. New coat of paint here and there, stripping wallpaper, staining some of the wood. Cosmetic stuff. Eve wanted a house that wasn't going to suck up all of our time. I was more excited to get in and get my hands dirty, but no, we didn't do a ton of reno work.

My notes say you were sleeping in the dining room when you first moved in? You must have been doing something if you weren't sleeping in a bedroom.

RYAN: That was because of the air conditioner. We only had one working air conditioner and we were painting the dining room and staining the floors in the living room. So we slept on an air mattress for a couple nights under the AC before we got another window unit for the upstairs.

Tell me about what happened in the dining room the first week, with the pictures.

RYAN: So the thing with the pictures was, I told Eve not to decorate before we finished the other work. You put all the furniture and rugs and shit down—sorry, sorry. Let me start that again. You put all the rugs down, then the furniture, then you decorate. But Eve has to hang pictures. She has this, like, *fear* of bare walls. But we're still tearing up carpeting. We're still painting. It didn't make any sense to hang pictures.

So you're sleeping in the dining room on an air mattress. It's the first night in your new home. You're excited to be there: new home, you're a lovely newlywed couple, and then what happens in the middle of the night?

RYAN: It's the first week in our new home, it's really hot, and
    we've only got the AC in one window. So we're sleeping on
    this air mattress in the dining room, and I wake up and for
    some reason I look at the wall where the pictures were. And
    there are no pictures. I guess it was on my mind because
    I had been arguing with Eve to hold off on the pictures
    until we're done everything else. But that girl gets what she
    wants—you know what I'm saying? I mean, she got me,
    heh heh.

*How do you feel when you wake up and see the pictures aren't on
    the wall? Are you scared, are you confused . . .*

RYAN: I'm lying there, thinking, like, *Where are the pictures?*
    Did she take them down? It would be pretty hard for her
    to get up off the air mattress, take down some pictures, and
    then get back on without me waking up. So I look across
    the room, and there are the pictures—clear across the room,
    like they must have flew over our heads and landed on the
    other side.

*That sounds really dangerous. That sounds like, you've just
    moved into this new home, and maybe it isn't safe for
    you?*

RYAN: Exactly. I'm lying there thinking, *What if they had
    fallen?* Those frames have sharp corners. What if some
    picture frame fell down in the middle of the night on top
    of our heads? That's when I was like, this is freaky.

*Did it make you question whether or not it's safe to stay in your
    home?*

RYAN: Sure. When you put it like that.

Can you give me one sentence that's like . . .

RYAN: Okay, how's this: If we can't figure out what's going on
    in our house, we're gonna have to move.

INTERVIEW—EVE

EVE: The pictures were down, yes. But they hardly flew across the room. We were in the middle of the floor, and the pictures fell, oh, five or six inches away from the wall. When we got up in the morning the pictures were on the floor. I hadn't hung them with nails—you know those little plastic hooks with the sticky backs? They were only supposed to be temporary.

Question

EVE: Ryan did seem alarmed about it when we woke up the next morning. But we weren't sleeping right there—the mattress wasn't up against the wall where the pictures were hanging.

Question

EVE: That's a bit dramatic, wouldn't you say? It's a house. Objects fall down.

Question

EVE: I'm *not* saying that—I've felt a presence in this house many times. But I never felt I was in any *danger*. This might sound strange to you, but to me it felt like something trying to connect.

——— · ———

After they'd slept together a second time, Eve decided to tell Ryan. There was something so giving about him, making love— from the moment she'd taken her shirt off he had been murmuring steadily, unable to control himself, exalting her voice, her breasts, the feel of her skin. She felt bathed in his attention, warmed by an otherworldly glow as he appraised her parts, finding none anything short of perfection. She had wanted to call out that she loved him, but that was ridiculous—it was their second date. She didn't think she loved him, yet she was astonished in equal parts by him and by the fact that she, after two years debating art history and critical theory in a jargon used by 0.01% of the population, had no words for her feelings. She was grateful, and she wanted to give something to him. Afterward, as they lay on their sides, she ran a finger down the line of hair trailing his navel. He feigned self-consciousness, sucking in his stomach, and she laughed, then pinched the tiny bit of fat that was there. He seemed in no hurry to get dressed.

"Want to hear a weird story?" she asked, the faux casualness of her voice coming out wrong.

"Sure," he said, and pulled her head to his chest.

She had told this story many times, to many lovers, in her head. She wasn't sure anyone outside her family knew it, and she suspected many within her family had forgotten. The fact that she was sharing it with Ryan might have been the moment when she "knew." She had the feeling then that she was telling a story she'd later tell as part of the mythology of their coupledom.

When she was ten, Eve's father got a job offer in south Texas, and the whole family moved. For reasons she could not remember—distance, perhaps, or anxiety about aging—her grandparents moved with them. Eve's parents, her older brother, Ben, and the family cat went in one car. Eve went with her grandmother, grandfather, and brother Simon in the second car. Her grandfather insisted on driving the whole way, as he did most family vacations. This was before cell phones, so the family mapped out the route ahead of time and identified motels where they would meet up at the end of each driving day. Her father had something of a lead foot and a death wish when it came to tractor trailers, but her grandfather promised they wouldn't lag too far behind.

The trip was mostly lost in her memory, though it lasted sev-

eral days, and must have been a fraught experience for someone
who had spent her entire life in the same state, not to mention the same elementary school, the same house. She recalled a
diner, mazes on a paper placemat, stubby crayons in a grimy cup
that even then she was too prim to reach for. What Eve remembered most, the heart of the story, was one night somewhere, she
thought, in Oklahoma.

Somewhere around Oklahoma, she said, watching Ryan carefully, her grandfather's age caught up to him, and he wanted to
rest. They were about a hundred miles from the next motel on the
itinerary, and he didn't think he could make it. He pulled over to
the side of the road and suggested they all try to sleep a few hours,
and then when he was feeling more alert he'd continue driving—
maybe all the way to Texas, he told the back seat, winking into
the rearview mirror. We'll beat your old dad yet.

Eve was always the last asleep at sleepovers or the night before
Christmas, and she was the last asleep that night. She sat for
hours listening to the steady exhalations of her family in the
warm car. She may have fallen asleep at some point, this part
may have been a dream, but her feeling then and now was that
she was awake when the crows appeared, throngs of them, pure
black against the green-black sky. They flapped their wings,
hovering just outside the car's windows. A few landed on the
hood and looked in, their eyes glinting as they assessed the car's
contents. They were huge, Texas-sized crows, and Eve tried to
remain very still, hoping their vision was based on movement,
that they wouldn't flap and peck unless something came toward
them first. She was the only one awake and she sat still for a long
time, thinking that whoever woke up next, she would have to
warn, *Sit very still. There are crows around the car.*

The next thing she remembered was daylight, her family
being woken up by a state trooper tapping on the driver's-side

window. Her grandparents blinked, coughed, rubbed their eyes. Her grandfather rolled down his window, letting hot, dusty air into the car.

"Are you the Malone family?" the trooper asked.

Her grandfather, who was prepared to defend his right to sleep in his car, looked to his wife before answering.

"That's us."

The trooper told them their car matched the description of a car that had been reported missing. Eve's father, mother, and brother had gotten to Texas four days ago, and panicked when the second car didn't arrive and hadn't checked in at any of the remaining motels along the route.

"Four days?" her grandfather asked, and Ryan echoed twenty years later.

"Weird, right?"

Ryan's heart rate had picked up, but he hadn't pushed Eve off him.

"What do you think happened?" he asked.

"I've thought about it a lot." In high school, the internet still a new thing, but, she knew, a place to find others like her, she had scoured chat rooms and communities for anyone with a similar story. She read about "time slips," but none of them mentioned crows. Though they might have been a dream, she felt that the crows were a necessary part of the story. The crows, somehow, would unlock the whole thing. "I can't come up with anything that explains it in a way that satisfies me."

"Is it possible you guys fell behind on your itinerary, and your grandfather didn't realize it, so you did only sleep one night, but were still that far behind?"

"But we met up with the other car each night at the designated motel. I only remember one night we didn't, and that was the night we slept on the road."

The state trooper radioed in that he'd found them, and wished them luck on the rest of their journey. They arrived in Texas safely, and lived there only a few years before her father was transferred back east, with a bonus high enough to hire movers and put the seven of them on a plane.

Ryan released her hand and reached over to stroke her arm. It wasn't the perfect response, though he seemed willing enough to believe her. Or, rather, he believed in the importance of this story to her. He didn't laugh. He didn't question the crows.

A couple years later, when preparing their application to appear on *Searching for . . . the Invisible World*, Eve brought up the story and wondered if they should include it—if she should paint herself as susceptible to paranormal events. She reminded Ryan about time slips: hiccups in the chronology, people from other centuries appearing, deeply confused, then disappearing as suddenly as they'd come. She imagined the car, the four of them in it, materializing on that same road in another era, strangers from a thousand years out peering in the windows, tapping on the glass. And what if something had come back through the slip with her, had been following her ever since?

Ryan set down the spoon he'd been stirring a sauce with on the stove. It was a Sunday night. Ryan always cooked on Sundays; it was a thing in his family. Eve's parents had no such rituals, and she found the novelty of it charming, though Ryan's repertoire was limited.

"Babe?" he started. "Did you ever think maybe, that night on the road, something else happened?"

"Like what?" This was the first she'd heard of Ryan having a theory.

"Something you don't want to remember." He screwed up his face. "Like maybe your grandfather . . ."

"My grandfather what?"

"He gave you a bunch of NyQuil and . . ." He looked at her, begging her not to make him finish the sentence.

"And . . . diddled me? For the better part of a week? Over the sleeping body of his wife and my brother?"

"It happens. Probably more often than anybody realizes." He crouched on the kitchen floor in front of her, put a hand on each of her knees. "People can't always talk about traumatic experiences directly." He told her about a special he had seen, about survivors who have blanks in their memories, how those blanks are protecting their minds from trauma. "It's a way for the mind to, like, preserve itself," he said, a clinical psychologist all of a sudden.

"You saw this on TV," the medium reason enough to discredit him.

Ryan continued, reeling off the victims' stories, but she wasn't listening. She was picturing herself the way Ryan had been seeing her all this time: as a fragile girl, assaulted by a family member, unable to speak about it, inventing fantastical metaphors for the experience. Ryan hadn't read Freud, didn't know the Wolf Man, but surely to him the crows represented her grandfather's pointy penis or something. For two days she didn't speak to her husband, found reasons to stay out of the house until she was sure he was asleep. In the mornings she rose only after Ryan had left for his stereo store, where he primarily oversaw the installation of subwoofers into muscle cars—shiny red (now throbbing) proxy genitals he manipulated without a hint of irony.

On the third day they had dinner plans with his parents and she knew she would have to at least be cordial. In the car on the way over she said simply, "I was never molested by my grandfather."

"Okay," Ryan said, exasperated, then "okay" again, softer this time, and reached across the shift to put his hand on top of hers and grasp it. "I'm sorry. It was a logical conclusion to make."

As opposed to, Eve thought, the highly illogical ones she had been seeking all these years. Their fight was over, but that night, watching Ryan interact with his parents, helping them program their DVR and load the dishwasher, she knew he lacked that quality of wonder, that hope that the world was enormous and strange and harbored secrets it shared with a precious few. Whatever was going on in their house, he would trust the least imaginative explanation, be it radio waves, underground vibrations, good old swamp gas. Eve had never felt more despairing than she did on the car ride home. Sex with Ryan that night was like watching a pornographic movie, the sounds and thrusts not connected to her at all, and she lay in bed long after he dropped off to sleep, listening to the house noises and evaluating them in her mind. None left any room for interpretation, none warranted slipping out of bed and down the hall to check. It was nearly light out when she fell asleep, to the sound of birds clearing their throats in preparation for another predictable day.

A week later the show called to tell them that their application had been accepted.

———————

Transcript: SIW-221a-2/CAMERA A, 11:26:13

INTERVIEW—EVE

Question
EVE: Because I didn't *feel* it was hostile, whatever it was. Even if the pictures didn't just fall down. I wasn't scared.
Question
EVE: Of course in the *moment* it's frightening and destabilizing—things moving on their own, who wouldn't

be frightened by that? But if I had to guess the emotional
state of . . . whatever it is, I would say it was curious.
Question
EVE: About me, about us. I imagine that it wanted to let us
know it was there, as a courtesy. As weird as that sounds.
Question
EVE: Because this isn't my first rodeo, so to speak. I had an
experience as a little girl—my whole family did—and ever
since then I think I've always been in the presence of forces
bigger than myself.

———•·•———

Sandra gestured to Ronnie to shut the camera off.

"Eve, you never mentioned a childhood experience before
now."

"You guys just got here."

"In your application, or the intake interview we did over the
phone." Sandra pretended to flip through her notes, but she
didn't need to: she knew exactly what Eve had said previously,
what lines the script was designed to get Eve to deliver.

"Ryan didn't think I should mention it." Her face darkened.
"You said the interviews would take three to five hours each.
What does it matter if I add something now?"

Sandra shook her head. Stories from the past, especially ones
involving extended family, were structured differently, and typically those family members were contacted and asked to participate. During intake, the couple had little activity to discuss, and
even with Alan's investigation the Hawthornes were slotted for
a B episode—split with another family's story, twenty-one minutes each, rather than the full forty-two minutes dedicated to
one house. The subjects weren't aware of the formulaic nature of

these shoots: her colleague Lisa was thirty miles away right then with a mirror image of Sandra's crew, asking some other couple the same types of questions, their shooting schedules identical down to the fifteen-minute mark.

"You have to trust me that over the years we've developed a good method of filming that minimizes the time we need to spend disrupting your lives. Part of that involves getting the basic elements of the story in place before we arrive."

Eve bit her lip. "This is such an important part of my history, I'd feel sick not to be able to discuss it at all."

Take it up with your husband, Sandra thought. "Our schedule is pretty tight, believe it or not. The information we gather during preproduction determines the production schedule and final episode outline. Anything we add now means something else we have to take out later that we won't have time for. And it doesn't sound like we're even at the most important events yet." In truth, there was wiggle room in the interview schedule, but anything Eve discussed that had not been blocked into the script already would most likely be cut, and Sandra didn't want to set herself up, once the episode aired, for an excoriating letter or a voice mail left over the weekend, the light on her phone blinking ominously when she entered her office Monday morning. Sandra could tell Eve had it in her.

"Okay." Eve put her hands up. "I'm sorry I said anything." She did not look sorry. She looked pissed.

Sandra took Eve in: her cheekbones were contoured, her hair was shiny in the light. This confident woman couldn't really believe she had been pursued by a ghost since her childhood, could she? Stiff, awkward people who needed an excuse for not fitting in to the world, Sandra understood. Give them a ghost, a companion for the long lonely nights. Something to explain feeling uncomfortable in their skins. And while Sandra could have respected Eve's desire not to compromise on her story, every aspect of this production was some sort of compromise for every single person involved. The mid-aughts had seen a surge in paranormal reality programming; *Searching for . . .* was attempting to heave itself onto an already crowded bandwagon. Investigators on bigger shows had become household names—at least in a small, creepy subset of households—with popular podcasts and invitations to speak at conventions, but Alan Purvis and his crew had not. And if Eve had applied to one of those other shows before *Searching for . . .* , Sandra would have been neither surprised nor offended.

It was Monday. By Friday, Eve would realize what she would gain from her participation: very, very little. She was fuel for a rusting, unwieldy machine, just enough for it to lumber forward a quarter of a quarter of an inch.

"Eve, would you like a glass of water?" Sandra jutted her chin at a PA, sending them scurrying.

"No, thank you." Eve's eyes narrowed. She looked at the curtain that hung behind her, the dust that had been revealed when they pushed the table against the wall and rolled up the rug, little poofs flying up whenever anyone walked through, then resettling. "When are the . . . ghost hunters arriving?"

"The paranormal team comes in the evening. They do their work at night, for obvious reasons." Sandra smiled, hoping to coax a smile out of Eve. Nothing doing. A glass of water appeared, and Eve took a sip.

Sandra looked at her watch. "Let's take a break for lunch. I think we could all use a little air. I should check in with my other camera operator anyway." Sandra didn't really have to check in with Macon. He was a pro and, considering he was on a break at the moment, wouldn't have anything to report anyway. She just wanted out of the dining room, which had started to feel muggy. "Let's stretch our legs, get something to eat, and then we can talk about the next part of the day."

Eve didn't move. Sandra felt awkward standing up and walking out of the room, but less awkward than remaining where she was, sitting across from Eve in silence.

———————

The cameraman who had been filming the interviews stayed behind in the dining room. He was tall—well over six feet—muscular in a ripply, unostentatious way, and a bald due two-thirds to nature, a razor the rest. Tattoos had been uncovered over the course of the day, as a sweater was removed and sleeves rolled up. When he turned to listen to a voice coming from the other room, Eve saw ink at the top of his neck that his shirt collar didn't entirely conceal.

Eve cleared her throat, a little louder than she'd intended. He turned back to her.

"Is it always like this?" she asked.

"Like what?"

Eve had assumed—naïvely, it was now clear—that the show would let her tell her story her way. She thought she would have control over, at the very least, the words that came out of her mouth and the order in which they did so. Her childhood experience in the car was just the start. She'd had all sorts of experiences, spanning her whole life, and she'd looked forward to the show as a venue to finally share them. But it had become obvious from watching Ryan's interrogation and now embarking on her own that Eve's lines had been written for her already, the sticky web of her experiences untangled just enough to be jovially draped over a window in anticipation of Halloween. It was like grad school, where critiques that were meant to be helpful instead gave Eve a clear picture of what her classmates believed was "good" art; they examined her work through narrow, entirely subjective definitions, with no allowances for anything they didn't personally prefer. Eve had never been chased by a slender figure draped in a sheet, had never tripped down the stairs of an old mansion, seeking escape, only to find the front door locked. She hadn't been capable of producing a decent painting then nor, it turned out, a decent haunting now.

"Are the other homes you film, are the other hauntings like mine?"

"Everyone's is a little different." A non-answer.

"But also basically the same, aka, delusions. *Hysteria*." Eve snorted. "You leave here, all of you"—she gestured to the residue of PAs that clung to the walls—"have a drink when it's over, and make fun of us."

"I can't speak for the rest. Myself, I've been sober eight years."

Eve believed this. "What's your name?"

"Ronnie." He extended a hand for her to shake. It was warm and dry, the skin surprisingly soft.

"Ronnie, my point stands."

"What do you want me to say? We're here to do a job. Everyone here is doing the best they can. For some of them it's not a dream job, but for others it is. You're going to meet a lot of people this week who will care about what you have to say and believe all of it."

The future tense seemed important: "going to meet." That excluded Sandra. That hurt. Though a blond man had been introduced to Eve as the director, Sandra was the one running interviews, the one members of the crew came to with questions. At one point, during a five-minute break, Eve had observed a young woman on the crew whisper into Sandra's ear. Sandra had nodded, reached down into her bag, then discreetly passed a tampon to the young woman, who had caught Eve's eye and skittered away. By contrast, while she and her husband were being interviewed Eve had watched the "director" wandering her home, eating leftover bagels, and noodling around on his phone with his feet up on various pieces of furniture. This had raised no eyebrows among the rest of the crew. As a woman, Eve felt, Sandra owed her more than professional neutrality. Eve longed to shake Sandra's skepticism out of her, send her tumbling into a world whose true dimensions she couldn't begin to fathom.

"What about you, though? Do you believe me?" Her face burned.

"I don't have an opinion either way."

"Bullshit."

"Pardon me, but it isn't."

"Do you want to see something?" She stood up. Her heart was pounding.

"What?"

"Something real." She nodded to outside the house. "I could show you."

Ronnie put his hands on his camera, as if to remind them both where his duties lay.

"You must be curious." She couldn't keep the suggestiveness out of her voice. At times, and she always hated herself afterward, it felt like the only power she had. "Come on. I want to show you." She held his gaze for a long moment, until he dropped his hands from the camera and nodded. She turned to the front door.

At that moment the door opened and the other camera guy, shorter, with shoulder-length hair in need of a wash, stepped in. He was twirling a keychain around his pointer finger and nodded to Ronnie.

"Lunch?"

"I could use a smoke." Ronnie flipped a switch on his camera, headed out of the room, then paused to look back at Eve.

Later, she mouthed. He saw, but did not react.

———————

Sandra found Patrick sitting at the kitchen table with his feet up on a chair, eyes on his phone, a couple of sycophants hovering nearby, yearning to be called into action. She was starving, even after the bagel at breakfast. Some local deli was bringing in sandwiches for lunch, and they were late.

"You ever have one of those days when the universe is trying to tell you you're in the wrong line of work?"

"I generally let those calls go through to voice mail."

She remained standing in the doorway. "What's wrong with the script this week?"

This got him to tear his eyes away from the screen. "What do you mean?"

If there was one thing that stressed Patrick out, it was having to manage. It was easy to imagine Patrick at a young age seeing a photo of Spielberg, maybe, or Kubrick behind the camera: a commanding presence, worlds spinning out from his fingertips. That image, black and white, often returned to, must have determined the course of his life. But the daydream never went any deeper. Patrick had no interest in the millions of tiny details that filming a show required. The distance between the finished product and the mundanity of being in these families' houses had disappointed Patrick to a lobotomizing degree. He let everyone else do his work for him, navigating shoots magnificently tuned out, his comprehension that of a college student's many bong rips in. It infuriated Sandra. They were too complementary a team: her mind was always weighing and chopping the world around her into a story she could use.

Sandra had majored in English literature at a small liberal-arts college and wanted to spend some time in The City before deciding what to do next. Four years later, she had a job in a bookstore and one room in a three-bedroom apartment in Brooklyn with two roommates from Craigslist. On her days off, which never seemed to be Saturdays or Sundays, she'd slouch on the stained, torn sofa left by a roommate three roommates back and watch the gigantic TV one of the current roommates had brought in. It was much too large for the space, so Sandra could lie down and the screen would fill her vision completely. She hadn't had TV in college, so those first years out were an education in the new world of the unscripted. In those days the word "bingeing" still had connotations tied to food; instead, cable networks ran "marathons" of their most popular shows, a whole season in one day. In this way, Sandra caught up: cooking competitions, fashion competitions, attempts to stay alive in the wilderness. Ridiculous dating scenarios, shows in which married women went to live in the households of other married women and imposed new rules. She'd watch from start to finish, cereal bowls accumulating on the IKEA end table, go to bed after the climactic finales, and dream of the people she'd watched. She kept a little notebook by her bed, where she wrote down their occasional moments of deep insight, the things they said without even realizing they were stating something powerful and true. And then one roommate moved out and another moved in who worked in the industry, who told her yeah, they were always looking for people.

"I'm not doing anything different than I normally do in my interviews, and Eve keeps looking at me as if I'm trying to put one over on her. She's bringing up stories she never mentioned during her screening."

"The husband seems game."

"That worries me, too. He and his wife can't agree on one single detail of the story, down to what they ate for dinner last night. When do we get them together? I'm going to have to block out extra time for that interview."

She began as a logger, transcribing the raw footage word for word so that editors didn't have to sit through hours of retakes or bumbling interviews to find the moments they wanted. It was tedious work, but Sandra kept an ear out for any gems for her notebook. Something about a raw, unpracticed insight resonated with her more deeply than any underlined sentence from the books she'd parsed in college. And in the meantime, she was fast and precise and personable around the office, and the editors quickly found new things for her to do.

"There is no couple's interview."

"Why not?"

"They never saw anything at the same time."

Sandra finally sat down. "And that isn't weird?"

Patrick raised an eyebrow: What about this job wasn't weird? Tucked in at the triple-digit end of the cable menu, it was a show about people who blamed ghosts for causing their dogs to bark at odd hours and rearranging their CD collections in the night.

Within a couple years as a producer, Sandra had had to admit that the people she was interviewing couldn't offer any truth that was bigger than themselves. Perhaps it was because the shows she was working on were small, had a small audience—a major network show with a 5 share in 18 to 49 would necessarily have a different sort of subject, one who was worthy of so many eyeballs. But it had been years since she'd quit the book-

store, and the shows she worked on were still small. She pivoted
her hopes away from individual subjects to asking herself, What
is the story the show *as a whole* is telling re America, its anxieties and obsessions? These questions guided her decisions. And
while her work garnered praise from within Roving Eye, she
could only confess her approach three drinks in on a Friday,
blushing furiously at the memory of it later, but in the moment
leaning across the bar to a colleague, gesturing earnestly while
he couldn't care less, was probably updating his LinkedIn as she
spoke.

A car pulled up the drive, and Sandra offered a quick secular
prayer that it was the sandwiches.

Patrick returned to his phone. "Before I forget: Alan called."

"Oh? How is he?" Sandra pretended to look at her phone.

"He said he can't make it out tonight."

"Did he say why?" Her face went warm; suddenly she had lost
her appetite.

"Watching a sick kid for a neighbor."

"I hope it's nothing serious. Should we push the investigation
back a night?"

"He said he'll be sending out his team and he'll supervise
the evidence review tomorrow." The "team" that made up the
Paranormal Investigators of Pennsylvania—PIP for short—was
small and scrappy, a couple of young people Alan treated with
avuncular care.

It was Sandra's turn to raise an eyebrow.

Patrick threw up his hands. "Just the messenger. I feel the
same as you."

But Sandra doubted that. She put her elbows on her knees
and her head in her hands. "What makes this shoot different
from every other shoot?"

Patrick was silent.

She looked at him. "What?"

"Did you forget what week it is?"

Uncharacteristically, she had. It was the week the network made decisions about next season—it might order up another twenty-two episodes of *Searching for . . .* or scale back to a cautious ten, taking them just to midseason with an eye on the numbers. Or, Sandra very well knew, the network might order none at all. The franchise was wearing thin, *Searching for . . . the World's Best Theme Park* having exhausted its source material after three seasons, *Searching for . . . America's Best Diner* lost amidst similar shows that aired on more appropriate (though saturated) networks. While the paranormal was trending, with numerous families applying to the show, *The Invisible World*, in keeping with the series's "roaming" format, lacked the recurring psychic of other shows like it, a personality to keep viewers and a visage to slap on a T-shirt.

"I might update my résumé, is all."

"I'm sure you already have."

"You know I'd be delighted to bring you along with me wherever I end up. We make a great team."

Sandra withheld a derisive response. She wasn't sure how to feel about the show potentially being canceled. She was reasonably confident she'd find another job; turnover in the industry was high and she had enough connections who'd be willing to bring her on to some other project. But she felt an unexpected sadness at the thought of never doing *this* again. Though she'd never believed any of it, there was an undeniable thrill to stomping around these modest homes at night, awaiting some knock or hand on the shoulder, a disembodied voice in the ear. A minimal amount of research turned up a surprising number of tragedies connected to each home, regardless of location or date of construction. She wasn't pretentious enough to claim they were "exposing the dark underside of the middle class," or anything so grandiose, but she'd taken the job with a renewed interest in uncovering *some* truth. If she walked away now, could she say she had found one? And what if she never saw Alan again? Her heart clenched emptily at the thought.

Meanwhile, Patrick had been talking, the gist of which was that Sandra had more power than she knew, more agency than he did, maybe, when it came to the future of the show. "Not to put too much pressure on a single episode, but we should try to make the argument that we've still got new stories to tell. Even if, to us it looks like . . ." He gestured, let her fill in the rest: *same shit, different day.* "Just need to generate some buzz," he finished, sounding like a dad trying out the lingo for the first time.

"Of course," Sandra said, unsure if that was an appropriate response, not really caring either way.

And then, at long last, a tramping through the front door, the heavy footsteps of the laden. Sandra leaned back to survey the boxes and bags coming in. "You want some lunch?"

"Six-footer?"

She squinted. "Looks like the usual size."

"I'll wait."

She stood to leave. "Keep chasing that white whale, my friend."

"Pennsylvania invented the six-foot sub!" he called out as she walked down the hall to pay for the food. But Sandra, based on everything Patrick had claimed thus far, wondered where he'd heard that one.

———•—•———

Ryan wove through the living room, between sandwiches being passed overhand and underhand to the crew, down the hallway. On his way he tucked a stray cord under the runner, piled a few empty cups and plates into a stack. When he was sure no one was paying attention to him, he opened a door between the kitchen and living room and slipped down the stairs to the basement. He yanked the chain to turn on the light, pulled an energy bar from his pocket, and unwrapped it.

As far as he knew no one had been in the basement yet. Didn't all this shit usually start there, where angry ghosts rose up to rattle their chains at whoever slept above? How could these clowns have overlooked where every supernatural event originated? He remembered one episode of the show he and Eve had watched together. It was about ghost monkeys in the attic of a store. Ryan found that acceptable. Animals lived in trees, so maybe their spirits came down from the trees and entered houses through the roof. But humans were buried in the ground, all of them, and if they wanted to come back they needed to start from the bottom.

The basement was unfinished, with a poured-concrete floor and cinder-block walls, and contained a couple of crawl spaces where he and Eve stashed old stuff—Christmas tree ornaments, cases of wine from her parents that neither of them wanted to drink. In one of these crawl spaces, up against the wall and behind a box of Zinfandel, Ryan had placed some stereo equipment, a little something he had been tinkering with during slow days at the store these past couple weeks, using parts from old boom boxes. He had built the contraption to make three different sounds: a sort of low wail that his buddy Jake had insisted was too cheesy and everyone would see through; an arrhythmic thumping that was frustrating as hell, your brain trying to make the beats line up; and a harsh static that Jake had thought was a mistake but that Ryan actually liked. It was the sound of equipment malfunctioning. He could see their house on the TV screen, the ghosts suddenly getting angry and shutting off the cameras. The third sound would be the soundtrack. The box was connected to a digital clock with a timer. The whole setup looked like a bomb with a couple of speakers attached, and Ryan had sweated like crazy driving it home from the store, worried he'd be pulled over for some taillight bullshit and find himself en route to Guantánamo. But in the safety of the crawl space, he admired the project.

Feet crossed the floor above him.

Ryan pressed the button to play the thumping noise. He turned it on low and spent a few minutes walking around the basement, adjusting the volume, seeing how it sounded in the walls. It shouldn't be so loud that its source could easily be traced, but he also didn't want it lost in the hubbub of TV crew and ghost hunters.

"Hey, you hear that?" he said aloud. "Wait, guys, stop, listen for a sec. You hear that?" Ryan paused. *Whump. Whump-whump-whump.* Corvette idling at a stoplight, giant subwoofers vibrating the cars around it. *Whumpwhump. Whump.* Long pause. *Whump.* Perfect.

Ryan hadn't told Eve about the machine. He considered it an insurance plan. All week she'd been worrying: *What if nothing happens. What if they don't believe us.* Ryan wanted this week—this invasion—to be a one-and-done. *Here's some spooky shit. Now get the hell out of my house.* According to the schedule Sandra had given them, the paranormal team would begin their investigation around nine. He set the timer for ten fifteen. He turned the machine off, cranked the volume all the way to the right, and went upstairs to join everyone else for lunch.

Transcript: SIW-221a-4/CAMERA A, 15:30:46

INTERVIEW—EVE

EVE: For me, everything started in the guest room. Not long
after we moved in, a friend from grad school came to visit
and stayed a couple days. After she left, I was changing
the sheets on the bed, and I had a very sudden and
unmistakable feeling of being watched.

Question

EVE: It wasn't . . . this is one of the things we were talking about,
actually, when my friend was here, how impossible it is to be
objective during a critique because your classmates are also
your competition for grants and scholarships and stuff. So
there's so much ego vandalizing going on, it's impossible to
sort out the useful critique from the personal attacks.

Question

EVE: "Ego vandalizing" means everyone else wants to see you
doubt yourself, see you give up. So you'll retreat to the sticks
where there's absolutely no one around to see your work, to
bestow their imprimatur on it . . . Sorry, is that word too
difficult as well?

Question

EVE: What I'm trying to say is that in grad school you both
need the feedback—art needs an audience to be real—and
you need to protect the art-making part of you from the
feedback, and there's no way out of the loop. There's nothing
anyone can say to you in that environment that doesn't
make you suspect their motivation, but when I felt this, this
presence in my guest room, it was entirely dispassionate.

Question

EVE: Sure. So I'm folding the sheets, whatever, tidying up,

and I have this very strong feeling of being watched, and
that whatever was watching me was doing so without
judgment. And for just a second my consciousness, like,
leapt into this other space, and I saw myself from behind:
folding sheets in this old summer dress I used to wear.
I saw *everything:* the way my hair looked swept up, the
strands that had fallen out of place. My tag sticking out of
the back of my dress. And then it was over, and I was back
in my own head.

Question

EVE: I wasn't afraid because I didn't know how to process it.
Like I said, it didn't feel hostile, just *there* . . . this other set
of eyes. When I looked up the word "discarnate" later, that
felt exactly right. A presence without a physical body. I felt it
for another second or two, kind of hanging behind me, and
then it went away.

Question

EVE: Not exactly.

Question

EVE: Because how would I describe it to him? Even what I just
said to you now, how scary does it actually sound? As a kid
I had these nightmares that, if I described them out loud,
would sound so benign, but they were *terrifying*. Something
about the quality of the light, an uncertainty about the laws
of physics . . .

Question

EVE: But that's why we called you, to figure this out. It felt
paranormal but not, strictly, like a ghost. Or at least not
what I thought living with a ghost would be like.

Question

EVE: I know I can't talk about the show on-camera. I'm just
trying to explain myself. As a person.

Question

EVE: Right. The second time was in our bedroom. It was a little more by the books. I was having trouble sleeping, sort of going in and out of consciousness. At one point I woke up and saw a figure at the foot of my bed. This time it looked more like a ghost: a vaguely human shape, sort of gray and shadowy. Like a shadow with . . . density.

Question

EVE: No, I didn't.

Question

EVE: I didn't wake Ryan because . . . it's complicated. I know you want me to run screaming from the house like in some slasher movie, but that isn't how I felt.

Question

EVE *(snorts)*: I'm sure he did.

Question

EVE: Look, he said that for your benefit. He loves this house. We both do. We're not selling it.

——— · ———

During their lunch break Eve had gone upstairs to slather a detoxifying mask on her face then reapply her makeup, her bathroom Bluetooth speaker wailing what Ryan thought of as her "leave me alone" mix, a playlist of female singer-songwriters that elicited snide comments from the crew. Ryan busied himself in the kitchen while she sat for more interviews, her face a little pink and shiny. He had chopped some vegetables and set a chicken on the counter, though he had not yet turned the oven on. It was too early to start making dinner—the smell of raw onions and deli meats wafted in from the living room still.

Eve walked into the kitchen and leaned into Ryan's back,

wrapping her arms around his waist and placing her cheek on his shoulder. She radiated unhappiness.

"That took a while," Ryan said, piling carrots carefully so as not to nudge Eve away.

"Sandra wanted to ask me a few more questions."

"Why?"

"I'm not giving her the story she wants."

Ryan put the knife down, swiveled to face his wife, and put her head on his shoulder. He thought of his machine in the basement. *Say it now*, he commanded himself.

Ryan exhaled. "I can't believe how many of them there are. I found two of the guys up in the bedroom, messing with the blinds. They said they were trying to get the light right for shooting, but there were drawers open and stuff on the floor."

"It's like I'm incidental to this whole thing. Like I'm here just to deliver lines they wrote for me. Is this or is this not my story? She won't let me into it."

"We still have the ghost hunters coming."

"I should have taken a nap."

"We should go to a hotel."

"God, I would love that." She slipped out of his arms. Ryan put water into the pot for rice, turned on the stove. Eve sat at the kitchen table, chin in one palm.

"No, really, Eve, let them have the house. Let them do their investigation and we can stay at the Marriott and come back in the morning not feeling like we want to kill all of them." He eyed his wife. "They could still find something when we're not here."

"We invited them. We still have four days left."

"We can rent a pay-per-view movie and get a room service breakfast."

"We can't afford any of that." Eve stood and walked over to him, looking out the window.

Ryan followed her gaze to a few members of the crew taking a smoke break in the yard, including the tall, tattooed camera guy, who made Ryan feel insecure in a way he didn't want to explore.

"This is nothing like I thought it would be."

Eve didn't reply. Sandra stuck her head in the kitchen door.

"Eve? We have time for a few more questions."

Ryan looked at his wife, who seemed not to have heard. "Give us five minutes?"

Sandra looked at Eve a long moment, then retreated.

"Babe?" he asked.

"They're taking a dinner break at six, according to the agenda." Eve scooped the carrots into a plastic tub. "We'll leave a note."

Ryan slipped an arm around her waist, pulled her to him. He kissed her deeply.

"I'm sorry I brought them here," he whispered into her hair.

But Eve didn't reply to this, either, just strode into the dining room and clipped her microphone back on, giving Sandra a smile only someone who knew her well would be wary of.

"Ronnie!" Standing outside the house, Patrick waved to the A-cam operator as the crew was piling into their vans to go to dinner. "Why don't you ride with me?"

Sandra, talking to some of the crew, gave Patrick a quizzical look. He gestured for her to climb into one of the vans and held open the passenger door of his Mini Cooper for Ronnie, who, ever the good soldier, folded himself in.

Patrick pulled out of the driveway, then realized he hadn't bothered to ask anyone where they were going, so he idled while the two vans organized themselves and started rolling. He and

Ronnie sat in silence a long moment. To Patrick the cameraman would not have looked out of place bouncing for a Manhattan club, or smashing your car window with a crowbar if you owed his boss some money. While Patrick saw this job as a stepping stone to working on a real show, he imagined that for Ronnie it was the redemptive conclusion to a roller-coaster life of abjection, truths too gritty for most people to bear. Though, logically, Patrick knew he must have some technical training. One does not simply kick the dragon and then find oneself behind a camera.

"Something you want to talk about, boss?" Ronnie asked once they had been on the road a few minutes.

"I'm not going to supervise the shoot tonight," Patrick said. "Sandra's had a tough day. I think I'll take her out for a drink. I'm leaving you in charge."

Ronnie didn't say anything. It was not uncommon for Patrick to skip out on night shoots, though he typically did not announce it ahead of time.

"Ted'll be with you, and get a couple of the PAs to stick around. I don't care which ones." In truth Patrick wasn't sure what most of the PAs' names were. "We can pay them overtime. You know the drill." But there was no "drill" on night shoots. The ghost-hunting team scouted the location and stated their preferences for which rooms they wanted to investigate. Then it was up to Patrick and a producer to arrange the setups, watch for continuity errors, assure the families that an extra take or two didn't constitute "lying." Typically there were two producers on set, but Lisa hadn't come out with them this week, a last-minute change in the scheduling of another family's story that had spread the staff a little too thin. Still, how hard could it be? "Oh, one other change: the ghost-hunting guy Alan called out, so he's not going to be on set either, just the other two."

This, Ronnie protested. "Boss, they're teenagers."

"Let them deal with it in post."

Ronnie paused. "What about the Hawthornes?"

Patrick turned his head. "What about them?"

"Shouldn't someone be there, to . . ." Ronnie searched for the word. "Oversee?"

His question didn't seem to come from a place of pure responsibility, but Patrick couldn't fathom what else might have motivated it. A desire to tick off the boxes, perhaps. Too many experiences of things gone awry.

The largest evidence Patrick had of Ronnie's checkered past was a set of tattoos, a list of dates, in script, starting in the mid-eighties and running down a bicep. People who had died, almost certainly, but there were no birth dates, no names, just the frightening regularity of an event too terrible to describe, a personal September 11 a dozen times over. The most recent was less than two years ago. Whatever the dates signified, Ronnie had outlasted. Though Patrick had no fears about an actual supernatural event taking place, he figured that during the worst that could happen—one of the kids cuts his hand, they screw up a couple of shots—Ronnie would remain coolheaded. Patrick ached, deep within himself, for an hour alone with the guy, to hear some stories. He was sure Ronnie had them.

"I trust you."

Ronnie didn't reply to that, either.

They had arrived at a diner. Patrick pulled into a space and watched the crew jump out of the vans, Sandra among them, stepping out of the front seat in her heels, adjusting her skirt with a look of annoyance. He wanted Ronnie to say something else to him, some reassurance that Patrick was making a good decision for the group as a whole.

"That it?" Ronnie asked.

"Yeah, that's it." Patrick took his keys out of the ignition. "Let's eat."

—·—

"But the results changed based on what people wanted," Caitlin insisted from the back seat, where she was checking the batteries in the tape recorders.

"How so?" Charles looked at her in the rearview mirror.

"More people guessed correctly when the pictures were kinda sexy and the people guessing were . . ."

"Kinda horny?" Charles finished for her. Caitlin reddened.

"It's called retrocausality. And it's physics!" She beamed, triumphant.

"That's not the kind of thing they teach in your average Intro to Physics class."

"Ask your professor. He'll know."

Charles didn't respond. In fact, Professor Stoughton might have been aware of the studies Caitlin referred to, discussed on the internet and rarely elsewhere. He seemed knowledgeable, tolerant. But Charles had not yet outed himself as a paranormal researcher to anyone at school.

He lifted a sheet of directions off the passenger seat. "Right on Turner," he read, "then left on Shopping Mall Lane. Do you think that's the original street name?"

"It's the big one, you know, with the Applebee's and the Sports Authority. This is real close to where the twins live."

"Jesus, that was ages ago. How do you remember how to get there?" Charles asked as they swung by an Applebee's, then a Sports Authority.

"Dunno. Just do."

The twins had been eleven or so, old enough to recognize

their function as pawns in a protracted, messy separation, not old enough to do anything about it. Monetized and fungible, why shouldn't they have lashed out at their parents by insisting on a monster in the closet? There was, to be sure, a monster in that house, probably two of them.

"They should have let us go back," Caitlin said, following Charles's line of thought. "We needed one more night."

"They didn't want us to find anything. It was some kind of latent rage in the girls. I think the parents knew it." Charles had been taking psych courses and lately found those interpretations coming to him more readily than supernatural ones. He watched his classmates streaming out of lectures, in the dining hall, in the dorms: they seemed happy enough. All things being equal, what if he could be, too? Charles had previously operated on the premise that all things weren't equal. But his fixation for the past six or so years had isolated him from his classmates at the huge state college, where football dominated the discourse. He was reluctant to share this aspect of himself, and this reluctance became the foundation for other withholdings, a neat circle of stone that went all the way around. Charles hadn't told anyone on his floor he was spending spring break ghost hunting, and he hadn't told Alan or Caitlin he was thinking about winding down this part of his life for a little while. To focus on his schoolwork, he'd say. Alan, at least, would understand.

"We got that EVP!" Caitlin leaned forward, putting her head right next to Charles's. "That sounded like a kid screaming."

"That house was old. It could have been anything."

"And houses have memory." Caitlin's studies, meanwhile, had only gotten more esoteric. She exhilarated over schools of thought that believed stone and water had "memory," could make recordings and play them back. She pushed Alan for equipment he couldn't afford that was viewed skeptically even within the community. Not yet old enough to vote, Caitlin had a reputation among some fringe types online, and Charles occasionally worried for her on behalf of her largely absent parents.

"Memories of all the hot air that's blown through them." He also loved to goad her.

Caitlin thumped back and crossed her arms over her chest. "They should have let us go back."

The van slowed in front of what surely had to be the Hawthornes' house, with the visible clutter of two rooms' worth of furniture packed into one room whose picture windows, unfortunately, faced the street. "Be that as it may," Charles said, pulling into the driveway, "every investigation is a chance to start fresh and do right by people who don't know what's going on in their homes." The lecture was more for himself than Caitlin. Anything could happen, he told himself. That was why he was here.

Caitlin threw open the van door, leaving Charles to gather the equipment while she marched up to the house and knocked.

Charles removed a soft picnic cooler from the back seat, old blankets protecting the wireless webcams and digital cameras within. The longer he'd been in the field, the less equipment Alan used: these days it was just a tape recorder and his Trifield EMF Meter reader. But the show suggested that each member of the team carry some device, and Alan acquiesced, for reasons Charles couldn't fathom. And Caitlin, for all her interest in place memory, for all the value she gave to her dreams, loved reviewing the smeary footage the next day.

"Where is everybody?" No one had come to the door.

"Maybe they went to get something to eat." Charles peered into the living room windows. He didn't see any movement.

"So, we wait?"

He plunked down on the step to the front door. "It shouldn't be long—they knew we were coming."

Caitlin sat beside him, though she had been bouncy in the back seat, dying to get out and look around. She leaned back, trying to get comfortable on the bristly welcome mat.

"Huh," she said, flipping it over to reveal a couple of keys on a ring. "Could we be any more obvious?" She stood up.

Charles grabbed her ankle. "We never enter the home without the owners present."

"Maybe they left it out for us."

"Alan would have told me."

Caitlin opened the screen door and inserted the key into the lock. "There's a first time for everything." She slipped her leg from Charles's grasp and looked inside. The house was dark. "Hello? Mr. and Mrs. Hawthorne? Is anybody home?"

Charles stood up. "Wait," he said, nearly in a panic.

"I could make a blueprint," Caitlin said, a concession.

Technically Caitlin already had too much information about the Hawthornes to make a blueprint, which should have been gathered without expectations. But the cat was away—all the cats were away—and Charles knew Caitlin would argue until he relented.

"Ten minutes," Charles said. "And if I call you, for the love of god, answer; it means someone's back."

"If you never see me again, tell my family I—"

"Yeah, yeah, yeah." He shut the door.

Caitlin paused a moment, feeling the space. She stood between the living room and what was probably the dining room, with two facing chairs and the black interview curtain against one wall. The windows were closed, though the air outside was lovely, promising a warm and fruitful spring. She took a step, and the floorboards creaked beneath her.

Caitlin walked through each room on the first floor, her hands buzzy, her heart pounding too joyously to truly listen.

She loved these cases, could barely sleep in the months between filming and when the episode finally aired. She had loved being in PIP from the moment Alan had asked her, two years ago, if she wanted to put a group together. But the show—the easy jocularity of the crew; the unstated, omnipresent audience— made everything they did more real. On TV, the investigation looked the way it always had in her mind: slightly pixelated and thrumming with anxiety. The show could take a dry investigation, a Class-C EVP, and explode the tension Caitlin knew had been there all along.

Seeing herself on TV for the first time, in her favorite green hoodie, her eyes aglow in the night-vision cameras during a Q and A, had opened in Caitlin a chasm, very wide and deep, that left her unable to go to school for two days. It was overwhelming—the secret principle she had organized her life around suddenly there for all to see. When she did go back to school—her face a little more puffed and pink than usual—she was greeted with such astonishment from her classmates, such awe at the fear on her face, in a shot in which she whipped her head around before they cut to commercial, that it sent her spinning right back to her bed. Her hobby, which before no one had bothered to ask her about except maybe the goth kids, had raised curiosity even among the jocks, the prettiest girls with long gleaming hair. Caitlin, who'd always despised the very idea of popularity, began to suspect that people who were watched lived above the rest, their feet barely skimming the ground on which everyone else plodded. The world looked brighter, sharper. Caitlin had more confidence in her readings during sessions. The "regular" cases they handled, as Caitlin came to think of them, became dry runs for filming nights, when the houses were humid with bodies, absolutely chaotic with signals.

She ended up in the pantry, eyeing a box of those chocolate

mints they used to leave with the check at restaurants. They were individually wrapped in green foil, even. The front door opened. Caitlin slipped a few mints into her pants pocket.

"What'd you get?" Charles called to her from the living room, where he was unpacking his laptop.

"Nothing." Caitlin shrugged and joined him.

"The guest room?"

"Oops." She hadn't gone upstairs at all yet. She offered Charles a mint.

"Oh, man." He took two. "I used to love these." He ate the first one. "So you got nothing? No temperature changes even?"

"What can I say? It's pretty quiet. For now," she intoned devilishly. "Want me to set up these webcams?"

"One in the basement, one in the guest room . . ."

"One in here, one in the Hawthornes' room?"

Together, they barely needed to discuss anything. Once the TV crew arrived, Charles would stiffen, second-guessing his instincts, tamping down her enthusiasm with every comment. But when it was just the two of them, they thought alike, moved with a shared purpose.

Caitlin had taken one step toward the stairs when the front door opened and two guys walked in: one of the cameramen— tall, tattooed, generally silent—and Ted the boom operator. Normally the TV crew arrived like a soccer team, shouting and jostling, but Ted closed the door quietly behind him.

The four stood a moment, looking at one another.

"The Hawthornes here?" Ted asked.

"Nobody's here," Caitlin said.

"Where's your boss?"

Caitlin started to reply, *I'm the boss*, but Charles put out a hand to stop her. "He's not going to make it tonight."

The cameraman looked at his watch.

"Patrick bounced?" Ted asked him. The cameraman nodded.

"We don't need those other guys," Caitlin said. "Charles and I have a strategy for the investigation. We're putting wireless cams in four rooms and will be conducting Q and A sessions in each. You two can follow us like you always do."

But Charles knew the crew didn't follow them; the director preceded everyone into a room, setting up shots, telling them when to begin speaking, asking them to stop and repeat themselves, throwing off the rhythm of their investigation. If these two and only these two—were here tonight, deferring to PIP, the investigation might approach something authentic, might yield evidence Charles could trust.

"We have all done this a thousand times," Charles said.

"Without the family?" Ted asked his coworker.

The cameraman shook his head. "I'm turning over three hours of footage in the morning, no matter who's in it. Just don't break anything, and we'll be fine." He stuck his hand out to Charles. "Ronnie," he said, then shook Caitlin's hand as well, as firmly as he had Charles's. Caitlin felt her face go warm.

Ted shrugged. "Give me a minute to set up."

"Me, too." Caitlin practically skipped up the stairs with the wireless cameras in hand.

The Hawthornes' bedroom was understatedly romantic. An old wrought-iron bed stood in the middle of the room, with mismatched antique nightstands on either side. Mrs. Hawthorne's was piled high with books, jewelry, scraps of paper, and tiny, fancy knickknacks. Mr. Hawthorne's was spare: just a lamp, an alarm clock, and a stale glass of water on a coaster. Mrs. Hawthorne slept on the side closer to the window, and from her place in the bed could see the backyard, the old tree. Mr. Hawthorne's side faced his boring closet, where his T-shirts were hung on hangers, his pants folded on shelves. Caitlin wondered what it would be like to share a bed with the same person night after night. If they woke up in the morning, with their bedhead and morning breath, and he turned to his wife and told her she'd never looked more beautiful. She thought of Charles's hand wrapped around her ankle, the anxiety in his eyes as she went into the house alone.

Caitlin moved a couple of bracelets to make room on Mrs. Hawthorne's nightstand for the webcam, pointed toward the door. A door slamming with no person around to push it would be spectacular. She took one last look around the room. A bird skimming by outside drew Caitlin to the window. She put her hand to the glass, and it shifted under her palm. She stepped back. Pulling the curtain aside revealed clear tape sealing a space between the glass and the old frame. She ran her finger up the tape along the side of the window, then, when she reached the top, peeled it away. It came off without protest—dust had gotten in and loosened it—taking with it a few chips of paint, leaving the glass wobbly in its slot in the frame. Air streamed in from outside. Caitlin balled up the strip of tape and shoved it down into her pocket, then moved the camera to the dresser, facing the window, making sure the curtain was dead center. She switched the motion-detecting switch to "ready" and left the room.

NIGHT 1

(Caitlin sits in the Hawthornes' living room, making notes on a pad that rests on the coffee table.)

RONNIE: We're rolling.

CHARLES *(entering frame)*: Normally we'd start on the first floor, but the space in here is a little . . . compromised.

RONNIE: It doesn't look natural.

CHARLES: My notes say the Hawthornes had activity in the dining room. Where are they?

CAITLIN *(standing)*: Can we do the flashlight?

CHARLES: You know Alan doesn't approve of the flashlight.

CAITLIN: Alan's not here! Nobody's here!

CHARLES: Okay, do the flashlight. Photograph orbs and vortexes, too. Let's ignore all the rigorous approaches devised over the years and revert to the silliest, most easily disproven.

CAITLIN: God, when did college make you so boring?

(Ted chuckles off-screen.)

CHARLES: Can we start?

CAITLIN *(peering at laptop screen on the coffee table)*: Hey, check this out.

CHARLES: What is it?

CAITLIN: Looks like curtains moving in the master bed. Maybe we should start there?

CHARLES: You get started. I'll join you in a minute.

CAITLIN *(taking the stairs two at a time, singing on her way up)*: I'm bringing the flashliiiight!

Magnetic Tape #HAW-08-04-1,
courtesy Paranormal Investigators of Pennsylvania

CAITLIN: It is April —. We are in the master bedroom of the Hawthorne home in Ninebark, Pennsylvania. My name is Caitlin. I am joined by Ted and Ronald.

RONNIE: Ronnie.

CAITLIN: Ronnie. We are not here to hurt you. We want to get to know you. Can you tell us your name?

(Twenty-second pause)

CAITLIN: Are you a former occupant of this house?

(Twenty-second pause)

CAITLIN: Do you have a message for the Hawthornes?

(Twenty-second pause)

CAITLIN: I'm going to put this flashlight down on the floor. If you can, please turn it on, to let us know that you are here.

(Thirty-second pause)

CAITLIN: I made the request, but the flashlight did not change its state. You can come in.

TED: I think you guys have this covered. Maybe I'll go back downstairs.

RONNIE: We didn't mike the kids.

TED: *(curses indistinguishably)*

CAITLIN: Please, watch your language. We don't want to offend the spirits. Spirits, Ted is friendly and apologizes for his comment.

TED: My bad.

CAITLIN: Is there something you would like us to know?

(Twenty-second pause)

CAITLIN: You guys are real patient.

(Pause)

RONNIE: Who, us?

CAITLIN: Yeah, you're just standing there, waiting. Why don't you come in?

RONNIE: I'm not gonna sit on the floor with you, kid.

CAITLIN: Ted?

TED: I'm good.

CAITLIN: How long has it been?

RONNIE: Since we came upstairs? About . . . seven minutes.

CAITLIN: I'm supposed to stay here for thirty. I thought Charles would come with me. It creeps me out that you're both just standing over me like that.

TED: You're trying to have a conversation with a ghost, and we're creeping you out?

CAITLIN: You're just standing there, not doing anything.

RONNIE: We're doing our job.

(Pause)

CAITLIN: Let's get Charles and go into the guest room. That's where Alan said there was activity.

(Break in recording)

Magnetic Tape #HAW-08-04-XXX, courtesy Paranormal Investigators of Pennsylvania

CHARLES: It is April —. I am in the basement of the Hawthornes' home in Ninebark. It is approximately nine fifty p.m. I am alone, for the moment. Am I alone? Is anyone with me tonight?

(Thirty-second pause)

CHARLES: Can you tell me your name?

(Twenty-second pause)

CHARLES: Are you a previous resident of this house?

(Thirty-second pause)

CHARLES: Maybe I should ask: Are you a current resident of
this house?

(Thirty-second pause)

CHARLES: Are you having trouble passing between the worlds?

(Thirty-second pause)

CHARLES: Or maybe you *want* to stick around here.

(Longer pause)

CHARLES: What are you looking for here? Why don't you move
on? Do you have a choice?

(Ten-second pause)

CHARLES: It's not too late, right? You can, if you decide to,
choose something else?

(Thirty-second pause)

CHARLES: Tell me someone is here. Tell me I'm not talking
to myself in a dirty basement, no different than any other
Monday night.

(Very long pause)

CHARLES: Tell me what you've learned, where you are. Give me
one word. Is there one word that you wished you'd heard at
my age, that would have brought it all into focus?

(Caitlin's voice, far away but distinct, can be heard on the tape.)

CAITLIN: Charles! Want to do the guest room?

CHARLES *(quietly)*: Fuck. I fucked this up. *(louder)* There in
a sec!

(Tape ends.)

Transcript: SIW-221a-8/CAMERA A, 22:25:03

*(Charles and Caitlin are in frame. Caitlin is sitting on the
bed, Charles in the desk chair. There is a small hand-held
tape recorder on the bed beside Caitlin. She sets a flashlight
on the floor. Charles holds an EMF reader. Ted stands in the*

*doorway and can occasionally be seen stepping into the room,
at the edge of the frame, then out of it.)*

CHARLES: Did you try that thing in the bedroom?

CAITLIN: I told you I would.

CHARLES: Did you get anything?

CAITLIN: Nah.

CHARLES: I'm running the Q and A.

CAITLIN: Fine by me. Gentlemen, you might want to make
sure you get this in your shot, in case something amazing
happens.

(She bends over the flashlight, unscrewing the back slightly.)

CHARLES: Are we ready?

CAITLIN: One . . . sec. Okay, ready.

(The flashlight is off.)

CHARLES: We are in the guest room at the Hawthornes' house.
It is ten twenty-seven p.m.

CAITLIN: Oops. I forgot the time stamp earlier. See, this is why
I need you with me.

CHARLES: My name is Charles, with me tonight are Caitlin,
Ronnie, and Ted. Is anyone else present with us tonight?
*(Twenty-second pause. Caitlin stares at the flashlight on the
floor, and Charles occasionally glances at it as well.)*

CHARLES: What is your name?
(Twenty-second pause)

CHARLES: Are you a former occupant of this house?
(Twenty-second pause)

CHARLES: Do you know the Hawthornes?
(Twenty-second pause)

CAITLIN: Charles?

CHARLES: Go ahead.

CAITLIN: There is a flashlight on the floor. If you can, please
touch it to let us know you are here.

(Thirty-second pause while everyone stares at the flashlight)

CHARLES: Do you have a message for the Hawthornes?

(Flashlight flickers.)

CAITLIN: Did you see that?

CHARLES: I had an EMF spike, too.

CAITLIN: Do you want the Hawthornes to leave this house?

CHARLES: Negatory, Caitlin.

(Flashlight blinks, on and then off.)

CAITLIN: Why do you want the Hawthornes to leave?

CHARLES: Caitlin, stop it.

(The flashlight blinks several times, then rolls an inch toward the door. A rumbling, like distant thunder, can just be detected.)

TED: Holy . . .

CHARLES: Are you in pain?

(Twenty-second pause, the rumbling intensifies.)

CHARLES *(voice rising)*: Is there anything we can do to help?

(Twenty-second pause)

CHARLES: Can you tell us anything about yourself?

(Thirty-second pause, in which the background noise lessens)

CHARLES: It went away?

CAITLIN: I'm not feeling anything.

CHARLES: You could try not to rile it, you know.

CAITLIN: It responded, didn't it?

CHARLES: Caitlin . . .

CAITLIN: Evidence is evidence.

CHARLES: That's not what we—

CAITLIN: What if right as that flashlight rolled we got an EVP that said "Get out" or something?

CHARLES: That's so entirely—

TED: Folks?

(The flashlight is blinking, on-off on-off on-off, though no one is touching it, and wobbling back and forth.)

CAITLIN: Are you getting anything?

CHARLES: A little. It's weird because—

> *(His words are cut off by a banging: WHOOMP WHOOMP WHOOMP.)*

CHARLES: What the hell—

TED: Where is that coming from?

CAITLIN: Sounds like the back of the—

> *(Caitlin stands and the camera follows her out of the bedroom and down the stairs. Rest of footage is indistinguishable jiggling.)*

CAITLIN: Where is the—

?:—sounds like—

> *WHOOMP*

TED: —inside the—

CHARLES: —get to—

> *WHOOMP*
>
> *(Tape ends.)*

COMING UP:

EVE *(interview footage)*: Nothing on this scale has ever happened before.

MADAME MANDAYA *(interview footage)*: We are dealing with energies and forces much stronger than we thought.

VOICEOVER: For the second night in a row, the Hawthornes host an uninvited visitor.

CAITLIN *(investigation footage)*: If there are any spirits here with us tonight, please give us a sign.

EVP *(subtitled)*: *Here.*

VOICEOVER: Eve and Ryan may be in danger . . .

EVE *(investigation footage)*: Why me? What do you want from me?

VOICEOVER: . . . but nobody's safe in Ninebark.

CAITLIN *(investigation footage)*: What the—
(The camera bounces and cuts out.)

VOICEOVER: Next, on *Searching for . . . the Invisible World.*

DAY 2

INTERVIEW—CHARLES

Question

CHARLES: You ask that as if I've slept.

Question

CHARLES: Look, let's get one thing clear. We have a fundamentally different idea about what constitutes a haunting. What am I basing this on? I'm basing it on what evidence you choose to present, what you ignore, and what you *invent*. There, I said it. I don't know how you decide what's legitimate and what isn't. You decide with plenty of confidence, though.

Question

CHARLES: What I'm saying is, you've never shown any sense of responsibility for me, for Caitlin, for the expertise or reputation of our group. So it's a little rich that now you want us to be responsible for someone on *your* team.

——— · ———

The morning hammered on Sandra's skull with the insistence of a high school health teacher on the topic of responsible drinking. She swallowed with some difficulty and leaned across the bed to silence a jangling, her body moving in ways her brain hadn't caught up to yet.

"Hello."

"Sandra, good morning."

"Alan?" For a moment Sandra wasn't sure where she was, why Alan was calling. Her brain scanned through several possible reasons, only the last having to do with work.

"I'm glad I caught you. I wanted to apologize. I'm kicking myself for having missed what happened last night. This is way more than we thought going in. There's a malevolent spirit attached to that house, maybe even a poltergeist. I'm bringing a psychic with me today to see if she can make contact with it, and I'm calling every volunteer we've ever had to see who can come out with the works: cameras, lenses, tape recorders, EMF detectors, night vision; we'll put a three-hundred-and-sixty-degree perimeter monitor in effect and devices in every room of the house."

"Alan, slow down. What happened last night?" Phone pressed against her ear, Sandra buried herself deeper under the comforter, closed her eyes, and tried to will her body into alertness.

After dinner, Patrick had generously given Sandra the night off, oblivious to the fact that there was no other producer on-site for the shoot. But Sandra decided not to point this out, and to accept Patrick's offer of a drink at Winebark, where one gin and tonic had turned into four, and that was before the karaoke started. Sandra hadn't sung karaoke in she didn't know how long, but if she had to guess, she would say the little TV they rolled out with a mic on top was God's present to her for having made it through the day. Out here, in some town she'd never visit again, she wasn't afraid to belt out the standards from her youth: REO Speedwagon, Joan Jett, and a run of three Genesis songs once the locals had started to drift back to their cars. Shots had been ordered, and Sandra didn't remember Patrick singing anything, although he did match her drink for drink and always had a fresh one waiting for her when she came down from the little platform that served as a stage.

"That's what we're trying to figure out. The readings my team got weren't so great. They didn't set them up in the most optimal locations, but I promise you that tonight I will be there and I will monitor every step."

Sandra sat up, one piece of information meeting its target. "We don't have another investigation scheduled for tonight."

Alan took a breath. "But you can schedule one?"

"It doesn't work that way. My team worked a very long day yesterday. Day two is always lighter: a couple of interviews recapping the investigation, some research into the history of the house." Then Sandra would call her editors in New York and give everyone a good night's sleep. "Your team reviews what you captured and makes suggestions for what might be the source. Day three or four, even, we can do another night shoot, assuming the family gives us permission. What does Eve think?"

"I don't think she knows about it yet."

"She wasn't there?"

"According to Caitlin and Charles, it was just my two and two of your guys—Ronnie and Ted."

"Alan, I need to call you back." Sandra was awake enough for the headache to emerge in full now, threatening to swell up and absorb the questions that arose from Alan's call. Squinting one eye—the most glare from her cell phone screen she could take—she scrolled through the crew's names in her contact list. Ronnie's phone went straight to voice mail. Ted was too smug; she wasn't ready for that yet.

Sandra flopped back, accepted the reality of the clock: nine forty-five. She should have been at the Hawthornes' at nine. She had slept through the alarm, or failed to set it. Her face and hair were greasy, like the fries that had been her only dinner. She couldn't entirely remember how she had gotten back to the hotel. She had an image of Patrick leaning across the bar to flirt with the bartender, waving her on as he so often did on shoots: *You got this.* On the bedside table, next to the alarm clock, Patrick's keys.

If she got up now she could be at the Hawthornes' in twenty minutes. Once she was in Patrick's car, she took a chance with one more call.

"Sandra!" Eve sounded well rested. In the rearview mirror, Sandra poked under her eyes. "This is quite a scene over here. I never expected . . . Caitlin and Charles told me a bit about what happened last night." She sounded like she'd won some sort of prize, the supernatural sweepstakes.

Sandra turned on the car. She tilted the AC vents and angled her armpits directly in the streams of cold air. "We can discuss this more when I get to your house, but I wanted to let you know that Alan Purvis is recommending a second investigation tonight with the paranormal team. It's not in your contract, so really—"

"It's fine. Ryan and I weren't even here last night, it didn't disrupt us at all."

Sandra pulled lipstick out of her bag, sitting up to apply it in the rearview mirror. "I have to urge you to discuss it with your husband first. When we plan the pacing of the week and the intensity of each day, we have at heart the best interests of—"

"And I'm telling you we want to do it. This feels too important not to follow up on, right?" Sandra didn't reply. "To be honest, I felt a little guilty slipping out last night"—she didn't sound the least bit guilty—"so I'm happy to be here and see the magic happen." Her voice dropped suggestively, in a way that no doubt had bewitched her husband not so long ago. But it threw Sandra—it implied that the show had *done* something, not merely captured evidence of activity that Eve was already familiar with.

As presentable as she was going to get, Sandra shifted Patrick's car out of park. There was background chatter coming through the phone, and Sandra couldn't make out who asked Eve what, only her upbeat "Hmm?" followed by, "Sandra?"

"I'll be there soon," Sandra said, hanging up and tossing her cell onto the passenger seat. She focused on the road. She needed coffee, a shower, and ideally thirty minutes in a diner to grill Ronnie and Ted. Whatever had happened last night, her crew's explanation would be the one she could trust . . . even as her mind wandered to the thought of breakfast with Alan instead, huge plates of French toast in front of them as he narrated to her, eyes shining. She extinguished the thought, switching into work mode. The closer she got to the Hawthornes', the more her headache receded, replaced by a list of tasks—the more mundane, the better.

INTERVIEW—CHARLES

CHARLES: We're all up in the guest room with the tape
    recorder. Plus a flashlight, which I haven't told Alan about
    yet, though I'm sure you'll want to use that footage.
    Question
CHARLES: Caitlin pushed for it. I think it's cheesy. I'm sure
    your audience will eat it up, though.
    Question
CHARLES: It's not . . . as far as our investigations go, it's not a
    form of evidence we can admit, because there's no guarantee

it was a discarnate manipulating it. Slight vibrations in the floor might be enough, and a moment after the flashlight started blinking, the whole house shook.

Que—

CHARLES: This is the first investigation I've done without Alan, I should say, so I can't promise that all my decisions were perfectly sound. Sorry to interrupt you.

Question

CHARLES: Like a really big stick or bat or something being whacked against the side of the house. WHUMP WHUMP WHUMP WHUMP WHUMP WHUMP WHUMP.

Question

CHARLES: We looked out the window, but we didn't see anything. It was pitch-black out there.

Question

CHARLES: I'd say approximately ten fifty, eleven p.m.

Question

CHARLES: It was different in that most of the time on the first night of an investigation we capture very little. We use a couple devices at various points around the house, hoping to pinpoint something for follow-up. But we're never sure what to expect.

Question

CHARLES: We always start with a person's intuition, but feelings can't be recorded. Film and magnetic tape, though mechanical, are sensitive. Alan would say there are things human eyes don't want to see, things human ears don't *want* to hear. The tape is impartial. Which is what's so weird about what happened last night. No one who was in this house would deny that something happened, but our tape's a mess.

Question

CHARLES: WHUMP WHUMP WHUMP WHUMP
WHUMP WHUMP WHUMP.

Question

CHARLES: We took the investigation outside, to see if we could
locate the source of the sound. Although, to be honest with
you, I was pissing myself. Apparently they've never heard of
streetlights in Ninebark. We went back inside and waited,
staked out in different parts of the house with recorders,
seeing if it would come back.

Question

CHARLES: Your guy Ronnie stepped out around midnight.
It didn't seem like anything else was going to happen. He
said he was going to get some footage outside the house. I
couldn't believe he went out there alone.

Question

CHARLES: You don't have to use the line, I'm just telling you as
a person.

Question

CHARLES: I was frightened. We all were. It was louder and
more threatening than anything I've ever experienced. And
there's nothing on the tape to back it up. No proof. Just
static. *(Charles's head pitches forward, off-screen, and rests in
his hands, his voice muffled.)* Any other questions?

———— · ————

"Is that the last of the coffee?"
   "Taste this. What is it, pumpkin?"
   "I can't find a goddamn free outlet to save my life."
   "I think it's nutmeg."

"Unplug that guy over there."

To whom does a haunted house belong? Following Alan's strict instructions, Caitlin had locked the door and left the spare key under the mat when she and Charles left shortly before dawn to get a few hours' sleep before reviewing the evidence. When Alan arrived around nine, he was swept up by the crew piling out of their vans, streaming into the house and bustling about their routine, oblivious to the Hawthornes lurking at their edges.

"Do NOT unplug that one. Here, unplug this one."

"Nobody makes nutmeg bagels. It's gotta be pumpkin."

"Doughnuts, gentlemen?"

Alan Purvis, founder of the Paranormal Investigators of Pennsylvania, and possessed by the guiltiest conscience east of the Mississippi, elbowed into their midst bearing two pallets of chocolate, glazed, and Boston cream for the crew. He placed them on the kitchen table, and the sun was momentarily blocked by the swarm.

Thanks to a relationship between PIP and Roving Eye Productions, *Searching for . . . the Invisible World*, although technically based out of New York City, frequently shot in Pennsylvania. Without knowing that background, however, viewers of the show could easily come to believe that the secret history of Pennsylvania was rife with shady doctors performing black magic after hours; midnight coven meetings in any clearing in the woods; amateur scientists conducting medical experiments on chimps in basement labs; disfigured pariahs licking their chops on the edge of town just waiting for a child to stray; abandoned mental asylums and crumbling prisons that could never, for whatever reason, be razed; each turnpike exit between Philadelphia and Pittsburgh a veritable gateway to another dimension.

Alan wandered the first floor of the house looking for Sandra, then retreated to his car without introducing himself to Eve, who continued to eavesdrop.

"Did you hear about Jessie?"

"Like a rat leaving the ship."

"He's not that prescient. He got a job on McMurphy's new project, the lucky bastard."

"That's the kind of show I want to work on."

"Good luck. You think your old pal Jessie will bring you on? He's probably already changed his number."

"I got a friend worked on McMurphy's last show, the one about the time-traveling accountant."

"Actuary."

"Who cares? Point is, there's none of this traveling crap. Spending half my life on the turnpike, the other half in these podunk—"

"*Hmm-hm.*" Ted cleared his throat, unsubtly indicating Eve, curled over a mug of coffee by the stove.

"Good morning, Ted. Have a doughnut. They're vegan."

"I'm sure that's not—"

"We heard Patrick bailed, and yet you showed up anyway."

"Awfully responsible of you, Ted. Too bad it's too late to ask for a raise."

Everyone chewed in silence for a long moment.

"Wonder if we're shooting outside tonight."

"Remember that other one we filmed outside, those people who lived next door to the cemetery? That sucked."

"It was so fucking cold."

"When was that, like two years ago now?"

"That was six months ago."

"Man, time moves so slowly sometimes."

"That's because you're young. Pretty soon, time will start moving the other way. Then you'll have something to complain about."

"Behold, the ravages of age."

"Have another doughnut, kid. While your metabolism can handle it."

The chatter quieted as Sandra entered, her hair frizzy and her eyes sunken. She glanced at the doughnuts, then her eyes lit on the coffee, not the fancy stuff from yesterday but a big box from a franchise.

"Is Alan here?" She eschewed niceties, as usual.

One of the PAs said, "He brought all this."

Sandra didn't seem to register the information. "Eve?"

Eve stepped forward, and Sandra turned to her.

"You put us in a bad position last night by leaving the site during filming."

"I might say the same to you." A flush climbed Eve's neck, staining her cheeks. "Apparently two members of your crew and a couple of teenagers were the only ones here."

Said crew dissolved into the walls. Sandra opened her mouth to reply, but Eve wasn't done.

"This is a little overwhelming for Ryan and I. We needed space." And why didn't Sandra sympathize? Normally she would have at least pretended to. "I know it was a bad decision, and we're prepared to follow your schedule from here on out. But this is my home, it's my . . ." Eve's what—her haunting? Her decision to bestow it, or not, upon the world? So many of these families thought of their experiences as accidents of real estate, tragedies that brushed the sides of their faces before gliding away, disrupting family dinners just long enough to mutate into stories they'd retell for decades. They didn't look inward, even as Sandra believed more and more that their hauntings were projections, disfigured manifestations of their traumas and secrets. Eve wasn't like them. Whatever doubts someone might have had about Eve's experiences, Eve herself had had, and sat with, and emerged surer than ever. And that awoke something in Sandra—a previously dormant antenna began extending outward. But Eve shook her head and left the room without finishing her sentence. Sandra looked around, remembered her coffee on the table. She refilled her cup. She wondered if anyone could see her hands shaking.

"Ted, Ronnie? Can I talk to you guys for a sec?"

Ted rematerialized from just outside the kitchen. "Ronnie's not here."

Sandra looked at the wall clock, which seemed to have stopped. "Where is he? Where's Patrick?"

Ted cleared his throat. "Um, Sandra? I think we should talk."

———·———

Transcript: SIW-221a-10/CAMERA A, 11:30:22

INTERVIEW—CAITLIN

CAITLIN: There are two major categories of hauntings—intelligent and residual. Residual is your classic ghost, a spirit trapped on this plane. It can't do much, and what it does, it does over and over again until you release it.
Question
CAITLIN: Exactly. A residual haunting is a recording. It's the DVR of the afterlife.
Question
CAITLIN: Intelligent hauntings are way more interesting. That's when the spirit can interact with you—respond to your questions, move stuff around, et cetera. Like a poltergeist.

Question

CAITLIN: You better believe it. The Hawthornes' haunting is definitely intelligent.

Question

CAITLIN: Because the Hawthornes haven't experienced anything like this before, that's how I know. It's responding to this particular situation.

Question

CAITLIN: In a sentence? I think what happened last night is a direct consequence of all of us being here. Me, you—it wants all of our attention.

Question

CAITLIN: Yeah, but this is really special. I can say it in a different way if you want, but just take a second to think about how awesome this is. It knows we're here, and it *wants* to be seen. That's huge.

———— · ————

"What is this?" Sandra scanned through the footage. On the dining room chair beside her, Ted watched her face while she looked at the laptop.

"That's the last of it."

"The last of *what*?" Sandra couldn't soften the edge in her voice, her irritation at needing everything explained to her. She hadn't done anything wrong, she reminded herself—Patrick had—yet every hour of this morning she felt as if she were being punished.

"The last of Ronnie's footage." It showed the living room, Caitlin and Charles on the couch, tape recorders in hand. They looked around them. Occasionally they asked a question. Sandra jumped the footage ahead: at one point Caitlin was lying on the floor, tape recorder on her stomach rising and falling with her breath, and Charles had his feet up on the coffee table. "We were waiting to see if anything happened again. And then, when we only had about twenty minutes left in our shift, Ronnie swapped in a new memory card and said he was going outside to shoot B-roll."

"In the middle of the night?" Sandra rubbed her face. "You two could have shot some interviews—"

"We couldn't have. We didn't have any questions. No one was here." Ted's voice rose, an edge of boyish panic. And what did he have to be afraid of?

"Okay, so Ronnie said he was going to shoot B-roll. Then what?"

"That's it. He never came back. I stayed inside and started packing up my gear. At one a.m. I called him and he didn't pick up. So I left."

"He went back to the hotel without you."

Ted shook his head. "The van was here. I drove it back myself."

"He called a cab."

"Maybe." Ted waited.

"What else could it be?"

"Have you been able to reach him today? I've called him at least seven times."

"Ted, it wasn't . . ."

"I'm not saying it was."

But it was what he was implying. Sandra's most vivid memory of Ronnie was one Friday night at the bar following a shoot in upstate New York. After much prodding by younger members of the crew who had heard it before, Ronnie told a story about having been carjacked by a couple of junkies, forced to drive them around for hours and then pay for their drugs once they'd located their dealer. The crew was in stitches at the thought of a couple of skinny junkies picking the first car that looked promising and finding it belonged to a lumberjack like Ronnie—inked skull with glowing eyes on the back of his neck—but going through with it anyway. Ronnie dryly concluded the story by saying it was not the worst thing that had happened to him. No one doubted that. A man of Ronnie's mien did not walk off into the haunted suburbs, never to be seen again. He took a cab back to the hotel. His phone died on the way. He was sleeping it off as they spoke. And in the meantime, the footage was terrible: boring, monotonous, Eve and Ryan absent from every shot. If they were going to incorporate it into the episode they would need to intercut it with whatever they could get from PIP. She was about to tell Ted as much when Alan entered the house, giving Sandra a cautious wave.

"Alan, wait," she said, before he went down the hall. The teenagers trailed behind him, eyeing her on their way to the kitchen. The house was crowded, floorboards creaking under the constant stream of traffic in and out the front door. "Ted, talk to Charles about what they got. Maybe we can zip it and send it back to Cameron this afternoon."

Alan gave a friendly nod as Ted left but remained standing just outside the dining room. He looked different in the day, fresh. Sandra was used to seeing Alan after nine p.m., when, with a five-o'clock shadow, his graying blond hair ruffled and shirt untucked, he looked like a weary archeologist from the movies. First thing in the morning he looked too groomed, shiny, with comb tracks in his still-damp hair. He looked like any other man on the subway, albeit a little shorter than average. He still made her heart thump. She wondered if he had any idea.

"How are you?" she asked, waving him in.

"I'm good, yeah. It's nice to see you," he said, and she wasn't sure how to read it: if he was being courteous, or if he meant it.

"It's been a few months," she said, trying to recall the last episode they worked on together. A family with a bar in the basement, barstools being pushed around by invisible hands. Or was it the kid who claimed his dead grandmother was sitting at the foot of his bed, telling him about things that hadn't happened yet, that he couldn't possibly know? After a while, they sort of ran together.

"I'm sorry I wasn't here last night. I didn't anticipate—"

"None of us could have," she reassured him. "But I'm not sure whether we can use it in the episode." Alan's eyes widened. "The couple wasn't here. The footage my team got is terrible. What did your team pick up?" She laughed once. "Save us, Alan."

Alan shook his head. "I've only heard what they told me, I haven't seen anything yet."

Sandra patted the seat Ted had vacated. She hit play on her laptop and perched it between them, her thigh flanking Alan's, creating a line of heat. It was too easy to imagine them sitting side by side like this somewhere else: a darkened movie theater, almost empty, the other patrons far enough away to give them the space they needed, the demands of her job a distant memory. Alan's hand brushed hers as she reached for the play button, and he apologized unnecessarily, shifting his eyes back to the screen.

But the movie they were watching was so dull: Caitlin sitting cross-legged on the floor in the Hawthornes' bedroom, talking in the direction of a tape recorder in front of her, looking around the room between questions. She fidgeted, glanced at the camera too often, played with the many bracelets on her wrist. Sandra wished for some *thing* to fill those spaces—a disembodied growl, for example, instantly translating into terror on the girl's face, instead of this semi-boredom.

After a few minutes Caitlin's gestures indicated she was finished, and Ronnie switched his camera off. When he started rolling again, Caitlin and Charles were sitting in the guest room, framed slightly better, though still just sitting. If Sandra had been there, or Patrick, they would have encouraged the kids to move through the house more. Ronnie hadn't even bothered to capture them transitioning from one room to the other, something they could have used to make it look like these investigations consisted of actively *investigating*, rather than sitting around, waiting for ghosts to show up.

Alan was leaning forward, though, one trimmed fingernail extended toward the screen.

"Caitlin," he muttered. Sandra leaned over to see what he was pointing to. There appeared to be a flashlight on the floor, turned off. While Sandra was looking at it, trying to figure out why it upset Alan, it blinked. Sandra gasped.

"I didn't notice that. What does it mean?"

Alan shook his head. "Any number of things could set it off."

On-screen Charles and Caitlin appeared to be having an argument. To Sandra's annoyance, Ted's voice could just be discerned when the flashlight started blinking rapidly. Sandra turned the sound on the laptop as high as it would go, and Alan leaned in further, his cheek an inch from the screen. He jumped back at the banging, a beanstalk giant clomping to open a fairy-tale castle door. The camera shook and exited the room after the kids, which was a decision Sandra would have made, too, if the clatter of shoes on the stairs didn't all but drown out the noise they were chasing. Once on the first floor Ronnie's camera swung around the living room while Charles and Caitlin stood between the living and dining rooms, looking at each other and around them. For the next two minutes, nothing happened: Caitlin and Charles breathed, scanned the area. Ronnie's camera panned back and forth, letting the workings of the show—the interview setup in the dining room, extra furniture jammed into the living room—occasionally into the frame. And then, for no discernible reason, the tape ended.

Sandra let Alan consider the footage. The front door opened and Patrick entered, sheepish, relieved to see her there. Sandra shot him a look and he recoiled, reached for his phone. She wondered what he'd heard, if the desperation he exuded was to find out what had gone on in his absence, or to take his mind off the mistake he'd gone home with the night before.

"What do you think?" she asked, loud enough to both acknowledge Patrick and discourage him from drifting any closer.

Alan shook his head. "It's extraordinary." He gestured for her to rewind to the moment when it started, Ted at the edge of the frame as Charles and Caitlin argue, then duck reflexively at the noise.

"The sound is lousy. Ted should be ashamed."

"It's drastically atypical." Alan sat back, running his hands over his scalp. When he pulled them away, his hair was sticking up in places, betraying his use of some product, a vanity she wouldn't have guessed of him. "We don't see things like this . . . I never see things like this." It was when he was least composed that Sandra liked Alan the most, when his thoughts came out in fragments only she heard. He would give her the sound bite in interviews, but off-screen, between takes, his raw thoughts were a door she wanted to walk through, a room she wanted to poke around in. "We think of presences trapped in the house, or ones that come with the owners. This is coming from outside the house and appears to want to get in. Who wants that?"

"Eve has already told us like six different stories on-camera. We have to be able to connect it to something she's said. Otherwise, we scrap it." Sandra's days were already spent balancing the wants of too many: homeowners, editors, sponsors. All she needed was the undead demanding a say.

"We can't determine whether or not it is connected to them from this one incident. It may not be that simple."

It needed to be, though. No one back in New York was eager to rework the Hawthornes' story, nor, did Sandra find, would they much need to.

In college, on a whim, Sandra had taken a 3D art class. They did a unit on stained glass and Sandra was astonished at how thinly you could score a sheet of glass for it to break along the lines you had drawn. Couples arrived to reality TV production pre-scored: all scenarios could fit the standard episode outline with minimal fuss. She needed only press her thumb to the weakness and watch the parts split.

"Alan," she tried to sound apologetic, "last night was so far off protocol. I could get in a lot of trouble for it."

Alan nodded. "Once I review our evidence, I'll be in a better position to make a recommendation for what to do next." He looked sad, and for a half second Sandra's heart ached at the thought that she had disappointed him.

She spoke quietly. "I know if we weren't here, it would be different." She was not supposed to admit that to anyone who appeared on the show. "You'd have more freedom to conduct your investigation as you see fit."

Alan shrugged. "If we didn't have the show, we wouldn't have the exposure, either. I'm not sure PIP would still be around without it." He smiled ruefully. "A haunted house wouldn't be haunted without the living there to notice, even if it seems to drive the living away." It wasn't unkind of him to say, but it left Sandra to wonder: Of the two of them, who was the living? Who the ghost?

—— · ——

Ryan found Eve in the backyard, sitting in one of the Adirondack chairs, a paper cup of coffee gone cold on the arm. Ryan placed a fresh mug, hot, beside her elbow and kissed the top of her head.

"Thank you," she said, staring ahead of her. The backyard was Ryan's favorite part of the property. Although the yard was not especially large, the rough wooden fence that delineated it could easily be overlooked, and beyond it lay a swath of some old farm gone to seed, bordered at its far end by a line of poplars. It was nice to sit out here in the mornings, surveying the acres and pretending to be master of all within sight.

"Pretty crazy, huh?" Ryan said, sliding into the chair beside her. "What do you think happened last night?"

Eve shook her head, still not looking at him.

"Everybody is talking about it nonstop. This might be their scariest episode." He sipped his coffee. "Too bad we didn't get to see it."

Eve snorted. Skeptical of what, Ryan had no idea. The story Ryan had told Eve, back when they started dating, was less dramatic than hers: childhood basement gave him the creeps. No one ever wanted to go down there, including his parents. What was up with that? After they'd moved out to a bigger place, his mom told him that the previous occupant of the house died in the basement. Killed herself after her baby died. They found her swinging from the rafters.

"Jesus," Eve had said. "She told you that? Just sat you down and said, 'It's time you knew'?"

"No, it wasn't like . . . it wasn't like that." Ryan had paused, gazing into the past. He had read once about when people are lying: Do they glance to the right, or to the left? What if you're left-handed, is it the opposite? Ryan wasn't, but Eve had a painting called *Left-Handed Devil*, a slash of red in a terrain of rocky black, a lick of fire coming out of a cave. She was waiting for an explanation.

"I must have asked her about it. Maybe we were playing in the basement in the new house, and I asked about the old one."

"Why did your parents buy the house, if they knew?"

Ryan had shrugged. "It was probably cheap." His father loved a bargain, bought soap on sale whether they needed it or not, until the stacks of Irish Spring reached eighteen bars, a new one ready the moment the old had melted away.

"It was *cheap*?"

"No, we . . . we didn't know right away. We were living there a few years. And then a neighbor told my parents what happened."

"And then you moved out."

"Not right away." Ryan began to feel uncomfortable, felt as if he were betraying his childhood home, which had given him and his brothers years of good times.

Eve had leaned toward him. "How long did you stay after you found out?" Something in her eyes, some need, unsettled him. "Were they afraid?"

"It was just a story. They told me a story that somebody had told them." He'd tried not to sound annoyed. Eve had shared with him, and now they were even. He wanted to move on. Allison had accused him of withholding, right around when he found out she was sleeping with another man, a personal trainer they'd seen in a regional production of *Barefoot in the Park*. They'd run into him in a local pub a week after the performance, and Allison gushed. Ryan guessed that's when the affair had started. Six months later, in what would be the final weeks of their marriage, she had provided him with a laundry list of his faults, accumulated practically since they'd first met.

"I'm just glad," Ryan said now, trying to share his feelings, "that the show was able to capture what we're going through. Maybe they can help us get rid of it."

Eve turned to him, her eyes two gray stones.

"This is *not* what we're going through."

Ryan's heart pounded. "Then what is it?"

Her voice rose. "It's like if it doesn't happen their way, it didn't happen at all. Sandra told me she doesn't think they can use it in the episode, because we weren't here." Eve ground the heels of her hands into her eye sockets. "Am I crazy? Why doesn't anyone . . . ?"

"You're not crazy." Ryan reached over to take her hand and squeeze it. Later he'd understood all of those things Allison had said were her justifying her actions to herself. At least, that's what Eve had told him, and he wanted to believe her. But he also found himself from time to time saying something or doing something from Allison's list, then searching Eve's face for whether he'd done wrong. Did he not share enough, express his own preferences often enough, did he assume she could read his mind? Eve never mentioned it. If she kept her own list, it was a mystery to him. "Maybe it'll happen again tonight,"

Eve shook her head, her lips pressed together. Ryan sensed that it would be a mistake to tell her about his stereo right now.

He thought of the day they'd signed the papers on the house. Eve had walked the empty rooms, a hand lightly brushing the walls. He'd assured her that it had no secrets.

"It's old," she'd said. "Who knows what might have happened here." She said it not with reservation, but with an uptick in her voice, and Ryan, for the first time since he'd met her, felt a bubble of fear in his gut. But then Eve pushed her body against him, her mouth on his, her hand already at his belt. They fucked right there on the floor, and he quashed his alarm, trying not to think that he was doing exactly what Allison had chided him for. He told himself, *This is different, it will be different, everything is going to be fine.*

————•—•————

Caitlin watched Charles unplug and pack the equipment a little too angrily. Caitlin knew she should offer to grab the rest of the webcams, to finish the packing up they'd put off at the end of the night, but she still felt faintly blasted from the event, an investigative hangover. It was not an uncommon sensation for her.

And, in fact, she sought out these nights the way so many of her classmates sought out parties with alcohol. Her squirming fascination with the macabre began with a collection of fairy tales, decidedly not the Disney versions, obtained at a yard sale when she was nine. The Grimm book was eye-opening, a peek at another world behind the colorful cartoons. This world revealed itself further with the arrival, as if from Destiny herself, of the Time-Life Books series Mysteries of the Unknown, which came at the tail end of one of her father's whims, to become a DIY master. The Home Repair and Improvement series, ordered via 1-800 number one night when he'd had too much to drink, arrived dutifully, a volume a month, though few were ever opened. Occasionally one might appear in the bathroom, its cover mottled with water droplets after one of her father's baths, but the sinks continued to drip unabated, the front porch continued to slant. When that series was completed, the first Mysteries of the Unknown book arrived, much to her father's outrage. He promised to call the next day and cancel the damn thing. He didn't call—his threats always severe and rarely seen through—and Caitlin learned to anticipate when the next book in the series would arrive so she could squirrel it away in her room. She'd read them under the covers after lights-out (though in her house there was no official lights-out, neither parent particularly interested in enforcing any rules save those against violence). Something about the blanket setup, the flashlight, intensified the scare for her, the feeling that outside the boundaries of her nubbly duvet was a pitch black populated by indescribable creatures. She would awake in the morning safe and secure, having survived unseen horrors, and thus began a lifelong habit of draining flashlight batteries. In this manner she accumulated and read every book in the series, then called on behalf of her father to cancel the subscription when the first Classics of the Old West arrived.

As she got older, and the world outside her bedroom firmed up, she continued putting herself in thrilling situations, right at the porous boundary between the known and everything else. Middle school was boring, predictable; high school doubly so. Ghost hunting returned some of the rattling unfamiliar to the world. And Alan, without knowing it, had become the duvet, that permeable but all-important barrier between her and inky darkness.

Charles had stomped upstairs to collect their equipment; Caitlin remained plunged in the couch. Ted, the boom mic guy from the night before, poked his head into the living room.

"Your buddy in here?" he asked.

"Charles," Caitlin said. "He's upstairs. What do you need?"

"I was wondering if we could take a look at your footage from last night. Ours wasn't so great."

"Oh my god, of course." Caitlin sat up straight. She turned on the laptop that Charles had already shut down, and Ted sat beside her. "That was wild, right?"

Ted shook his head, rubbed his face. His fingers were long and slender, nearly hairless, the nails rounded carefully. Caitlin queued up the footage from the bedroom webcam.

"Not that one," Ted said, "we were up there. What about in here?"

"Sure," Caitlin said, and was about to open the living room file when Charles clomped back downstairs.

"Hey!" Charles exclaimed, then recomposed himself. "It's better if we do our review first and make assessments. It is our property, after all."

"Relax," Ted said, "I'm just taking a look. You guys got some better angles than we did."

"Thanks." Charles was temporarily chastened. Caitlin had a potent desire for the three of them to go out for milkshakes and ask each other everything: what happened last night, and where was Ronnie, and what's the craziest thing you've ever seen?

"Actually, I was hoping we could copy some of this and send it back to our office. Our editors want to take a look, too."

"I need to take it back to our office for a review," Charles said. Caitlin knew this wasn't strictly true—Alan encouraged them to put space between an investigation and the review, to not let high-running emotions influence their interpretation. But Ted surprised them both.

"Maybe I could come back with you and make a copy there?"

Charles didn't look at Caitlin's face, didn't need to. The hope radiated out of her, the knocking of her heart as loud as anything they'd heard from outside the house.

"Why not," he said, looking more tired than Caitlin remembered seeing him. "What's the worst that could happen?"

"Sandra?" Patrick roamed the second floor, calling her name. "You up here?" A door to the master bedroom opened and Sandra stepped out, wearing the clothes she'd been wearing when she arrived, but smelling quite a bit fresher, a bit like Mrs. Hawthorne even, and her curls were damp.

"Did you just take a shower?"

"Did you get in touch with the psychic?" Sandra asked, reaching up to pat the top of her head with one of the Hawthornes' towels. She was ever so faintly smiling. It was such an obvious no-no that Sandra had never even had to tell the crew not to do it, though she had to tell them not to do any number of other things, the most common being not to steal prescription drugs from the families' medicine cabinets. But she had become aware, in conducting interviews about the previous night, of how sticky she felt, how with each shake of her head the smell of the bar came wafting out of her hair. And how easy it had been to turn the water on, how good to step in.

Patrick nodded. "Right on. I just wanted to let you know that Ted's leaving with the ghost hunters to make a copy of their footage from last night. The psychic said she can come in a few hours. Should we get some questions ready for her?"

"Ted's going to the PIP office?"

"Do you . . . want to go?"

"I've never seen it before."

"I've never seen a . . . ," Patrick started, some cheesy line he had at the ready, and then caught himself. "Hurry back, okay? Things get weird when you're not here."

———— • ————

As soon as Ted announced to his colleagues, much to Charles's chagrin, that he was going to the offices of the Paranormal Investigators of Pennsylvania, a spontaneous field trip was organized, with most of the younger gofer-type guys raising their hands to come along. The caravan started with Alan's economy car, then the PIP van, driven by Charles, with Caitlin riding shotgun. The rest of the crew followed in their own van.

Charles normally found the crew taciturn, focused on some schedule PIP was never privy to but expected to follow nonetheless, to keep to the bottom line. That was what he imagined them saying to one another in New York, that it was *all about the bottom line*. None of them had ever exhibited the least amount of interest in PIP's findings before—the electromagnetic field readings, the EVPs, none of these raised an eyebrow a scant millimeter on any of their foreheads. Then their cameraman walks off with their footage and suddenly they're curious, solicitous. Kind. Charles knew exactly how this thing would end. They'd collect more evidence, or they wouldn't, and at the end of five days the crew would depart and it would be up to him, Alan, and Caitlin to clean up the mess they left behind—to recommend a spiritual cleansing led by a local psychic or faith healer; to put the family in touch with other families who had gone through such things before. A week or two later the PIP office would get a call from some assistant, no one who'd actually been in the house with them, asking if there had been further activity. The information Charles or Alan relayed—the person calling never bothered to ask who she was speaking to—would make it into the final ten seconds of the show, a one-sentence update superimposed over a solarized shot of the house. The wooden creak of a mummy emerging from his coffin, or whatever ridiculous sound cue the show threw in, and roll credits.

Charles had watched, with disgust, every episode of the show, whether PIP had been in it or not. The show failed to recognize the irony of its own continued existence: at the end of each episode, the paranormal was determined to be, unequivocally, the source of the family's experiences. The invisible world, thus found, should have meant the show would disband, sending everyone away in search of something else. And yet it soldiered on, ever expanding its roster of investigative teams, geek squads brought in against the chaos of night vision and slo-mo. They reduced an ethereal dimension, hovering just a breath away, to *data*. Sometimes Alan looked like that, too, Charles was sorry to say. His face was never framed in a flattering way and in the clips Alan came across as stiff, tactical.

But maybe Alan buttoned up in front of the cameras on purpose. Charles had seen Alan genuinely scared—before the group had Caitlin, or a name—in the house of a woman who lived alone somewhere inside of four enormous bedrooms. The house was spanking new, decorated straight out of a catalog, all the tchotchkes color coordinated in a dull red, white, and antique blue. None of them were quite sure how she could afford it, or why she'd want to. There were no photos suggesting children grown up and moved on, no photos at all. But no matter how firm and fresh the flooring, she had something fearsome banging around in her basement, clanking the pipes and sending howls of anguish up through the floor. When they went down there—Alan, Charles, and Alan's then wife, Lauren—it was stifling, the fire breath of a thousand demons clogging the air. No crew with lights and cameras had followed them, only the woman, in thick black eyeliner, heavy gold jewelry, and breasts Charles was willing to bet she didn't grow on her own. She wasn't scared, either. She tramped right down to the basement with them, shouting expletives into the dark, and Charles could feel the temperature of the space rise in response. Alan tried to calm her, tried to get her to see that the supernatural, like the living, react in kind to what you offer them, but the woman waved that off.

"Fuck it," she said. "Burn the whole place to the ground. I'll move out before I show this piece of shit an ounce of respect." And Alan, in contrast, was struck dumb. At one point while in the basement—Charles knew, intellectually, they couldn't have been down there for more than a few minutes, though it had felt like hours—Alan fell to his knees, staring ahead with his mouth open. Charles stepped in front of him to help him get up but Alan looked right through him, maintaining eye contact with whatever presence he'd connected to. Lauren had dragged him back up the stairs—the only creaky part of the house, still smelling faintly of pine—and a moment later he'd come to. In the track-lighted kitchen, being offered both coffee and vodka simultaneously from the owner, Alan began to shake. Sweating, incoherent, he grasped whatever he'd seen only once they were above ground, though he wouldn't describe it, not once he'd calmed down, or later. The next day the house was on the market. The owner had hired PIP the way she'd hire an exterminator, with no interest in the life cycles or habits of the thing she wanted gone.

That was three years ago. It was the last case Lauren went on and had marked the beginning of the end of their marriage. In the months after Lauren left, Alan had leaned harder into investigating, bringing Caitlin on weekend sessions and printing T-shirts, hoodies when it got cold. The show had contacted Alan through PIP's website about helping out with an episode shooting nearby and he'd agreed, though they'd been hired on few actual cases since making the group official. Alan had said it was because he wanted Charles and Caitlin to focus on their schoolwork, but Charles had been aware of the stories going around. Alan's "hobby" had been tolerated with bemusement, but once it got in the way of a marriage—of *family*—it became another issue. The show didn't know any of that. The producer,

Sandra, and the blond guy who Charles thought of as a Rod or a Hank, didn't know anything except that Alan investigated in the area.

"It's one of those sleazy 'reality' shows," Charles had argued. "The ones that don't care how real it is at all."

Alan had gestured for Charles to relax. "I'm going to help them the way I'd help anyone who called me. They're honest enough to admit they don't understand what's going on in this house, aren't they?"

But Charles had never found anyone on the show willing to admit to anything they couldn't understand. They chomped their gum while Alan discussed his readings during interviews, made fun of PIP when they thought no one could hear. The show had raised PIP's profile enough that they got calls from people in other states, the big leagues in this line of work. Nevertheless, it was a dog-and-pony show PIP was doing, and now that Alan had been in consistently good spirits for a while, Charles longed for him to stop taking Sandra's calls—though he suspected Alan had a thing for her.

Alan pulled into one of the five parking spaces behind the office building PIP shared with a therapist and an attorney, and Charles parked beside him. Charles turned the engine off, but didn't move. Alan walked toward the van to help them unload, but Charles waved for him to go on ahead, they'd take care of it. The crew had pulled into the last empty spot in the lot; they were piling out of their van amidst a flurry of jokes and junk food wrappings, Sandra among them. They didn't notice Charles at all, though he was the one with the tapes they had come for.

Caitlin remained in her seat, not sure why Charles hadn't undone his seatbelt yet, but attentively waiting for him.

"What do you make of all this?" Charles asked her. He glanced at the rearview mirror and for the first time noticed they had a hitchhiker—one of Roving Eye's PAs who had clambered in the back, uninvited. He was tapping away at his BlackBerry, oblivious. Charles jutted his head toward the back seat; Caitlin turned her head, then looked at Charles in confusion.

"The banging? Could be lots of things. As Alan said, poltergeist . . ."

"Not the banging." Charles pulled the key from the ignition. "The excitement. These guys coming out to the office. They've never wanted to before."

"They've never caught anything this righteous before."

The van's extra occupant lifted his head, made eye contact with Charles in the mirror.

Charles shifted in his seat. "This isn't the most intense thing we've ever experienced."

"It may be the scariest thing that *they've* experienced."

"Are you scared?"

"Aren't you?"

Charles shook his head. "I don't know." In the light of day, what had happened the night before seemed impossible, though while it was happening it had felt more than real: totalizing, the only thing that existed in the universe that banging, and the agonizing silences between.

"Charles, you know me. I've felt the cold spots, gotten objects to move, I've captured the most EVPs myself, during Q and A's I've conducted." This was true. The spirit world, for all its flightiness, had a fondness for Caitlin and opened right up to her like an old lady on a bus. Two minutes in an attic with Caitlin and the invisible photo wallet came out. "Remember the haunted barn? I had a fever for two days. Something got *inside* me. And still that was not like this."

"And that doesn't seem odd to you?" Charles turned to look Caitlin in the face. She had too much makeup on, as always, blue eyeliner smudged thickly and her lips a garish orange. Her nose stud glinted in the sun. Her strawberry-blond hair was pulled back in a series of barrettes and ribbons, but the night spent sleeping on the Hawthornes' floor had pulled strands out and they wafted, halo-like, around her face. She looked incredibly young to Charles, a baby, her surety a mask that had fallen away. "I mean what are the chances they'd be here with us, on this case, when we get the most aggressive appearance we've seen in years?"

"They come with us on like half our cases now. So the chances are fifty-fifty." Caitlin paused. "You think one of them was out there, banging the outside of the house?"

"All I'm saying is, all of sudden they're interested in seeing our offices and making copies of our tapes when before all they wanted from us was a couple of sound bites. Those episodes aren't filmed, they're . . . created, built in their editing lab. The show is nothing like the work we do. So don't you think it's a pretty weird coincidence that these two things would happen at the same time?"

The last word had barely left his mouth before Caitlin was out of the van, slamming the door behind her and stomping up the walk to the PIP office. Charles put his head down on the steering wheel and sighed.

"I hear you, dude," the nameless lackey said from the back seat. "But we'd have no reason to put one over on you like this. What's our motivation?"

"Higher ratings?" Charles looked up to make eye contact in the rearview mirror, but the kid's head was pointed down. He appeared to be as absorbed in his phone as ever. When he spoke again, his voice emerged more from the walls of the van than his mouth, which did not open.

"But our footage sucks. That's why we're here. If we'd manufactured the event, why wouldn't we place ourselves in a more optimal spot to capture it?"

Charles studied the apparition, subtly feeling his jacket pockets for his tape recorder. "To deflect suspicion?"

The voice chuckled. "We have better ways to spend our time."

Charles snorted. How would he know that? In all the months the show had been calling PIP, in all the investigations they had done side by side, not once had anyone from the show bothered to strike up a conversation with Charles, to solicit from him anything but the barest minimum of information.

Before he could respond, though, he saw in the rearview mirror that the back seat was empty. He turned his head to confirm it: no one was there. With a shake of his head, Charles got out, coming around to the side of the van to remove the bag of tapes Caitlin had neglected to carry. He slammed the van door closed and headed inside to join the others.

———

Ryan gave Eve a kiss and watched her drive off to run an errand. Everyone was gone, half to the ghost hunters' office, the other half to get lunch. He stood in the driveway a moment, making sure nobody was coming back, then went inside. He busied himself about the house, tidying up, arranging certain foods in the fridge for easy retrieval, appearing beyond suspicion to anyone looking in, but carrying in his head an intention, like a man with a date and time to meet a woman at a motel.

Satisfied with how the first floor looked, Ryan went down to the basement. The light flared and burned out when he hit the switch, sending him back into the kitchen for the spare bulbs, the flashlight under the sink. Ryan reached up to replace the bulb at the foot of the stairs, forgetting he had left the switch at the top of the steps in the on position. The bulb sprang awake before it was fully screwed in, bursting in his eyes and causing him to drop the flashlight from between his teeth.

The basement, lit by the exposed bulb, was a world of indistinguishable shapes and shadows, dark corners harboring any number of frights, both otherworldly and rodential, and on a visual level Ryan was again disappointed the show was letting the setting go to waste. He moved the wine and leaned into the crawl space to look. His machine was dark. The red standby light should have been lit, and when Ryan hit the power button, nothing happened. He hit it again. Still dark. He followed the power cord from the back of the stereo, behind a few boxes, to the outlet, which the plug lay below, on the floor. But he had plugged it in. He had tested it. Ryan felt a chill, the kind ghost hunters yapped about into their tape recorders. But it wasn't a spook—someone in the house knew about his stereo. Someone from the TV crew, or one of the kids who had been running around his house with their little devices, unsupervised. No one had spoken to him that day; no one had given him so much as a glance. They circled around Eve, they interrogated the teenagers for every detail of the night before. But somebody had something on him, information that threatened to pull the plug—so to speak—on the rest of the week.

Ryan climbed the stairs uncertainly, not bothering to push the boxes back into place. Outside, the sun was too large for shadows; it baked the basement smell into his skin. Ryan ran his hands over the wood on the side of the house: not a dent or indentation marked it, at least not at the level a man would be able to hit with a heavy object. Ryan hadn't thought, when he'd heard the tape, that his machine was capable of producing such a noise, but he'd never listened to it from upstairs, had no idea how the house might carry and release its reverberations.

He stood under a storm window he'd been meaning to take out for weeks now, looking at the pure white siding of his home. It was unmarked except for some faint dirt and dust, completely normal for this time of year, when it had been a long time since it had rained.

A slurping brought Ryan back to the present. The short, long-haired camera guy, the only one who had shown up today, was walking up to him with a huge plastic cup of soda, the reusable kind they sold at the gas station, with a lime-green bendy straw. Following his appearance, Ryan became aware of other sounds and presences: van doors opening, bodies jumping out. The half of the crew that had gone to lunch was back. Ryan's heart pounded as he eyed the man, in a plaid flannel shirt and old jeans.

"Hell of a thing," the man said. "Nothing like this has ever happened on the show before." Ryan couldn't tell by his tone if the man meant the noises, or being duped by the homeowners. "Scary enough to send one of our own packing, even. Wish I had been here to see it." He scratched the top of his receding hairline, then extended the hand for Ryan to shake. "Macon," he said. "I believe that's the first time I've ever said that."

"Come again?" Ryan asked, hoping Macon didn't notice how clammy his hand was.

"That I wish I'd seen something I hadn't. Usually it's the other way around, especially when it comes to television." Macon leaned forward and touched the wood siding ever so gently, as if the trauma of the night before had left internal wounds. "You know?"

Ryan nodded vaguely.

"I heard you and the missus excused yourself from the party a little early."

"We needed some space." Ryan's voice was weak, cracked on

exit. If they left now, if Eve didn't get what she wanted from this and they had to start over . . . He willed himself to pull it together.

Macon nodded. "No doubt. Still, if it was my house, I'd want to be sure. You going to be around tonight?"

"I don't think we have a choice," Ryan said.

"That makes two of us. Or, really, eight." Macon indicated the crew congregated in the front yard.

Ryan knew it was his turn to speak, but he failed to come up with anything. He shrugged as if to say, *The more the merrier*, the opposite of how he felt.

"We'll be out of your hair soon enough," Macon concluded, clapping him on the shoulder, as if it were the crew who brought the event with them, bottling it when they departed to unleash on the next couple of rubes who thought a TV show would clean their family laundry. Macon ambled back to his people, soda in tow, but Ryan remained staring at the side of the house, unwilling for the moment to go back in, for the first time since they'd moved there truly unsure of what awaited him inside.

———·—

Sandra expected the PIP office to be small. Hell, the offices of *Get Her in the Gown*, the first show she'd worked on as a producer, were small, and that was for a staff of twelve. Three shared desks—rotated between day and evening shifts—two tiny offices, one for her and one for Jonathan, a few phone extensions, and a fax machine were all it took to put together a show about reluctant brides. It was nice to have moved up to Roving Eye, which had a stable of shows in a similar format. But though *America's Best Diner* was in its sixth season, its stability did not spill over to *The Invisible World*, whose every episode felt slapped together from scratch. This may have been due in part to high turnover in the industry, which also kept Roving Eye's offices, though spacious, a little impersonal: no one really settled in. Perhaps that was the reason Sandra, arriving at the same time every day for a year, never got a nod or smile or any indication from the guard that she was different from anybody else who waved their pass by his nose on their way to the elevator bank. When she stopped arriving each day, she realized with a jolt, her absence would go unnoticed. The show itself would blip out with hardly a ripple—if ten years from now she saw its name on some nostalgic listicle, she'd be astonished. She'd eat the heels she was currently wearing, which scraped at the skin over her Achilles tendon.

There was no security between the outside world and PIP's one room, which contained two desks—a full-sized one, with their computer and editing equipment, and a smaller one, an antique that was just a little too big for the corner it had been shoved into but a little too small for the piles of papers and notebooks that it held. Wires snaked around the perimeter of the room and along the base of metal shelving overstuffed with books, files, tapes in plastic boxes, and old newspapers. A corner was filled by a mini-fridge, by the door hung a key for a bathroom down the hall, and behind the big desk was a window overlooking the parking lot they had just come from. One phone, no fax—Sandra wondered if the computer her staff was circling around even had a broadband modem. It was all so, so tiny. When she stepped into it she had an image of Alan, mouth agape upon arriving in New York City, skyscrapers flinging themselves out of the ground in front of him, the steel and glass a terrifying vision he'd be glad to leave. It was ungenerous of her—in fact, in their conversations Alan had alluded to trips he'd taken to New York, his voice betraying no particular reverence for her ability to live there nor any scorn at the crowds, the searing subways. But Sandra had the same mood-swingy reaction to Alan as she did around her exes, despite the fact that they'd never been together. Sometimes she felt warm, comfortable in the presence of one who knew her and accepted her on her own terms; other times she found him irritating, a silent reminder of some personal inadequacy, his voice chipping ever so persistently at her sanity.

Ted sat down at the desk, running a hand over PIP's editing deck. "This is a nice piece of equipment you have here," he said, gently turning the scroll wheel. "Practically vintage." In contrast to Roving Eye's decks, which were slim, black, hardly larger than a keyboard, PIP's was bulky, gray, a VCR on steroids with square buttons and a big black wheel to speed up or slow down playback. It was one more thing that didn't fit in the space, and Ted's fawning over it made Sandra uncomfortable, like he was patronizing Alan's team. "Man, I miss these old decks. So tactile. You really feel like you're doing something, you know what I mean?"

The PA Sandra liked the least laughed. "I have no fucking clue what you mean."

"Yes, you do. Like, our deck in the office, it's so efficient. It's all quiet clicks and shortcuts. You don't get that satisfaction of pressing two buttons at the same time to record. It's one step away from being able to manipulate it with our minds. Sometimes I think one day, computers won't need us at all. They'll just . . . go."

An awkward silence followed his prediction, and Ted, a little red-faced, focused on the screen again.

"Okay, here it is," he said, pausing the tape. There wasn't any room around the desk—there wasn't any room in the office at all, with all of PIP, half her crew, and herself—but Sandra cleared her throat and some of the guys stepped back, allowing her to shove up next to Ted, her thigh pressed against the desk as he hit play.

No one was in the shot when the tape started; it was grainy and calm. A cliché in the genre: seemingly empty room, and then!

Then what they came for became audible, a knocking rolling around the house, bowling balls bouncing in a colossal spill. A moment later, feet pounded the stairs.

"Fuck was that?" Ted's voice on the tape was an octave higher than usual. Watching himself from the PIP office, Ted's neck went pink. On-screen, Ronnie whipped his camera, still mounted on his shoulder, around the living room.

Ted touched the wheel to back up the tape and let them all hear it again more slowly, each *WHUMP* distinct, but rounded, too, the sound not only of impact but of air around it being displaced. *WHOOMPWHOOMPWHOOMPWHOOMPWHOOMP-WHOOMPWHOOMP.*

"This is why I don't think it's a person making the noise," Ted said, answering a question no one had asked and backing up the tape. "Listen to how loud it is, and how quickly it moves. You can't even . . . here." He bent under the desk and from inside his bag produced a set of headphones. He plugged them into the monitor and without looking up handed them to Sandra. "Listen to the way the sound moves."

Sandra put the headphones on and nodded for Ted to play it again. It was over in seconds as the noise traveled from one end of the house to the other. It was how Sandra imagined it would feel inside a thundercloud, a sound so huge it blocked light.

Ted paused the tape and swiveled to look at Sandra. "A person couldn't run that fast and hit the side of a building with that much force. How would you do it? Slam a brick on the side?

There isn't time to pull your arm back and slam it again before the next one."

Sandra removed the headphones. "It's irrelevant. Eve and Ryan weren't there. They can't respond to it in interviews. We ignore it."

Protest erupted, fast and loud, from her crew: "You can't mean that." "This is the wildest shit we've ever—" "I will personally see to it that—" "Sandra, what about Ronnie?"

Sandra raised her hands for quiet. "Fine, we'll work it in. We'll take a look at the side of the house when we get back. Alan, you go with Eve and Ryan to examine on-camera. Maybe there will be something there to react to." Out of the corner of her eye, she saw Alan glance at his phone, a missed call.

"Madame Mandaya is on her way," he murmured.

"Okay, we have to head back."

"Um, Sandra, I still need to copy the tape. That's why we came here."

She finally looked at Ted. "How long is that going to take?"

Ted looked to Charles.

Charles shrugged. "A little while."

"I'll drive you to the Hawthornes'," Alan offered.

"Come as soon as possible," Sandra told Ted. "I'll prep the psychic and have her fill out the paperwork, but we need you for the walkthrough." If they left now and Alan drove a little over the speed limit, the psychic wouldn't arrive at an empty house, wouldn't have time to concoct some story too good for the cameras.

Unlike the crew's van or Patrick's Mini Cooper, both way stations for food garbage, discarded script pages, empty coffee cups and soda cans, with a fine silt of gum wrappers and crumbs underfoot at all times, Alan kept his little Kia spotless, smelling faintly of a pineapple air freshener stamped with the name of an auto-body shop. Sandra ran a finger over the dashboard to call attention to its cleanliness, but came away with a fine sprinkling of glitter.

"Caitlin's," Alan said. "She puts on her makeup on the way to school."

"You drive her to school?"

"From time to time." He pulled onto the highway and, to Sandra's satisfaction, gunned it. "I'm friends with her parents. They're good people, but a little scattered." His face clouded, and Sandra assumed he was being nice about Caitlin's parents, wanting to protect Caitlin from any shift in Sandra's esteem. "I sold them their house, and they invited me over to dinner after they moved in. It became a sort of tradition, and then I found out Caitlin and I had similar interests. It was when Caitlin came on board that PIP became official."

"So this isn't your full-time job." Finally it made sense. Caitlin, his proxy daughter. He did it for her.

Alan laughed, warmly. "God, no. I don't even charge. It would be unethical. If families want to give me something afterward, I leave that to them."

"You don't charge anything? Expenses, gas?" She gestured to the car, cringing at the thought of how poorly the show compensated him, how much he probably drove.

Alan shook his head, smiling.

"Why do it, then?" The question was out of her mouth before she could stop it.

"Not everything in life comes down to money."

Sandra flushed. "Yeah, no, of course."

They sat in uncomfortable silence a moment. Sandra looked out the window. The highway came at them and slid by, sound-absorbing walls on either side blocking the homes from view. She could smell Eve's lavender body wash on her skin.

Alan cleared his throat. "I'm sorry again about my absence last night. You seem frustrated."

"It's a problem that Eve wasn't there."

"Or Ryan."

"Right."

"For you," Alan amended.

"Me?" Sandra was offended. What did any of this have to do with her? Her personal feelings were irrelevant. Even if the activity had been unusually intense, Sandra wasn't going to lose any sleep over whether or not—

"For your team. But not a problem for mine. It's unusual to have such unambiguous activity without the homeowners present. That changes our approach. Can it change yours?"

Sandra snorted. There was a reason she delivered the schedule to them, printed and binding, in advance. The stated mission of the show was to capture the unseen, though this was done indirectly, with description. The unstated part was to do it as cheaply as possible. Families were shuffled through a format, the details of their stories slotted into segments of predetermined length. The structure of the show was so embedded in her brain that sometimes before Sandra fell asleep at night she heard voiceover recapping the events of her day; voiceover narrating in a ten-second teaser what she had coming up the next.

"We can pull together an investigation for tonight, sure, but we can't rework the script."

"Don't you have an obligation to show"—he paused—"what actually happened?"

What did happen? she wanted to ask. There had been a moment in Alan's office when she saw why Ted felt so strongly that the footage should be included in the episode, should maybe even shift the course of the episode. She caught herself wondering, if she had been there, if she might have been scared. Would she have braved the darkness, more frightening in that moment than the house? Never before had she pictured herself in this way: in the dim of the living room or descending the stairs, her blood throbbing cold.

"Of course." Her professional demeanor slid into place and she welcomed it like a contact lens: the world was instantly clearer. The format worked, almost without exception. The only mystery left was why it worked, what larger stories these individual stories were telling. For Sandra to figure that out, Eve—and everyone else—needed to fall in line. "Charles gives a decent interview. With the footage your team got I think we can cut something together that captures the . . . essence of it. What do you recommend we do tonight?"

Alan frowned slightly. "Now that we know some activity is taking place outside the home, we can put a team there," he said. "Maybe put one group outside, and one in. Where's your man who shot the footage? He didn't come to the office."

"Sleeping in, I guess. We haven't heard from him."

"Aren't you worried?"

"About what?" She smiled at Alan, daring him to say it.

"Is it typical for your employees to disappear in the middle of making an episode?"

"Nothing about this episode is typical," Sandra muttered before she realized what she was saying. She swallowed. "We hire a lot of young guys, recent film school grads. This isn't what they want to be doing in the long term. Reliability is not their strong suit." When it came to Ronnie, none of those things applied. But it reassured Sandra to hear herself say it.

"Sandra," Alan said, firmly this time. "What do *you* think caused the banging?"

"That's your job to figure out." She laughed once. "Not mine."

"You've filmed a dozen episodes with us by now." He looked right at her; he didn't glance away. "You must have some opinion."

"Eight."

"Sorry?"

"Eight cases with PIP." A prickle ran over the surface of her skin. She blamed it on low blood sugar; she'd had only coffee. "I can't . . ." What couldn't she do? Conspire with him on the investigation, follow each lead where it took them, sponsors be damned? Come back to New York with a hundred hours of footage to be sorted through and edited at leisure into some new kind of episode, messy and sprawling, an ambiguous ending they'd get phone calls about? Impossible.

Alan pulled up in front of the Hawthornes' and they both sat a minute, not looking at each other. Alan turned the engine off even though he made no move to get out, sparing the environment those few moments of idling. He was so careful. Sandra wanted to fuck him somewhere filthy, like the Hawthornes' basement, their crowded garage. She wanted Alan's hands around her hips, for him to emit sounds he couldn't control as he ground into her.

She unbuckled her seatbelt. "Shall we?"

Alan smiled. "You said 'cases,' just now. Not 'episodes.'"

"Did I?" Her face went warm. Alan's mouth opened, like he wanted to say something else, and her heart pounded in anticipation. He gazed out the windshield a moment, then shook his head.

"Come on. Let's go in," he said, looking embarrassed, and got out of the car.

———•———

Regina generally began by delineating the space in her mind, eyes closed. An image would take shape around her, each room and hallway stripped of furniture, framed photos, pets, and she would see the space as it existed permanently, sense the permanent inhabitants. Houses that had undergone extensive renovation made this difficult, since they transmitted their original floor plans, and walls could surprise you, jumping out where they didn't belong. The Hawthornes' house hadn't had any major structural work done, but all the furniture was clumped together in one room so the TV people could do their nasty business. Regina had to crack her eyes open a bit to keep from knocking into random end tables and hutches and rolled-up rugs. The matriarch, Eve, had told her that there was some concern over the dining room, some hostility between residents on different planes. But Regina didn't want to do a reading of the space with all those men standing around in their jeans, hips jutted. She said the profligacy of electricity in the room disrupted her perception of its energy. Eve looked upset at that, but Regina was pleased with how it sounded and whispered to herself "profligacy, profligacy" as she gingerly, eyes shaded, took the stairs.

"This is where I felt a . . . presence for the first time," Eve said at the doorway to the smaller bedroom.

A camera looked over Eve's shoulder, its unblinking eye trained right at Regina. "I feel a presence in here."

"Right now?"

"Hmm." There were so many signals whizzing by her head. Who could tell the dead from the electronic? Sweat beaded her upper lip.

"It's always backward," Eve went on. "Hot in here when the

house is cool, cold when the house is warm. Something with the ducts, I guess."

The medium stepped farther into the room, putting space between herself and the cameras. She had been told it was a guest room and it was decorated in cream and gray, with a few uninteresting books on a shelf and a plastic-framed mirror on the wall. She didn't get the feeling the Hawthornes hosted much. The air in the room felt static, thick. But when Eve stepped into the room, Regina felt the energy coalesce around her in a tight embrace.

"It means you are doing something backward. You need a reversal of yourself, to bring everything back to right."

"Is that what the spirits are telling you?" Eve asked, allowing her sarcasm to leak through.

Regina inhaled, recentered. "Spirits feed off the energy in a home. They thrive on aggression. The less you offer them, the faster they go away."

Eve averted her eyes.

It only got worse—the more Regina relaxed into her role, the more the tension between her and Eve grew. Sandra had encouraged the psychic to share as many impressions as she could, in the hopes that something she said could be massaged into linking the banging to Eve and Ryan's experiences. Regina tried to play along, sketching out anxious husbands in precarious marriages; a lonely child who perpetually scampered down the hallway, seeking connection; an angry spirit bent on destruction. All the while, she watched Eve out of the corner of her eye. The more outlandish the story, the more mistrustful Eve looked. There were moments when Regina hit on something, though, saw a flash of recognition in Eve's eyes as she wrapped her hands around her neck in the master bathroom, simulating a noose.

"That's it?" Eve asked, when they were back on the first floor.

Ted was clipping a microphone onto Regina's shirt, delicately adjusting her scarves around it.

"What did you expect, dear, for me to start speaking in tongues? I can only tell you what I receive. It's up to you to decide how you want to move forward." She took a chance. "Is there something specific you want to talk about? Sometimes the living need me more than the dead." She raised one eyebrow.

"No, no," Eve said, waving a hand as if to bat away an insect. "I'm sorry. I should be more open to this. I hate people who try something only to be able to criticize it later." She was dissembling, but Regina could take her at face value, leaving open the possibility for a true conversation later. Off-camera.

———·———

Transcript: SIW-221a-11/CAMERA A, 15:31:02

INTERVIEW—MADAME MANDAYA

MME. MANDAYA: My name is Regina Ubyivovk. I am a psychic medium and educator.

Question

MME. MANDAYA: Madame Mandaya is my professional name, but it isn't my legal name.

Question

MME. MANDAYA: Oh, sure. I am Madame Mandaya, fortune teller to the stars!

Question

MME. MANDAYA: Well, I'm sorry, but I find this whole thing a bit ridiculous.

Question

MME. MANDAYA: The Hawthornes didn't call me—Alan did, on your behalf. I am here to help them, not advertise myself.
Question

MME. MANDAYA: As you wish. I educate people on opening their psychic gifts. We all have gifts; how we utilize them depends on whether or not we acknowledge them. Some people see things, others smell particular scents associated with distinct experiences. My abilities are rooted in history and place. I have a direct spiritual relationship with my ancestors going back five generations, right to a Civil War–era general I am a descendent of. Union general. My mother's side. I'm sure you'll want your viewers to know that.
Question

MME. MANDAYA: There are different ways of "seeing." Eve described seeing a gray figure at the foot of her bed. That's a visual kind of seeing. My seeing goes deeper than that, and even the word "see" should be considered insufficient.
Question

MME. MANDAYA: There are a lot of energies in this house vying for attention.
Question

MME. MANDAYA: We send out energies while we're living, energies that houses retain. And this is a very busy house.
Question

MME. MANDAYA: I felt a strong female presence throughout.
Question

MME. MANDAYA: I find it generally more helpful to start from a place of openness, of listening. Whether or not Eve is in tune with her gifts—and I do believe she has them—she knows her house better than you or I ever could. I see my job as building upon and deepening what Eve herself already knows.

Question

MME. MANDAYA: No, I did not "see" a spectral presence during
the walkthrough. I felt a specific feminine energy, very close
to this house.

Question

MME. MANDAYA: I'm not saying she's wrong, only that she isn't
listening to what her own house is telling her about herself.
And I'm sure the presence of you lot isn't helping. Is there
anything to drink? Diet Coke?

Question

MME. MANDAYA: Thank you. I have some in my car, but it's
probably warm by now.

Question

MME. MANDAYA: I'm doing my best to give you what you
want without compromising my principles. How's this:
It's possible that the presence Eve is aware of and the one I
perceived know each other. There is drama in this house.

Question

MME. MANDAYA: I couldn't make any predictions. I only listen
to what's here, dear. I can't get them to perform any tricks.
Nor would I want to. Let sleeping dogs lie, I say, and even
better, sleeping dead dogs. Dead sleeping dogs. Let dead
sleeping dogs lie.

Question

MME. MANDAYA: I've been asked to go. *Quelle surprise.* I'll
just emphasize while the cameras are still on that there
are many energies in this house competing for attention.
Favoring one very well might anger another. I don't think
anyone here is truly prepared to confront the forces already
in play.

———•———

Charles rewound the tape again. After copying PIP's footage, the crew had cleared out of their office, and Caitlin had gone to buy sandwiches. Ted had forgotten his headphones. Charles would return them later, but now he was using them, backing up to the seconds before the noise started, stopping just when they all came crashing down the stairs.

Charles listened to the *WHUMPWHUMPWHUMP-WHUMPWHUMP* on quarter speed, trying to detect any nuances, any secondary sound he might have missed in the moment. That was why they had the tape, along with methods to ensure the tapes wouldn't be tampered with. Whatever Charles felt later, whatever doubts or regrets, didn't matter. Only the tapes.

He was about to back the tape up again, watch it for the third, twelfth, three hundredth time, when Caitlin blew in bearing hoagies in white paper and sodas in sweating paper cups. Charles flipped the monitor off, though Caitlin had had a chance to see what he was doing. For once, she didn't say anything. She hadn't said much earlier, either, only slumped in the corner while some TV show took the first crack at their evidence.

They chewed in silence for a few minutes, the long night starting to catch up to Charles. When his Dr Pepper was almost drained, he cleared his throat.

"Listen, Caitlin, I'm sorry about what I said before. About the crew and maybe the whole thing being a hoax."

"So you don't think the show is faking it?" Caitlin was engaged in removing the onions from her sandwich, but she couldn't keep her voice from rising.

He thought of the PA who had appeared in the back of the van. Whose lips didn't move when he spoke. A fully formed apparition, speaking to him, invisible to others, counted for little without evidence. But the guy had a point. "Logically, it wouldn't make sense." Charles half expected to turn around and see him in the other desk chair, head bent toward his phone, sending emails into the ether.

She sat upright. "What are we going to do tonight, do you think?" Just like that, he was forgiven. Charles had always seen it as a symbol of her maturity, the way she put things behind her so easily, but he suddenly felt protective of Caitlin, saw a future in which she was hurt over and over again because of her refusal to stand up for herself, to say, *You acted like a jerk before.*

"Same as ever, probably. Alan'll get you to do a Q and A and maybe we'll have somebody filming outside the house. I think where the cameras are will depend on what they want, but we should do it the way we always do a second investigation."

"I guess there's a chance they were making that noise. Like, if they don't want to shoot outside the house, but then the noise happens again, what does that mean? They knew it was going to happen and they didn't want to capture it on-camera, because then we'd see it's one of their goons with a really big stick?" She considered this. "Maybe we can put one of the webcams in a window on the second floor, pointed outside, so we could see if somebody runs by."

Charles smiled and nodded at the concession. "Sounds like a plan." He crumpled up the sandwich paper. "Come on, I'll drive you home."

Though they seemed to have made peace, Caitlin barely spoke on the ride, replying to Charles with distracted one-word answers. Her family's house was white with green shutters, set back from the road by an untended lawn, with a garage and driveway on the right. It looked like the house where the protagonist of every film lived, but Charles had been inside. Her mother, a ceramicist, and her father, who worked "sometimes," encouraged Caitlin and her sister's creative endeavors and filled their home with mismatched furniture and "found items" Charles might more accurately classify as garbage. The wall next to the kitchen phone was scrawled on with numbers and messages; bare feet picked up the grit of migrating kitty litter and crumbs from the packaged snack foods her parents had not gotten the memo on denying one's children. Charles did love pigging out on sodium-rich cheese crackers and sandwich cookies when he went over there to play video games, but the house gave him a vague uneasy feeling as well, as if Caitlin had spent her childhood one phone call away from Protective Services.

The van idled in the street. Caitlin had not yet opened the door.

"Why do you hate them?" she asked in a small voice.

"I don't hate them. I don't," he repeated in response to one of her standard looks, the *duh* stare. "I just think that they want something different from what we want when we go into a home, and I don't like how they always win."

She squinted. She didn't ask what it was he thought the show wanted, nor did they much discuss, in a larger way, what they did. They could move through an entire investigation, right down to the final report, without making generalizing statements about their mission, perhaps because of the way words, once spoken, became inadequate for what they were meant to express.

"*It's not a contest, Charles,*" Charles said, high and squeaky, trying to elicit a playful smack, her tinkly laugh.

But Caitlin only gave him the finger as she stepped out of the car toward her house, her Hydrox, the TV that was probably tuned to some gory movie the family had watched together when the kids were five and six and now rewatched out of twisted nostalgia.

"See you at eight!" he called out behind her, though he knew that Caitlin wouldn't arrive until eight thirty and she knew, much as she loved to play the mature-for-my-age card, that nothing would get started without her.

Charles didn't hate *Searching for . . .* , but he hadn't told Caitlin the full truth about why he resented their intrusion into PIP's investigations. He knew how much Caitlin loved the show—she had recorded, on her family's grimy VCR, every episode that the Paranormal Investigators of Pennsylvania had been in. But in all her rewatchings, she never once realized what Charles saw every time: that the show determined what evidence was real, what wasn't worth mentioning, what EVPs needed "enhancement," what a lens filter could do. Voiceover of precisely edited interviews accompanied footage of a different moment, and via the power of montage viewers "saw" something that never actually happened. Even worse than the deception, though: they made paranormal investigation seem easy, when to Charles it had always been hard. So little that was definitive ever happened, but the show offered week after week of undeniable evidence. It made Charles feel like a failure. Although he knew the show was faked, it *looked* real, and so tantalizing. He had been there, been in those houses, said those words, but the episodes never aligned with what he remembered. It was crazy making, and he didn't know how Alan could stand it.

Charles rarely had nightmares, even in the thick of an investigation, but when he got home and fell into bed he was asleep almost immediately and in his sleep found himself followed by a man in a long coat who read back his life to him, verbatim transcripts of conversations he could barely remember from years long past, a keeper of posterity who wanted him to know that the experiences we hope are the least important are the ones that somehow dog us to the end.

Eve watched from the front window as two members of the crew broke off from the flock to film B-roll down the street. Houses were few out here, the remnants of a farming county in which nobody had farms anymore, or any idea what to do with their land. And so they had this: massive yards, of which they mowed a fraction and let the rest grow wild, to harbor rumors of pumas and fornicating teenagers in the fall.

Ted looked up as she approached. He wasn't holding any of his sound equipment and appeared to be outside just to keep the cameraman company. The show transitioned between scenes with time-lapse shots of clouds going by, the sky darkening rapidly, plants knocking about in a manic breeze. Camera two was set up in the middle of the road, pointed west as the sun went down, the Hawthornes' home at a severe angle in the frame.

"Mrs. Hawthorne. Funny meeting you here."

She had a plate of sandwiches, hastily assembled, though the meat and mustard were artisanal. Nothing in her house came presliced. She proffered the plate. The cameraman took one gratefully and nodded thanks; Ted was more wary.

"We all need our energy for tonight, right?" Her voice came out wrong, high and falsely girlish.

Ted didn't reply, and she had run out of small talk.

"Ted, what do you think about last night?"

"I don't—"

"You were there."

"It isn't my job to—"

"Is that the line you're all told to say?"

He reddened, then surprised her. "What happened to Ronnie?"

"Why would I . . . ?"

"If you're so worried about what's going on in your house, why aren't you worried about him?" The cameraman reached out to touch Ted's elbow, but Ted pulled it away.

"You think I . . . ?" A muscle in her neck she hadn't even been aware of holding taut relaxed. Finally, *finally*, someone besides her was willing to say out loud that something weird was going on in her house.

But Ted collapsed into himself. "I don't know." He rubbed his face with one hand; the sandwich, one bite removed, hung limp in the other.

Eve tried to soften her tone. "I'm sorry about your friend." She paused. "So this sort of thing *is* unusual."

Ted nodded.

"How long have you been at this job?"

"About six months."

"You like it?"

"I do." His response seemed genuine.

"Has anything like this ever happened before?"

"Being bribed with soppressata? No."

Eve smiled. "I mean, what's the activity like in the other homes?"

He looked to the cameraman and raised an eyebrow. The cameraman shrugged one shoulder, barely: *Up to you*.

"We're not here to capture activity, despite the name of the show. Ninety percent of what we film is interviews and reenactments. We do an investigation or two when the activity has been more recent, but even that is"—he screwed up his face—"a sort of reenactment."

Eve's heart started to pound. "How so?"

"Because we don't expect to 'see' anything. The investigative team goes back and fine-tunes their tapes and tells us what they found, but the truth is, we mess around with their tapes, too, and most of what you hear on the show happens in post—editing—more than in the houses."

Eve swallowed hard.

"I shouldn't be telling you this."

"No, you should. I need to know why I'm here. Not to be helped, but to . . . *perform*."

Ted backpedaled: "Look, Alan and PIP take you seriously."

"Sandra doesn't."

Ted looked past Eve, toward her house, then back to her. "A lot of people think the show is here to fix things, because when you see it on TV, it'll be fixed. But all that fixing happens . . ." he waved down the road, in the direction of New York, a few hundred miles away. "People you'll never meet do that part. But Alan will be here after we're gone. That's what you need, right?"

Eve sat down on the curb. It wasn't. She saw how Ryan looked at Alan and the kids, could already hear his assessment: *a kook*. She had thought that the show would validate the malevolence of her home, that the crew would leave in a cloud of sympathy mixed with relief at getting away: *It's bad in there*. But it wasn't bad to them—it wasn't anything. Even after Madame Mandaya's departure—when they'd sat Eve down for her post-walkthrough interview, and all the batteries on all the cameras instantly, inexplicably drained, pausing production for a few hours to charge—they didn't see how the house was hindering *their* creative process as well. True, the crew were mostly men, and men were accustomed to denying a reality inhabited by women, brushing off any suggestion of menace as imagination. But Sandra, out of all of them, should have understood.

Ted looked back to his coworker, who was closing up the camera, collapsing the tripod and setting it in a case. Ted leaned over, put his hands on his knees, and looked right into Eve's face.

"I hope you figure this out. I really do. Between you and me, that was one of the scariest things I've ever experienced." He held her gaze. It occurred to Eve that they were probably not that far apart in age. He may have had a master's degree as well; in another life she could be dating someone like him and laughing at people like her, sprawled out on a bed in a Williamsburg loft, watching TV on a laptop and pitying the sorts of people who invented ghosts to give their lives meaning, objects onto which to project feelings they weren't reflective enough to explore within themselves.

But that wasn't her life, and she wasn't one of those people. This thing in her house was not an excuse; it was a hindrance. Eve could have borne it if she had been able to *use* it—been able to retreat to that critical distance that allowed her to see, understand, mine for creative potential. But this thing, whatever it was, seemed to come from inside her, and she couldn't get far enough away to see it clearly.

Ted helped his colleague pack the rest of their equipment and they stood in front of her, shoulder to shoulder, awaiting orders. Eve didn't want to talk anymore. She nodded for them to go ahead. The sun had set but the sky was still aglow, a brilliant pink-orange that might have broken her heart with its casual beauty if she wasn't imagining that the closing of the screen door behind them was the click of a detonator, the sky lit by a more localized fire, her whole house gone up in flames, not a single survivor to be found.

———·—·———

"Are we all here?"

They sat on chairs and on the floor. They stood, leaning against the walls and in the doorway. Sandra and Patrick sat on the couch, no one else inclined to join them, though there was room for a third. There were too many of them in too tight a space, but the decision to have the pre-night-shoot crew meet-

ing in the Hawthornes' house felt like a deliberate one on Sandra's part. Ted assumed the hotel had a perfectly serviceable
conference room, but by having the meeting in their home, the
crew was probably meant to feel a deeper sense of responsibility
toward the couple.

"Priority number one tonight is getting Eve and Ryan on-
camera." Or maybe Sandra just wanted to keep them from slipping out the door. "They should be in frame at all times. I'd
love to end up with something that can be spliced together with
last night's footage. Though that may be a fantasy on my part."
She smiled tightly. One of the PAs raised his hand, a thing she
repeatedly asked them not to do. Sandra nodded.

"Wait, but where's Ronnie?"

"It's safe to assume that Ronnie won't be joining us this
evening."

Murmurs among the crew. "Where is he?"

Sandra shook her head. "I haven't been able to get in touch
with him."

"Are you worried?"

Sandra sighed at Ted. He had asked her this half a dozen
times already today; he'd only hoped that an audience would
prompt a different response.

"Ronnie's an adult. He made a decision last night. He left
with one of our cameras and whatever footage was on it. Now
we're down to Macon and our backup camera, which will sit
on a tripod in the basement while one team conducts their
investigation." She nodded to their B-cam operator, promoted
by virtue of having stuck around. "Tomorrow we'll get another
cameraman to come out. But since we didn't have this investigation scheduled originally, I appreciate all of you being so
flexible. I don't expect any noticeable difference in the caliber of
this evening's work."

"But, like," another PA spoke up, "is he *okay*?"

Sandra looked to Patrick for support. Patrick was pretending to consult his notes. "What happened last night was a severe break in protocol, for which I take responsibility. If we'd all been doing our jobs, myself included, it wouldn't have happened." This did not satisfy anyone who had seen the tapes, or been told about the tapes by someone who had seen them. The murmuring returned, took shape, swelled in the room like a bubble. Sandra raised her voice above it. "Anyone abdicating their responsibilities from here on out can expect their contract to be terminated as soon as we're back in New York. I don't care what your title is."

That shut them up.

"Patrick?" Sandra said, turning the meeting over to the director and sinking back into the couch. Ted saw a flush rise along her neck.

"We'll put one team outside, led by Albert—"

"Alan," Sandra muttered.

"Alan. Macon will shoot, with Ted on sound. We'll have Mr. Hawthorne in the yard, plus the psychic. The other two ghost hunters will be in the basement, camera on a tripod and in-camera sound, plus whatever those two get on their tapes. Mrs. Hawthorne will be with them. I'll be in the basement as well, keeping everyone"—he cleared his throat—"in frame." Patrick assigned PAs to both locations and the meeting dispersed.

Ted found Macon and clapped him on the shoulder from behind. "All eyes on you, buddy. Better not—what was the word? *Abdicate*." He smiled. Macon and Ted liked each other, surprising them both. Ted came to work with an enthusiasm and curiosity befitting Norman Rockwell. Macon, on the other hand, had been working in television long enough to have become disillusioned with the entire human race, especially anyone who wanted to be on TV. He had worked for seven years as camera one on the execrable *Jimmy Tikoff Show*, a vestige of a time when people could be shamed publicly for their weight, their class, their incestuous impulses rather than urged into a course of treatment. It was a show that had taught the crew that when women come on the stage to fight, they start by removing their shoes, a gesture that was repeated among the *Searching for . . .* guys whenever Macon began to disagree with one of them. Macon bore it all, and even bought coffee for whoever rode in his van when they stopped on the turnpike to fuel up. If he wasn't entirely good-natured about it, he hadn't told anybody to cram it yet, either. He worked with a purpose, never engaging in pranks with the younger crew or drinking so much at the end of one day that it jeopardized the next morning's wake-up, as if he could, via sheer work ethic, bring about the end of television and the beginning of whatever was next.

"So, tell me: should I be scared?" Obviously Macon was joking.

Ted caught Macon's tone, but raised an eyebrow anyway. "You saw the footage. It wasn't . . . it was something else."

"And yet you're going outside."

"Maybe better outside than in," Ted said, chin jutted toward the basement. They had said nothing about Eve's sandwich ambush. Ted had overheard her conversation with Ronnie the day before, and she was right: the crew made fun of the families. They were merciless. Some of them, every time they went out to celebrate a wrap, brought up the same anecdotes from past shoots, hammering their stories into fine points, to say: these people are nothing like us. But Ted knew these guys, knew their talents, and most of them wouldn't have a chance on a better show. Ted participated in the jokes as often as he abstained, and had already weighed in on this week's assessment: Eve was bangable, little else. He should have felt more shame than he did, was mainly uncomfortable in that way—shame for his lack of shame.

The ghost hunters arrived and Sandra brought them up to speed. All together, they moved into the yard. Alan and the psychic looked to each other and around them, waiting for a thing they could not know how to anticipate, neither of them having experienced it the night before.

"Where's Ryan?" Sandra asked. A moment later he came stumbling out of the house.

"Just went to change my shirt," he apologized, and Sandra's face hardened. His clothes should have matched the ones he was wearing in the interviews they shot earlier. Another continuity error, the snags in this shoot already outnumbering the things that had gone well.

Ted turned to Macon once more.

"Okay, seriously, what about Ronnie?"

Macon nodded. "I thought about reaching out to his girlfriend, but I don't know her number. Besides, I don't know if it's worth it."

"You mean, to worry her?"

"Is there anything to be worried about?" They held each other's eyes for a long moment.

"Sound?" Sandra called across the yard, and Ted nodded, breaking from Macon's gaze.

"Are we rolling?" Sandra asked.

"Rolling," Macon said, his voice cracking and too loud, and everyone turned to look at him.

NIGHT 2

(Foot-shuffling noises as the recording begins; someone backs into a bookcase and a small wooden box clatters to the floor. Cursing.)

PATRICK: Mrs. Hawthorne, I'm just going to ask you to step into the frame over here. Can I get you two to stand on either side of Mrs. Hawthorne? Just—perfect. What's that for?

CAITLIN: It's a flashlight.

PATRICK: We've got enough light for the look we want.

CHARLES: He's right, we don't need it.

CAITLIN: It's not for *illumination*. It's for *communication*. Ghosts can turn it on and off.

PATRICK: No shit? Can I get Mrs. Hawthorne to hold it?

EVE: I'd rather not.

CAITLIN: It's supposed to be on the floor.

PATRICK: We're not filming the floor. Here, let me . . . on or off?

CAITLIN *(softly)*: Off.

PATRICK *(hands the flashlight to Eve)*: On looks better. Just for a few minutes. That looks great, actually. Really spooky. I'm going to step back, let you three take it away.

CAITLIN: Gee, thanks. Are we ready?

CHARLES: Why not.

CAITLIN: It is Tuesday, April —, nine forty-six p.m., our second investigation at the Hawthorne home. My name is Caitlin. With us is Charles, Eve, and Patrick. Are there any spirits with us here tonight?

(Twenty-second pause)

CAITLIN: If there are any spirits here with us tonight, please give us a sign.

(Twenty-second pause)

CAITLIN: EMF?

CHARLES: Nada.

CAITLIN: Is anyone else here with us?

(Twenty-second pause)

CHARLES: I'm getting something.

CAITLIN: It's chilly now.

(Pause)

CAITLIN: We're listening to you.

(Brief pause)

CHARLES: Stronger. Keep going.

CAITLIN: Did you once live in this house?

CHARLES: Much stronger now. It's reacting.

CAITLIN: Do you have a message for us who are gathered here tonight?

(Pause)

CAITLIN: Can we put the flashlight on the floor?

EVE: Yes, please.

PATRICK *(off-screen)*: It looks great where it is.

EVE: Maybe I should hold it up under my chin and tell ghost stories?

Transcript: SIW-221a-14/CAMERA A, 21:35:15

(There are no streetlamps on the Hawthornes' block, so Macon's top-mounted light intensifies the contrast between each person and the darkness behind them. The effect is such that each speaker is visible through the dark only when they're speaking, and disappears as another voice speaks up and Macon turns to capture them. Occasionally he is not able to get a speaker in

frame before they are finished speaking, and their voice issues
out of the void.)

SANDRA: Let's get started. Madame Mandaya, would you like
to begin?

MME. MANDAYA: I'm not used to doing this *en plein air*. How
would you like me to begin?

SANDRA: Are you getting anything out here, a sense of a
presence?

MME. MANDAYA: Not yet, but to be honest it's been hard to
concentrate.

SANDRA: We'll be perfectly quiet. All of us.

PA *(off-screen)*: We weren't even talking.

ALAN: I'll start the Q and A. And then if Regina—excuse me,
Madame Mandaya—begins to sense a presence, we can
slow down and concentrate on that. Let's start by walking
around the yard. We can see if any areas register a spike
in electromagnetic activity. Ready? I'm turning the tape
recorder on. It is April —. I am with Ryan Hawthorne and
Madame Mandaya outside the Hawthornes' home. We are
accompanied by an array of TV people who are going to try
very hard not to speak and leave any false positives on the
tape.

RYAN: Nothing might happen, just from us being out here.
They're more afraid of us than we are of them, isn't that right?

MME. MANDAYA: I think that's spiders, dear.

(Brief pause)

ALAN: Are there any spirits here with us tonight?

(Fifteen-second pause)

ALAN: Are there any spirits here with us tonight?

(Fifteen-second pause)

ALAN: Are there any spirits here with us tonight?

(Thirty-second pause)

ALAN: Can you tell us your name?
(Thirty-second pause)

ALAN: Can you tell us your name?
(Thirty-second pause)

ALAN: Can you tell us anything about yourself?
(Forty-five-second pause)

ALAN: Can you tell us who you were when you were alive?
(Thirty-second pause)

ALAN: Is there anything you can tell us about yourself?
(Thirty-second pause)

ALAN: Did you previously occupy this house?
(Thirty-second pause)

ALAN: Are you trying to get back into this house?
(Thirty-second pause)

ALAN: Can you tell us anything about yourself?
(Thirty-second pause)

ALAN: Do you have a message for the Hawthornes?
(Thirty-second pause)

ALAN: What is your relationship to the house?
(Thirty-second pause)

ALAN: Is there anything you would like the Hawthornes to know?
(Thirty-second pause)

ALAN: Is there anyone among those of us gathered here tonight whom you would like to speak to?
(Fifteen-second pause)

MME. MANDAYA: Let's stop here. I'm getting something.

ALAN: What do you feel?

MME. MANDAYA: Someone has joined us. I'm getting . . . Tricia? Theresa? Does that name mean anything to anybody?
(Silence)

MME. MANDAYA: She is here for someone. She is quite young. Pretty. Oh, she's sad.

RYAN: Means nothing to me.

MME. MANDAYA: Perhaps someone from the show knows a Tricia? Alice, even?

SANDRA *(off-screen)*: Just try to ignore us.

MME. MANDAYA: I'm listening to whoever reaches out. I do not discriminate.

(Pause)

MME. MANDAYA: She's fading now, though. Disappointed. Last call for Tricia.

SANDRA *(off-screen)*: Let's move on.

ALAN: Sandra, if I may—

SANDRA *(off-screen)*: Macon, you good?

MACON *(off-screen)*: You bet.

ALAN: Pardon me. Are there any other presences here with us tonight?

(Thirty-second pause)

ALAN: Is there another spirit trying to reach anyone gathered here?

(Thirty-second pause)

ALAN: Can you tell us anything about yourself?

Transcript: SIW-221a-15/CAMERA B, 23:15:07

CHARLES: We are now in the living room on the first floor of the Hawthornes' house. After a considerable period of moving furniture for aesthetic purposes, we are ready to begin.

CAITLIN: So you get to be sarcastic, and I don't?

CHARLES: Do you want to get started?

PATRICK: One second. Eve, can you join them on the couch?

EVE: May I ask it a question? Since my presence is so important.

CHARLES: I don't think that's—

CAITLIN: Sure, why not.

PATRICK: It's a great idea.

CAITLIN: Start by asking if anyone is here, and then pause.

EVE: If anyone is here tonight, I want to know, why? Why are you here?

(*Twenty-second pause*)

EVE: Is it because of me?

CHARLES: I'm getting something.

PATRICK (*not off-screen enough*): This is good stuff.

EVE: Do you know me? How do you know me?

(*A few seconds of silence, followed by a scratching on the tape, a sound no one remembers hearing at the time.*)

EVE: How long have we been together? Can we exist without each other?

(*Long pause. Very long, in fact, long enough for the room to fall into silence, the gentle rotations of the tape at times the only noise, until its voice-activation feature automatically turns it off.*)

Transcript: SIW-221a-16/CAMERA A, 23:57:08

SANDRA: We've been out here a long time, I guess. It doesn't feel like it.

ALAN: It's just midnight now.

SANDRA: There's something hypnotic about the way you conduct your investigations. I feel sort of lulled.

MACON: Uh, Sandra? We're rolling.

SANDRA: Oh, my god. Am I in the shot?

MACON: Affirmative.

(*Sandra exits.*)

ALAN: Regina, what's your feeling right now?

MME. MANDAYA: I feel very alone.

ALAN: As in, there's no other presences with us at the moment?

MME. MANDAYA: If you like.

ALAN: We've been around the house several times. Of course there's still the evidence review we can do tomorrow, but for the moment, I'm not sure there's anywhere else to investigate outside.

MME. MANDAYA: If I may, what if we brought Eve out here? I feel quite strongly the activity is connected to her.

RYAN: You're not using my wife as ghost bait.

MME. MANDAYA: Good lord, child, you've seen too many movies. All I'm suggesting—

SANDRA *(off-screen)*: What would be better at this point is if we joined everyone else inside.

MME. MANDAYA: As you wish.

(The camera follows Ryan, Alan, and the psychic into the house. Ryan opens the door on Charles, Caitlin, and Eve gathered in the living room, seated around a tape recorder on the coffee table. Ryan bends to kiss the top of Eve's head and she reaches up to touch his cheek. He whispers in her ear, pointing to the crew and everyone tramping in after him, which causes her to turn and stare into the camera dead-on.)

CAITLIN: What on—

(Tape ends.)

COMING UP:

VOICEOVER: The Paranormal Investigators of Pennsylvania
find new evidence of activity in the Hawthornes' home.

CHARLES *(investigation footage)*: Tell me that you're here.

EVP *(subtitled)*: *Here.*

CHARLES *(interview footage)*: *Something* is going on in this
house.

VOICEOVER: And Ryan weighs his options.

RYAN *(interview footage)*: I don't know if it's safe for us here
anymore.

VOICEOVER: But the week is far from over, and the
Hawthornes may have to make some difficult decisions.

EVE *(investigation footage)*: Why is this happening to me? What
have I done to welcome this?

VOICEOVER: Next, on *Searching for . . . the Invisible World*.
(Commercial break)

DAY 3

INTERVIEW—ALAN

ALAN: It is very, very unusual for any kind of discarnate being to cause harm to the living. Mostly because they are incapable of it. The spirit lives on, but it is tremendously difficult to move physical objects in our world, even the slightest bit. And while I have felt myself in the presence of those who would wish to cause harm, that harm is generally emotional. It bears on the psychological space, not the physical . . . All I'm saying is, let's not panic.

Transcript: SIW-221a-18/CAMERA A, 07:22:29

INTERVIEW—CHARLES

CHARLES: Alan doesn't think it was a ghost at all, does he? Did you tell him denial's not just a river in Egypt?

Transcript: SIW-221a-19/CAMERA A, 07:57:46

INTERVIEW—CAITLIN

CAITLIN: I saw it! I mean, none of us *saw* it saw it, but I saw it happen before anybody. Sometimes I get this sense that something is about to happen. And then? It does.

Transcript: SIW-221a-20/CAMERA A, 08:24:41

INTERVIEW—RYAN

RYAN: Is he okay? I'm gonna be honest with you, I'm worried about malpractice. Not malpractice, what's that called? Negligence. Whatever. I signed a contract that I wouldn't sue you guys for breaking any of my furniture, but you're not going to sue us either, are you? Does that ever happen?

Transcript: SIW-221a-21/CAMERA A, 08:49:33

INTERVIEW—EVE

EVE: No, nothing. Nothing on this scale before. Even the picture frames—that was a hasty job, they were never supposed to stay up. This was a shelf, nailed into the wall. Ryan's a decent handyman. I was never worried about the security of the brackets to the wall. Whatever wrenched it free took some doing.
Question
EVE: Unfortunate, yes. Of course I'm concerned for the well-being of your cameramen. But coincidence? I don't think either of us wants to believe that.

Transcript: SIW-221a-22/CAMERA A, 09:11:38

INTERVIEW—MADAME MANDAYA

MME. MANDAYA: I've said it before and I'll say it again. You people are dealing with energies and forces much stronger than you, that you have no idea about. None of you has any idea what you've released here. Alan means well, but even he may have stepped into a swamp too murky to get out of. But maybe now you'll listen to me. I'm sorry someone had to go to the hospital to make that point. But as they say, it's all fun and games until . . . I'm sorry. That was crass. He is going to be all right, isn't he?

———— · ————

"Patrick's with Macon. They're holding him for a little while, but the doctors don't think—it sounds like they waited a long time to see a doctor at all . . . It was the middle of the night, where else were we going to take him? I don't care if he says he's fine. A whole shelf of books hit him on the head, followed by a very heavy vase." Sandra flashed Alan a nervous smile before resuming pacing the dining room, phone to her ear. Alan, sitting across from her in the living room, was scanning PIP's footage, trying to triangulate the moment the shelf collapsed with any of the readings his team had collected. Occasionally he looked up to the empty space on the wall, the holes left by the screws pinpoints of perfect darkness trailing rough arcs they slashed through the drywall on their way down. The shelf itself had been laid neatly on the floor, the books stacked nearby, the vase—more solid than it appeared—unscathed, set on top.

"I don't know." With the hand that wasn't holding the phone, Sandra reached up and massaged her forehead. "Do you want me to send him home? You can send Davon or one of the other guys down. I can shoot interviews while we wait . . . What about someone on Lisa's team? Maybe she can loan us one of her guys. Tell him we'll pay him time and a half." She wandered toward Alan, then turned down the hallway, to the kitchen.

Alan rewound the cassette and listened again to Eve asking,

"Why are you here?" He bent his ear toward the tape player, straining to discern through the mechanical turnings, the clickings of the machine, anything—a syllable, a scratch, a chuff of breath too close to the microphone to have been from one of the living. That faint hiss of empty tape had become an obsolete sound, cousin to the static of TVs after the programming day ended, radios out of broadcast range, delays during intercontinental phone calls made over landlines. Static contained potential: the chance for a signal, for the car to drive within another station's frequency, for the TV to suddenly, urgently blip back to life. No more. In the digital age there was something or there was null, a blank space without a quality of its own.

"Hey." Charles came in through the front door, startling Alan out of his reverie.

"I thought you'd gone."

"I dropped Caitlin off at her house. Do you want help with the evidence review?"

"I can take care of it." Alan was aware of Sandra lingering in the hallway just outside the living room. "It was a long night. Go home, get some rest. I'll call you if I find anything interesting."

Charles followed Alan's eyes, saw Sandra, now punching something into her BlackBerry, and nodded, leaving without saying goodbye. He let the door slam a little too hard, but Sandra didn't flinch, indicating, perhaps, that she was prepared for it.

She came and sat beside Alan on the couch, tipped her head forward into her hands, and sighed between her fingers.

"Is there coffee?" she asked.

Alan leapt off the couch to pour her the remaining inch from a pot someone had made . . . yesterday? They hadn't been to sleep yet, so maybe it didn't count. Sandra took it and thanked him but didn't sip, instead staring into space with the mug in both hands. Alan didn't want to disturb the planning and producing she was no doubt turning over in her mind. But they had been up all night together—Sandra had lost the freshness of the day before, her natural odor creeping through a faded layer of perfume. They were probably in the same weird headspace and he wanted to take advantage of the intimacy. He could say things now, attribute it to sleeplessness, feel better—sleep better, later—having said them.

But Sandra spoke first. "This episode is cursed."

"I'd say it's just the sort of event you were hoping to capture. Isn't that why we went inside, to see what activity would result from everyone being together?"

"I don't know if we can use it, we don't ever show the workings of the show on-screen. This isn't one of those meta-documentaries that suddenly becomes about the making of itself." She pointed to the tape player. "What did you get?"

"Nothing, yet."

"This episode is picking off my cameramen one by one—how is that possible?"

Alan shrugged. "It's not only possible, it's expected. The vast majority of the time we don't capture anything. Unlike you." He smiled teasingly, but Sandra didn't see it.

"We can't afford to waste any more time. Not this week." She pursed her lips. "I mean, doesn't it make you question everything, your whole . . . reason for being here, when all this happens and you have nothing to show for it?" She recoiled from herself, fell back into the couch. "I am so sorry. I'm overtired."

Alan had learned long ago not to take personally this type of anger, which normally came from homeowners. Behind the frustration was fear, perhaps a kind they'd never known before.

He reached out to place a hand on Sandra's arm, then thought better of it.

"No apology necessary."

"But you would prefer to get *some* evidence on tape?"

"The tape doesn't matter. The tape is not for the likes of us, Sandra."

"You and me?"

"Me and the other nutjobs. We've always believed. The tapes are for the skeptics, people who need proof. I don't need evidence to show me that another world exists, concurrent to this one, and that it can communicate with us when it chooses to. The evidence is for . . ."

Sandra looked surprised. "Me." She saw it, then, for the first time: the line they stood on opposite sides of. Double yellow, unbroken. For Alan it had always been there.

"What about you, Sandra? What do you believe?"

"It's not—"

"Because it sounds to me like you want the tape to yield something. Do you? Do you want to believe that shelf fell by some rule of physics and would fall again under the same circumstances? Or do you want to believe that something extraordinary happened a few hours ago?" He knew he was pushing her. They'd never spoken to each other this way before.

Her eyes flashed, a cornered animal. It made Alan a little sad. Her professionalism had almost squeezed the curiosity out of her.

Almost. A while back, following the second or third shoot the Paranormal Investigators of Pennsylvania had participated in, Sandra had asked Alan to recommend a place for the crew to get a celebratory drink and, when he named a popular sports bar, invited him to join them. After her third drink, Sandra had leaned in to confess to Alan that once, years ago, she'd gone to a psychic. A friend had put her up to it. The woman sat on the street with worn tarot cards on a little table. It had cost fifteen dollars.

"And?" Alan had smiled. "Did she know things about you? Did her predictions come true?"

Sandra had looked distant for a minute, then a little baffled, as if she hadn't, until this moment, considered the question. "Yeah," she'd said, taking in the crew crowded around their table ten feet away, shouting at the hockey game on TV, as if all this had been in the cards and she was just now realizing it. "They more or less did."

"And how does that make you feel?" He'd practically had to shout to be heard. It wasn't the ideal location for a conversation of this nature; Alan for the most part avoided bars.

"I mean, everything they say is so general, right? It could apply to anybody."

"That doesn't answer my question." He'd smiled.

Her breath had been hot on his neck. "She told me Thursday's a bad day for me. You want another beer?" She'd pointed to his half-full glass. Alan had shaken his head no, but she'd left to get herself one, and upon her return she'd moved on from the topic.

At the Hawthornes', Alan fought the urge to make some self-deprecating comment, a disguised apology for wanting, more than was reasonable, Sandra to believe. He tried to feel sorry for her, her world limited by the tangible. But he didn't feel that, either. He thought it would take so little for her to see: a moment or two without the façade, an experience she could neither explain nor forget. She was almost there. But then her phone chirped and she reached for it, and Alan began packing up their equipment to take back to the office, to prepare an assessment she'd want him to deliver later, on-screen.

———————•·———————

Eve was working in the yard. An inexperienced gardener, she'd tried it first ironically, as part of the whole homeowner package, then found she loved the feeling of her hands in the dirt, the sweat building up on her skin. The show had vacated the premises for an extra-long lunch break after the late night. Eve was happy to be alone for a few hours while Ryan checked in at the store. She could take advantage of the warmth to move bulbs from pots in the garage into the ground. On her knees, she made her way down the path that led to her studio without looking directly at it. She hadn't painted, hadn't done anything, in months.

Ryan had set up the studio for her as a gift. It was a small shed that had come with the property; he'd wired it for electricity and installed an old, deep industrial sink she could fill with the hose. The detail Ryan added that Eve loved the most was a skylight. It was needlessly luxurious, the roof angled so that Eve could sit at her table in the afternoons and without tilting her head too uncomfortably look up and see a segment of sky change color as the sun went down, or, if she was feeling ambitious, get started early and watch light from the sunrise fill the space. He knew what she was giving up, leaving New York, and he wanted her to continue to pursue her art.

At first, everything had seemed possible: the roominess here, the slowed-down pace, would afford her the luxury to reflect on her process, refine it. In time, the imaginary circle of critique she had lugged around in her head after grad school would fade, replaced by a space, vast and empty, untainted by the expectations of others. In that space her thoughts would be pure, and she'd return to her art with a joy she remembered from her undergraduate days, when nothing was at stake and she could bang away for eight-hour stretches without dehydration or lower-back pain to follow. There would be days when she would barely be conscious of the work taking shape before her, mornings when she would step into her studio surprised by what she'd painted the previous day. The great artists, she was sure, lived like this always—mere conduits, a stopping place for images on their way to someplace higher.

But what Ryan didn't realize was that Eve needed more than a room in which to work. The nearest museum was a history museum, and the history of the region consisted largely of mining disasters. Out here, the only conversations she had about art were with elementary-school children. Ryan had given her the studio, but he didn't actually care about her work—he never asked how it was going, wasn't sure how to reply if she brought up some problem she was working on. When she got frustrated, felt stuck, she reminded herself: she had chosen this. But on her dark days she wondered if she had chosen in a moment of anchorlessness, when her MFA was behind her and nothing awaited her in the future: no job, no gallery representation.

She tried to push through the doubts, the resentment that Ninebark was an unworthy venue for her talents. She assembled half a dozen new paintings and emailed a former professor with a few images of her work. He urged her to apply for a residency in New England—nine months, fully funded. He was on the board at the arts center and told her she'd be a shoo-in. The night she sent off her application, Eve was awoken by her bladder (too much celebratory wine) and in the bathroom mirror saw behind her the clearest vision she'd had yet—a bedraggled woman, gaping eye sockets and a line for a mouth, ring of notches around her neck, there and then gone when Eve turned around.

She had been in her studio when she opened the envelope from the residency center—a form rejection, not a word from the professor apologizing or offering any sort of explanation. She

didn't know whether to cry or scream, but she didn't have time
to decide—she heard a crackling behind her and turned to see
an electrical outlet shooting sparks, the leg of an easel already
aflame. Ryan brushed it off as a faulty connection between the
house's wiring and her studio's, and the easel was still usable,
but to Eve it reinforced what she already knew: forces conspired
against her.

"Baby," Ryan had said. "These are just unfortunate accidents."
Eve had spent the day lying on the floor. Ryan had brought her
out a sandwich and glass of lemonade midafternoon and found
her watching clouds through the skylight, every few minutes
the window becoming a frame for a perfect image she'd never
produce anything comparable to. He'd been similarly dismissive
of her encounter in the bathroom, writing it off as half drunken-
ness, half sleep. Some nights she shot up in bed and Ryan patted
her, patronizingly, *It's probably just the* . . . , before falling back
into unconsciousness.

"Unfortunate for whom?"

"For . . . you?" He looked confused.

"Yes, and why me? Why me, over and over again? Why not
your store—why did the fire start in my studio and not your
store?" She banged the floor with her fist.

"Eve," Ryan had crouched beside her, looking straight down
into her eyes, "this is a shed from, like, the eighteen-hundreds
with a couple of extension cords running from the house. It
wouldn't pass even the shoddiest, most lazy inspection. The strip
mall the store is in was built like twenty years ago, it—"

"Okay," Eve held her palms up to stop him. "I get it." The
problem was, Ryan didn't get it—didn't connect these "unfortunate accidents" to her attempts to work. Didn't see the pattern,
the forest for the trees. He hadn't finished college, but he'd been

raised with a work ethic that never faltered; each day she trucked out here only to doodle and rearrange stuff on the shelves widened the gulf between them. At a certain point it didn't make sense to pretend anymore; with no one to share her work with she stopped entering her studio altogether, let Ryan think teaching was taking up all of her time.

Her bulbs planted, Eve opened the door to the studio for the first time in months. That musty shed smell, which she had kept at bay with scented candles before the fire, had returned with a vengeance, as had the spiders laying claim to high corners. The last time she had been in here, she hadn't even tidied up before she'd left: the plate Ryan had brought her still sat on her work table, dusted with the few crumbs that hadn't been carried away by bugs. The lemonade glass was empty, sticky within, an ant traversing its base. Her sketchbook lay open on the table, a few freshly sharpened pencils ready to go. Eve set about straightening up, putting the dishes to soak in a bucket she filled from the hose, sweeping the spiderwebs from the corners. She imagined bringing the show into her studio, talking about those experiences in an interview. She imagined the paranormal team in here, the three of them with their tape recorders, asking questions in a tight circle as the cameramen elbowed for room. Then going back to their offices, listening to their tapes, finding nothing. *Sorry.* Shrug. She thought about Madame Mandaya telling her that a space responded in kind to what you offered it, wondered what she could do to make everyone else see it her way.

The room now tidier, Eve perched on her stool. She tilted her face up to the skylight and closed her eyes. She took a long, slow breath in to a count of four, held it, exhaled. She listened to her space.

"So what do you got for me, fucker, huh? Show me what you want to show me, it's now or never."

At that moment the clouds parted and a beam of sunlight inched over the frame of the skylight, flooding the room with brightness. Eve sat astonished—if it had been a movie, she would have rolled her eyes at such an obvious "sign." The beam bisected the room, a precise line that crossed the table where she sat, the floor behind Eve, all the way to the edge of the sink, where a glass soap dish balanced, the soap still a bit foamy. It rocked for a moment before the dish below it shattered, all at once.

Eve stood up. The soap remained in place, wobbling on a fragment of glass. The rest of the dish—clear, formerly fish shaped—was in a thousand pieces in the sink, on the floor; some had jumped to a shelf a foot away. Eve extended one finger to the soap, stilling it. It wasn't hot, and the glass she touched around it wasn't hot, either. The dish had simply, as if willingly, exploded, having given in to some rule of physics Eve was not aware of. It had sat in this very spot for months, the sun rose every day, and today was the day the two collided, with her as witness.

She sat back down, her heart pounding. Her eyes landed on a cup of brushes on the shelf, and as she stared at it, it began to rattle in place. It picked up momentum, rocking back and forth, its contents jostling in the glass, until it fell, smashing spectacularly on the poured-concrete floor, scattering brushes as far as ten feet away.

Eve gasped. She looked around her studio. There was glass everywhere: water glasses for drinking and cleaning paintbrushes; vases and bowls that had been wedding presents, displayed with found objects on the shelves; holders for the candles she lit while working. It all seemed to hum with trapped energy, its beauty merely a placeholder for its inherent danger. How easily a shard could become embedded in a fingertip or heel, how readily plunged into an artery. She had asked, and the studio had spoken.

She took a plate off a shelf, a wedding present from someone in Ryan's family, a dull brown sort of platter she supposed was meant for hors d'oeuvres. But who in Ninebark was worth having to dinner? Ryan's friends, who could talk endlessly about college basketball and little else? Eve raised the platter over her head and slammed it to the floor. It broke, but did not shatter. She tried again—a cheap glass vase that had come with a bouquet Ryan had bought her for some anniversary. It held half-used tubes of paint, which Eve tipped out onto the table before throwing this down, too, releasing with it a howl of anguish. The vase broke more dramatically, a shard bouncing up and grazing her cheek without breaking the skin.

Eve was panting. She took off a shelf the most precious object, a crystal vase from Tiffany that Ryan's grandmother had purchased for them. In the beginning, she had made a vow to regularly buy herself fresh flowers, eventually grow her own, and always keep them in sight, keep beauty only a glance away. She lifted the vase, *Lion King*–style, watched it capture sunlight, then lowered it. She wrapped the vase in a towel that hung by the sink and tucked it under her arm.

She stepped carefully over the shards littering the floor and stood a moment in the door to her studio, looking in. *Fuck you*, she thought, heart pounding. *Fuck you for making this place, my sanctuary, so fraught.* The room was still. It looked back at her, unconcerned, the only movement that of a bird passing over the skylight. She left the studio and went to call Ryan.

Charles opened the door to the PIP office and found Alan inside, head bent familiarly over the desk. Charles wondered if he'd gone home yet, if he'd taken his own admonishment to sleep. By his hair, his eyes, Charles guessed not.

"What's up?" he asked, dropping his keys on the desk to alert Alan to his presence. Alan got into these moods sometimes.

"Charles. Sit. I want you to hear something." They were normal words, the words Alan always used, but something made Charles's heart pound a bit as he pulled the second chair up beside Alan's. Their tape recorders were on the desk, and Alan had already digitized the recordings. He hit play on the computer, and Charles's voice, nasal and higher than he told himself his voice was, came through the speakers.

CHARLES: What are you looking for here? Why don't you move on? Do you have a choice?
(Ten-second pause)
CHARLES: It's not too late, right? You can, if you decide to, choose something else?
(Thirty-second pause)
CHARLES: Tell me someone is here. Tell me I'm not talking to myself in a dirty basement, no different than any other Monday night.

Charles blushed, wanting to explain, wanting his relationship with Alan to be one in which it was unnecessary to explain. He opened his mouth, but Alan lifted his hand to stop him.

"A little doubt is never a bad thing. And I didn't ask you to come here to have a heart-to-heart, Charles."

"Okay," Charles said, exhaling. "Thanks." Alan smiled, and in lieu of punching him on the shoulder or some other guy thing, replayed the segment, upping the decibels.

CHARLES: It's not too late, right? You can, if you decide to, choose something else?
(*Thirty-second pause*)
CHARLES: Tell me someone is here.

And then, a cough. Alan clicked back, upped the decibels again, played at half speed.

CHARLES: Tell me someone is here.

This time, the cough had shape to it.
A hundred decibels, quarter speed, Charles's voice low, drugged.

CHARLES: Tell me someone is here.
?: *Here.*

It sounded like a word. Not in the generous pauses Charles left after his questions, but the breath of space between his first statement and his second. A voice, likely male, definitely not with him in the basement when the recording was made. Alan backed up half a second, hit play again.

?: *Here.*

That was what Charles heard and it made sense, but in their line they didn't like to influence other listeners, who might have their own interpretations. When it was just Charles and Alan, this *you-first, no-you, no-please-I-insist* could go on for quite some time. Alan raised an eyebrow.

"Here," Charles said, and again his voice was just a tad higher than he'd like, a bit too whiny. He didn't put enough weight on the word, as if he wasn't sure where he was, or whether he had any right to be there. The voice on the tape—deep, assertive—needed only say that one word to claim all rights and privileges herein. Charles would always be a tourist, somebody's annoying guest.

"That's what I get, too." Alan was smiling. It was nice when their impressions lined up. Nice, too, to be back in the realm of the interpretive, a shared experience about which they could disagree. Forgotten was the fact that Charles made this tape alone in the basement, conducting a session in some kind of desperation rather than by the method Alan had tested and retested over the years. This was, they were finding, an assertive presence. Monday it had been outside, Tuesday it had—

"Wait," Charles said. "I made this tape on Monday, before the knocking."

Alan nodded, having grasped this some time ago.

"So whatever this is, it's separate from what was outside the house. We're dealing with more than one presence?"

Alan shrugged facetiously. *Who are we to say*, he loved to ask, comparing their work to that of lowly secretaries in a bureaucracy too complex to fathom, or monks copying scripture in years of dedicated silence. We don't run the meetings. We just take the notes.

"Do you want to hear it again?" Alan asked, as if he needed to, as if there was any possibility the recording did not need to be reviewed again in light of this greater understanding. The two men turned back to the screen, their faces aglow from the monitor, and listened.

———·——

As her crew settled into food court lunches, Sandra strolled the mall. She had proposed the field trip, since they had a long night ahead of them. She thought everyone could use a change of scenery.

The show typically shot twice at night, but Sandra had pitched to the office in New York an additional evening shoot. She had been FedExing memory cards back each day and had stated on her last check-in call that although everything they'd captured so far was a little messy, just a tad incoherent, they were on the verge of something more definitive. "Huge" was the word she'd heard come out of her mouth. Of course, her editors had no network sway; Sandra only needed to tell herself she'd done all she could. The pitch worked, though: she was given approval for a third night shoot. Sandra, who hadn't expected her bluff to be called, asked Alan for guidance.

Alan had recommended a séance, to give Madame Mandaya the chance to narrow in on some possible sources of the Hawthornes' disturbances. Her editors loved the idea—having everyone in one room would be easy to film and would practically guarantee usable footage. Lisa had given a cameraman up without protest. Everything was going smoothly on her shoot, she'd said on the phone; they might even finish up and ship out a day early.

"Great," Sandra had told her, staring down the barrel of another late night.

Though she'd suggested it casually, Sandra had an ulterior motive in taking her crew to the mall. She would never admit how much, since moving to New York, she missed malls. Missed the clashing music spilling out of stores, the selection a cue for who should shop there: the more clubby the atmosphere, the more svelte the clientele. Missed the wooden benches arrayed around large stone planters. Were the plants they contained real, or plastic? Sandra didn't care. She was tired of asking questions. She wanted to squeeze those weird pillows filled with tiny beads, sit in the massage chairs she would never consider buying, breathe in the rich leathery smell of the shoe store. She wanted women in blazers and pantyhose, their hair pulled back in tight chignons, to rush around bringing her shoes in tissue paper, kneeling to help her put them on. She wanted everything to look like exactly what it was.

Like the bookstore. It resembled every other bookstore of its name, with its brown and green color scheme, its lights dimmer than those of the mall proper, its smell refined. Within it, shoppers knew what to expect, no matter the mall or city. On the magazine racks, one cover after another bore images of those who had made their fame in Sandra's own industry. How would it feel, she wondered, dragging her fingertips across their surfaces, to work on a normal show, one that people had heard of? There were too many of them to keep track of, and to Sandra the stars all looked the same, the women with their long, wavy blowouts and Birkin bags. The men, few that there were, mainly white, rich, interchangeable nonentities.

INTERVIEW—ALAN

ALAN: When I enter a home for the first time, I assume nothing about what the family believes or does not believe. Almost universally they are doubting their own senses, and we start from a place of trying to detect any activity, without attributing it to one source or another.

Question

ALAN: It might be a chicken-or-egg thing, but if people are reaching out to me, there's a part of them that already wants to believe it's paranormal, even if they scoff at first and make a big show out of their skepticism. They say they've exhausted other options, but I often find they haven't. Once

I've spent time in the home and confirmed some of the
things they've experienced, they're more willing to open up.
They seem . . . relieved. They tell me about other things that
happened to them in the past. Little things that may have
seemed inconsequential at the time. But things they could
never explain, and never got over.

NEW AGE/Paranormal Exp. was tucked among the Bibles,
Spirituality, and the like, far enough away from the manga that
Sandra would not be bothered by teenagers, nowhere near the
display tables of new fiction and bestsellers. The bookcase turned
at one end, creating a cul-de-sac that did more than provide an
entire extra shelf for books on "The Law of Attraction," whatever that was. This was the corner people visited to sit on the
floor and read: shoved in with books about UFO sightings and
crystals were a biography of Nelson Algren, a celebrity tell-all,
and one of those slim volumes of hackneyed advice sold near the
registers. Sandra could imagine customers wandering, finding
this corner ideal to settle in and read a few pages before deciding
on a purchase. The New Age books themselves were barely organized, the Paranormal Exp. shelf a mishmash of everything in
the section. While she was looking for the title she had glimpsed
yesterday in the PIP office, a clerk came by, put a book back, and
walked away, uninterested in doing any tidying up. And when
Sandra found what she'd come for, it was not shelved alphabeti-
cally or near related titles. She felt a little sorry for the people
who had written these books, which were not afforded the same
respect as memoirs and YA blockbusters. Wasn't everyone really
into the supernatural these days, lusting over teenage vampires
and dressing like zombies for bar crawls? Since she'd joined Roving Eye, friends had sent her countless clips from similar shows,
each more low-budget than the last. It was a bubble, one that

had swelled far beyond what anyone might have anticipated, but now, at what had to be its precarious apex, Sandra thought the Paranormal Exp. shelf deserved to be located a little more centrally, tended to a little more carefully, even if she herself wasn't entirely sure what the "Exp." was short for.

INTERVIEW—ALAN

ALAN: We never fully know. There isn't one kind of activity you can point to and say, definitively, "This is paranormal." There's always an alternative explanation. Sometimes, as you suggest, people are working through real psychological issues, trauma and stress. I listen for what I think the families are really asking of me, and if they want it I lay a scrim of "data" over a well of intuition and belief. Just enough to give it a . . . a validity.
Question

ALAN: Of course. I'm biased—we all are—and so I want to ascribe this particular reading to every space I go into. I have to make a conscious effort not to jump to a supernatural explanation the moment something unusual happens. If you want it too much you'll see it everywhere, and that can be dangerous.
Question

ALAN: Because we still have to live in the real world. Whether or not you believe in ghosts, we have to function in a society in which most things obey the laws of physics, and most people want them to . . . The problem, too, is that I don't exactly want what the homeowners want. I never tell them this, of course.
Question

ALAN: They want no activity. Who could blame them? They
    want to feel safe in their homes. But when I find a home
    with a lot of activity—man, I could stay there forever.
    Question
ALAN: Just . . . listening.

Except the people who watched paranormal investigative
shows may very well have watched similar shows without gradu-
ating to books. The people who did read these books probably
got them from occult shops, the omnipresent internet. So if
these titles ended up among the detritus of the mall bookstore, it
was an accurate picture of where the occult stood in the culture.
And even Sandra grabbed two magazines almost at random to
place on either side of her book at the register and in the thin
plastic shopping bag she was handed. Never mind that the clerk
would never see her again. Never mind she wasn't buying hard-
core pornography or some self-help book by the social-media
famous, just *The Grudging Ghost Hunter: My Wary Pursuit of
the Supernatural*. She was ashamed of her purchase. She was no
better than the rest of the mall walkers, nor the reality stars with
their blowouts to whom she could never talk about her former
job, whenever this eventually became her former job.

INTERVIEW—ALAN

ALAN: We'll never know for sure until it's too late. This kind
    of belief is a choice that you keep on choosing. Most of the
    time we get nothing. And then, once in a while, we get a
    little something that could mean a lot. Just enough to keep
    going.
    (Pause)

ALAN: A couple years ago I attended a lecture on the shifting
    interests in monsters in our culture: vampires in the
    nineties, zombies in the aughts, et cetera. The speaker said
    every culture gets the monster it deserves. I've taken from
    that that every house gets the haunting it deserves, or really,
    the haunting it wants. So when I enter a home, I wonder,
    who in this house—living or otherwise—wants something
    very badly? And what do they want?
    Question
ALAN: What about you, Sandra? What would it take for you to
    believe? Isn't that what you really want to talk about?
    (Tape ends.)

——— · ———

Regina pulled her car up to the house before she realized she
hadn't called first; she didn't even have the Hawthornes' number.
There were cars in the driveway, but they could have belonged
to anyone involved with the show. Luckily when she knocked
Eve answered the door, and the rooms behind her were empty.
"Mrs. Hawthorne."

"Yes? Oh, it's you!" she said. "I didn't recognize you without
all the . . ." She gestured to indicate jewelry, scarves, etc. "Anyway, please call me Eve."

"Eve. Call me Regina." Eve looked a little amused about
Madame Mandaya's real name. "I know we have something
scheduled for later tonight, but I'd love the opportunity to talk
with you one-on-one first. Could we get a cup of coffee?"

"Okay." Eve held open the door.

"Ah." Regina didn't move. "I think outside the house would
be better."

Eve nodded; even, Regina thought, a bit relieved. "There's a place in town. If we drive we'll be there in three minutes."

"Lead the way."

Regina, though a business owner herself in the county, mostly avoided Ninebark, finding it on the whole bland and without personality, too subservient to the whims of shallow consumerism. She expected little from a local coffee shop, the pastry case and stock photography on the walls a mere placeholder for some future tanning salon or cell-phone store. But the café Eve led them to was delightful—mismatched Formica tables and vinyl chairs, old tin ceiling imported from somewhere, table by the door with alternative newspapers from Philly and a schedule of upcoming musical performances next to the menu. Paintings by local artists on the walls showed variety, if not exactly talent, and a chalkboard sign promised beer after four p.m.

They took their cappuccinos to a couple of armchairs, velvety and worn, in the back. Eve ordered a sandwich piled with cucumbers, tomato, avocado, and hummus, six inches high. Regina picked at the crumbs on her coffee cake while she watched Eve eat.

"I guess you want to talk about last night," Eve said, still working on a corner of bread. "Did anything you picked up on connect to what happened? The shelf?"

Regina tilted her head. "Why don't we start with what *you* think is going on. You've experienced the most activity."

"I was hoping you had felt something, could tell the show, you know, 'X, Y, and Z are definitely going on, definitely paranormal.'" Eve looked at her. Regina didn't reply. "You did see *something* last night?"

"We all saw *something*." Regina smiled. "But we may have different interpretations of what we saw."

Eve looked frustrated at this, her shining eyes skirting away.

Regina leaned forward, softened her tone. "Ryan has seen things, too?"

Eve pressed her lips together.

"What about when you're both in the house? What happens then?"

"Normally I'm alone, or the only one who's awake, when I experience something. Sometimes I worry I am moving objects around and forgetting, or switching to this hidden part of my brain that is sheltering me from . . ." She trailed off, hesitant to say aloud exactly what Regina wanted her to consider.

Regina nodded. "Activity like you've experienced tends to increase during periods of stress and upheaval—after a divorce, or the loss of a job. When did all of this start for you?"

"All of it? My whole life."

Regina didn't react—she had expected this. "But it's intensified more recently?"

Eve shrugged. "I guess."

"Tell me about Ryan. How did you two meet?"

She had just finished her master's degree in fine art, had two drawings and a painting in a group show at the school's gallery. One of her classmates had a graduation party, and Ryan was there, a friend of a friend. Newly on the prowl, Ryan chatted Eve up in the tiny Manhattan kitchen, the sink filled with ice into which bottles of overpriced beers were plunged, craft brews appropriate for an art-school party but too snooty for Ryan, who went digging in the fridge for something less hoppy. He owned a business, he was divorced. He seemed so much more adult than Eve's classmates, manic wanderers and directionless trust-fund babies blithely skipping off to residencies or living off grants, buying themselves more time. Ryan's problems were not born of a fickle market, the whims of Larry Gagosian. She was drawn to him and he was appropriately dazzled by her, the speed with which she took him to her apartment, her openness in listening to him talk about his ex the next morning over breakfast. They sat in a diner for hours, and when he told her he had to go back to Pennsylvania that night to reopen the store in the morning, but that she should come with him, she laughed and said okay. They both thought she was joking, both secretly hoped she was serious, and after a meaningful kiss outside his car, Eve went up to her shared apartment and began to pack her things. Before she'd even had a chance to tell Ryan of her intentions he texted her that a local school was looking for an art teacher for the fall. Nothing had ever seemed so clear to Eve: a whole life, readymade. She needed only step into it. They had a small outdoor wedding in the Poconos that few of her art-school friends bothered to attend. But everything, Eve told herself, everything going forward would be oriented toward what was real. Attainable. They'd moved into the house, she'd started her job, and one night just before she fell asleep she heard pounding in the walls, faint but rhythmic, the fists of protesting mice. That was the beginning.

"Noises at first," Regina said. "Did Ryan hear them?"

"He acted like he did. But overall I would say, no, he didn't hear anything. When we were renovating, he noticed things having been moved, but that's about it."

"Does Ryan feel any guilt about pulling you away from your work and your life in the city? You can't be terribly inspired out here . . ." Regina swept her hand to indicate the dog and flower paintings around them, acrylics applied with an exuberance to compensate for lack of vision.

"He gave me a studio to work in."

"So he does feel guilt," Regina confirmed. "The studio is consolation."

Eve's face shifted—Regina could see a tightening, the swift closure of automatic doors. "Staying in New York wouldn't have guaranteed anything. The competition is incredible, the cost of living insane. *Very* few make it as an artist."

"And yet so many continue to make art." Regina smiled.

Eve glowered. "I don't know why I'm trying to convince you. You don't know me. You don't even know what's going on in my house, which is literally the only reason you're here."

"So then let's talk about what's going on in your house." Regina did not feel insulted by Eve, nor was she intimidated. She had a feeling she knew more than Eve was comfortable with. "You've had quite a bit of activity, with a TV crew conveniently on hand to capture it all."

Eve looked at Regina steadily. She, too, was not intimidated. "If I was cooking this up, like those nineteenth-century women who kept ectoplasm in their vaginas, don't you think someone would have figured it out by now?"

Regina smiled. Eve had done her homework. "I don't think you are 'cooking' anything up."

"I wasn't even in the house Monday night."

"Your presence is not always required for such events to occur. The human mind is a powerful thing, Evelyn." The girl winced a little at her real name. Lucky guess. "Clamped down for too long, its needs will start to manifest themselves in physical ways." Regina took a breath. "Do you know the term 'PK,' psychokinesis?" She put a hand on top of Eve's; but Eve shrank back.

"That's like moving things with my mind."

Regina smiled. "That's putting it a bit simply. And I am not suggesting you have control over it."

"What do you think I'm trying to say that I can't say any other way, so that I have to do this bizarre dance to get people to pay attention to me? Why would I care what any of these . . ." She trailed off, exhausted at the thought.

"You tell me." She wanted to ask, *How much work are you really getting done in that studio Ryan gave you?* But she held back, softened her tone. "If it helps, psychokinesis is much more common among women."

Eve considered this. "'Asocial surrogates for docile selves.'"

"Pardon?"

"It's from *The Madwoman in the Attic*, a famous work of feminist literary criticism. You know *Jane Eyre*? Rochester's first wife was kept in the attic because he was ashamed of her, and then she burned the place down. The first wife represents the, like, Victorian repressed self. If psychokinesis is an updated version of the same anxiety, then I am my own madwoman, burning down my house to make a point."

"What point?"

Eve shook her head. "If I'm causing this, it means on some level I want it, even unconsciously. But I don't think I do." Eve's voice got faster, more insistent with each sentence. "It's keeping me from working . . . it's never been this bad. Cameramen keep walking out, and the ghost hunters want to move in, whether or not I'm even there. You asked about stress, but I don't have any. Ryan and I are stable, and happy. I have a good job and a funky old house, and nothing to complain about that really matters."

No, Regina thought, *what you have to complain about is the only thing that really matters.* But she nodded, pretending to concede. What Eve didn't understand yet was that the things she said were not mutually exclusive—everything could appear perfectly legitimate and frightening to a host of TV people and paranormal investigators and still be a manifestation of her will. Or, at least, something that wouldn't depart until Eve was ready to let it go.

Eve excused herself to go to the bathroom, and Regina stood to clear their table. A small painting hung over the bins for dirty plates and spoons. It was square, less than a foot on either side, and mostly black, though the paint had been slathered on so thickly it protruded from the canvas in waves. Pinpricks dotted the surface, and leaning in close revealed colors in the holes, bursts of pink and green and orange under the surface. The painting was called *Massive Compact Halo Object*, by Eve Beatrice Hawthorne-Malone. Regina smiled. She had been wrong. It wasn't Eve's artistic impulse that was sublimated. It was her *ambition*. Regina looked toward the restrooms in the back, eager for Eve to return.

⸺ ⸱ ⸺

Sandra was alone at the Hawthornes' when Patrick arrived, in her "office" on the enclosed back porch, a room with wicker furniture, a rusting bike. It had always smelled a bit musty, but the odor had intensified, bringing Sandra back to her first apartment with the giant TV, where a mouse had died behind the stove and took days to be discovered. Sandra had propped open the back door to air out the room, and her laptop was out, though she wasn't working. She had her new book in her lap, a thumb holding her spot.

Patrick stood in the doorway, looking down at her. "I'm back."

She didn't look at him. "How's Macon?"

"He says he's fine. He said he could finish out the week. I told him to get some dinner and meet us back here at nine."

"Eight."

"Eight?"

"We start filming at nine. We need time to meet and set up." She spoke slowly, a combination of irritation and exhaustion.

"My bad." Patrick took a breath. "What's the 'séance' looking like?" He made finger quotes around the word.

"What if we let the psychic run it how she normally would?"

"Just tell her, 'Take it away'?"

Sandra finally looked him in the eyes, this man she should have been closest to out of everyone on-site, but whom she had never fully trusted, while he trusted her a little too much. How many ghost stories began with the death of a woman, Sandra wondered. Her naked body, prone on the bed or the floor, plumbed for mysteries. Male detectives circled round, taking pictures, ready to explain. Women were the psychics, the tormented ghosts. Just once, Sandra thought, she'd like one of these stories to start with the death of a man.

"Would that be so terrible?"

Patrick considered it. "We should get an outline from her at the very least, and recommend a couple of beats for her to hit."

Sandra snorted. "The outside of the house was hit. Macon was hit. I'd say we're hitting every beat and then some."

"We've had a lot of bad luck this week, I'll give you that. But we've got Karl coming out, we'll do this séance thing tonight, and Vince and Cameron will work their magic in post like they always do. Before you know it, we'll be out of here."

"*Magic*," Sandra scoffed. "Did you ever wonder if maybe none of this is real because we never gave it the *chance* to be real? That we showed up with our script and our agenda and all our assumptions in place . . ."

"What the hell are you talking about? None of it is real because none of it is real." He crouched in front of her, angled for eye contact. He tried to read the title of her book, but she flipped it over, then slid it under her laptop.

"*Something* is going on. These families are . . . in a specific kind of pain. It's different from other families' pain. Why does it take this form? Why don't we bother to ask?" She felt on the verge of tears. It wasn't just these families, though, it was all of them, all the reality TV subjects she'd known over the years who thought visibility was the solution to their problems. Trapped in private hells, they were desperate not to free themselves, but to let others visit, show off what they'd done with the place.

"Because we're making a stupid show. That's all. We're here to do a job." The word ended her hypnosis. Sandra had a job to do, and she knew how to do it.

She exhaled. "I have gotten so little sleep the past few nights . . ." She shook her head. "Right. We'll shoot the séance in the living room. But we need everyone sitting around a table. Can you make sure there's room? Get some PAs to help you."

"Sure, sure," Patrick said, rising unsteadily and keeping an eye on Sandra as he stepped backward off the porch. "If that's what you want." He left Sandra alone.

What were the contours of Eve's private hell? What did she need to make visible? Not this ghost nonsense. Sandra slid the book into her bag. She opened her laptop, reviewed the script. It had been written last week, of course, before they'd gotten to Ninebark, so Ronnie's name was still all over it. Sandra reached into her bag for her cell phone. She'd tried calling Ronnie previously and it had gone to voice mail, so she wasn't sure why she was trying again, except to later say that she had.

Ronnie picked up.

"Sandra?" His voice came at her across a great distance, from the other side of the Grand Canyon.

"Ronnie? Where have you been?"

"Sandra, I—" His words distorted, wobbled. "—in the dark. I can see that you—" This time his voice didn't so much cut out, as with a dropped call, but was overcome by a rushing sound, something between a waterfall and TV static. "—be there for filming."

"Are you all right? Do you need help?"

"—be there," Ronnie repeated, and the line went dead.

Sandra sat a moment, heart pounding, then stood up to find Patrick.

In the living room, a half-hearted effort had been made to clear space for a table, with the couch pushed back and coffee table under the window. But Patrick was gone.

———— · ————

Ryan crouched on the floor of the studio, peering down at the ceramic platter. He lifted two pieces and fit them back together. "My mom's cousin gave us this," he said, with more sadness than Eve had expected. "She makes them. What happened?"

"I was just sitting here," Eve said, "when the sun came in through the skylight and started, like, exploding glass. First the soap dish. Look, the soap is still on it." Ryan looked. "Then the vase."

"I gave you that vase," he said, "for our anniversary."

"No, it was the little cup that was next." Eve realized her error. She gestured uselessly over the smashed glass on the floor—it was nearly impossible to distinguish what had come from the cup, what the vase.

"This isn't glass, though," Ryan said, still holding the two fragments of platter.

"I broke that," Eve said, softly.

"Accidentally?"

"In frustration."

"Frustration with what?"

"With the show, with . . . everything. With my whole, stupid life right now."

"I gotta be honest with you, Eve, I'm feeling a little frustrated myself." Eve's heart pounded. Ryan rarely got angry at her. "First you tell me you can't work out here, because this town is full of morons. Okay, fine. I won't take that personally. I build you this studio. Then you tell me the studio is the worst kind of present, like a treadmill, you said, because if you don't use it, you feel bad. Then you tell me you can't use it because it's haunted. Then you tell me you can't work in our house because *it's* haunted. What do you want, Eve? Want me to knock this down, start from scratch, build you a new studio? Want me to convert our garage, like that documentary you watched about that artist? All I want is for you to be happy, Eve. Tell me what you need to be happy."

But she couldn't. Confronted with everything she'd said to Ryan, she was struck dumb. All her excuses sounded feeble, ridiculous. They were things she believed, had felt in every cell in her body, but when put into words, they sounded so small. Any more words would have only further reduced the sentiments—complex, shaded—to a dark, sticky substance, bitter and burnt.

She swallowed hard. "I need to understand . . . I need you to try to believe me."

"I am trying, but it's hard, when you tell me that a ghost broke some of these things, but you broke the rest. How can I tell the difference?"

"How can *I* tell the difference?" Eve shouted, with a force that stunned both of them.

In the quiet that followed, they heard car doors slamming.

The crew was back, their timing impeccable. Ryan shook his head and ducked out of the shed, the pieces of his mother's cousin's platter under his arm, leaving the door open behind him. Eve didn't follow him out. She wasn't sure her legs would support her. She took a broom from the corner and began sweeping the remaining glass into a pile, half leaning on the broom as she felt strength return to her. She didn't have a dustpan or garbage bag, but she made as tight and neat a pile as possible until she saw a face at the door to the shed. One of the production assistants, a girl with a dirty-blond ponytail pulled through a baseball cap, stuck her face in and said cheerily that they had been looking for Eve, they were ready to get started.

———·—·———

In front of the house, Sandra was attempting to onboard Karl by orienting him to the couple and her own goals for the evening, glossing over the past two nights and the reason he was called in at the last minute. She wondered if the guys had said something to him, though, or if she wasn't as coherent as she thought, because he kept giving her small, funny looks as she spoke. Macon, to his credit, arrived at the Hawthornes' at eight, and Sandra let him take over. Usually at this point in the week she could see the end, but all of a sudden she was overcome by how much there still was to get through, just tonight. She excused herself from the cameramen and sat down on the porch. The light was diffuse, giving the world a flat, shadowless quality as everyone milled around the yard. At the house next door, a plastic toddler swing hung from an old tree, a blue-and-yellow shock of nostalgia too perfect to be real. Five deep breaths, she told herself, and closed her eyes. Take five breaths, then open your eyes and get through this screwy evening

She was exhaling her fourth, most relaxed breath yet when she heard the click of a lens cap being removed and opened her eyes to see Ronnie beside her, camera already in place on his shoulder, in the same distressed T-shirt he had been wearing when she saw him last, an image of a man's silhouette and string of words that read like either a band name or an awkwardly translated inspirational message.

"We about ready to go?" He peered through the viewfinder, adjusted the focus. Sandra's mouth opened, but the many questions she had for him jammed against one another: *Where have you been what was that phone call what the hell is going on?*

She looked around her. Ronnie's return had gone unnoticed by the rest of the crew.

"Where have you been?" she finally sputtered.

"You've been there." He nodded, then looked at Sandra again, as if realizing he'd mistaken her for someone else. "You will be."

"What?" Sandra couldn't process this. "Where?"

"I don't have much time, Sandra."

He turned his attention back to his camera and trained it on Ryan.

"You aren't going to finish out the week?" The words sounded stupid even as she spoke them, but she couldn't stop herself.

Ronnie shook his head. "Not this time. I need you to see something." He lifted the camera an inch off his shoulder and proffered it. Sandra stood up, shakily. She rarely did this during a shoot; often the first time she saw the footage was in editing. Ronnie lowered it onto her shoulder and nodded for her to put her eye to the viewfinder. He swiveled her shoulders to aim, but Ryan was blocked from view by some sort of black blur, ovoid but swirling, smoky wisps curling off and dissolving.

"It's out of focus."

"No, it's right," Ronnie said, and pushed down a little, keeping the camera in place. He turned it toward Eve, who through the camera appeared to be made of blue powder, bright like lapis lazuli, pure pigment in the form of a woman, but crumbling, a drying mud. Something glowed within, a golden light spilling through cracks that widened as she moved.

"What's going on?"

"What do you see?" He nodded for her to peer once more, this time at the center of the yard, where Sandra stood, surrounded by her team. Through the lens she wore a red dress covered in giant eyes, their irises sky blue and rolling every which way as they blinked. Her curls slithered over her head, extended outward, skinny serpents. Sandra gasped and pulled her head away. Outside the camera, she was wearing a navy blazer, slim jeans. She was here. There, her double was something out of Greek mythology.

She heard Alan's voice, did not want to see whatever he looked like in the camera's view. "I can't," she said, struggling against the weight of the camera before Ronnie removed it.

Sandra's hearing got fuzzy. Her vision vibrated like a projected image. She told herself to breathe. No one was looking at her, concerned, Alan had not rushed over to catch her because she looked like she might faint. She needed to sit down, talk to Alan, talk to Patrick, leave. But Patrick wasn't there.

"Sandra?" Eve asked expectantly, and Sandra, feeling like she stood six inches to the right of herself, called them into places for a brief reshoot of the night before.

"Are there spirits with us tonight?" Madame Mandaya stood with her hands above her head, bracelets clanking in benediction.

"I'm not getting any readings out here," Alan, ever the trooper, recited along with her.

Sandra couldn't look at them without fearing their alternative, monstrous forms.

"We got sound," Ted said and nodded toward Macon and Karl. He didn't see Ronnie; no one saw Ronnie.

"Are we rolling?" Sandra asked mechanically.

"Rolling," Ronnie said, quietly, and when Sandra looked, he was staring right at her.

NIGHT 3

Patrick wandered Main Street, Ninebark, carrying several small gift bags of candles, purchased for the séance. When he first noticed the bar, it didn't particularly excite him: a green-and-brown faux-Irish pub, tin Guinness signs standing in for actual longevity. He went in to have a place to sit down. Fifteen minutes, he told himself. One beer, then back to work.

The place already had a pretty good crowd when Patrick arrived, so he hung his jacket on a small open table, then went to the bar to order. The menus were large and sticky. Flat-screen TVs hung around the room, tuned to basketball. The bartender—male, deferential with that barely sublimated rage decent bartenders carried—was a welcome relief from the bartender he'd spent Monday night with, a twenty-four-year-old redhead all eagerness and glinting nose stud. Patrick ordered a lager and a burger and fries before he remembered he'd planned to stay only a few minutes.

Then he noticed a chalkboard sign, which, in addition to the beers on tap, listed upcoming games. His alma mater was playing that night in the semifinals. He looked at his watch, thought about the séance. He told himself he would leave after the first half.

———— • ————

After the reshoot, Alan found Caitlin in the Hawthornes' living room. She stood by herself in a corner and wasn't running through her usual pre-investigation warm-ups—rolling her head on her neck, bending over to touch her toes. *Keen body, keen mind*, he'd told her once, though he found her mind to be one of the keenest, requiring little support. She looked a little pale now; he attributed it to lack of sleep. A line from Shakespeare ran through his brain: *So shaken as we are, so wan with care.*

"I think this should go well tonight. They're giving Regina a lot of leeway to run this like a normal séance."

Caitlin looked wary. "They've never let any of us call the shots before."

Alan placed a hand on her shoulder. "They're trying to . . ." He searched for words. "There's concern about our footage—"

"Concern?"

One thing that didn't seem to concern people much was the friendship between a thirty-eight-year-old man and a sixteen-year-old girl. Alan suspected it was because in the minds of most people their shared interest was too geeky to be sexual. Caitlin's parents never balked at sending their daughter out on investigations; she never reported any arguments after he dropped her off at one a.m. Once Alan had pulled into her driveway, very late, to see Caitlin's father smoking in an old lawn chair, his robe a little too short and a little too open for sitting outside. Alan readied an apology, but Bill only waved, unperturbed as Caitlin climbed out of the car, the ember on his cigarette a gash in the dark.

"The Hawthornes weren't here Monday night."

"You weren't here, either. You didn't feel—"

"This is the Hawthornes' home, so in terms of how it gets shown on-screen, they want—"

"*She* wants," Caitlin clarified. "*Sandra* wants."

Alan felt his face go warm. The other reason he sensed people weren't concerned about Caitlin's association with him was because of him. Because he was *harmless*. "We should be grateful they're stepping back a little. You and I both know how intense the activity in this house has been. Whatever's here, it wants to be known. We have to trust it to speak for itself." Caitlin's shoulders relaxed. "Plus, Regina is smart, and she's on the same page as us," he said. "We're all on the same page," he amended, though he knew neither he nor Caitlin truly believed that.

———— · ————

Ted had reported some feedback from Eve's microphone, so he'd dug an old one out of the van and pulled Eve aside to the dining room to rewire her.

"Sorry about this. Shitty show, shitty equipment." Eve wondered if he genuinely felt more comfortable with her now, more open to disparaging his employer, or if he was just trying to soften her up. Perhaps he'd been deputized by Sandra to deliver some bad news. Eve had barely seen Sandra all day.

"I remember my first job in New York," Eve said, leaning forward in her chair so Ted could clip the battery pack inside the back of her pants.

"Oh, this isn't my first job," Ted cut in. For some reason this made Eve blush. He gestured for her to continue.

"It was at this fairly prestigious gallery but, like, behind the scenes the place was so disorganized."

"I know what you mean."

"Sometimes I'm astounded the world keeps running, with people being the ones to run it, you know?"

"I definitely do." They smiled at each other, and Eve blushed again.

Regina approached them. Eve had seen her hovering by the front door, but hadn't made eye contact.

"Eve," she said, her voice back in psychic mode, deeper and more sonorous than the voice she'd used in the café earlier. "How are you feeling about this evening?"

"Fine?" Eve said, embarrassed to be having this conversation in front of Ted, who was gently trying to tuck the microphone inside her shirt while making as little contact as possible with her skin. She didn't look up at his face. "How should I be feeling?"

"Vulnerable," Madame Mandaya said confidently. "But trust me, if you acknowledge to yourself those things we were discussing earlier, aspects of yourself you know to be true, you will notice a difference . . ." She waved her hand in a large circle, bangles tinkling. "You have the power to 'clear the air,' so to speak."

"I can't control what happens tonight—"

"I'm not saying that, dear, I just—"

"Excuse me." Eve stood up, knocking into Ted a little, for which she mumbled an apology. "I should go to the bathroom before we start."

Ted took a half step after her, calling out something about the microphone and her pants, but she didn't listen as she closed the bathroom door behind her. She gripped the sink, the porcelain chipped but stable under her weight. She stared at her reflection, thorough and brutal in her self-assessment: lines were forming around her eyes and mouth, more noticeable every time she looked for them. The skin on her face was thinner, her cheeks less full. She analyzed her features for the person the psychic saw, searching for what she imagined that sort of woman would look like: wild-eyed, wild-haired, lips always moving in ongoing incantation. That person wasn't in the mirror. Eve looked and looked, leaning in closer and closer to the mirror until it burst its clips, sliding down the wall. She caught it before it tipped over the sink, then peered into the holes left by the screws, searching for tiny, mischievous hands.

Ignored as the crew organized themselves, Charles went down to the basement, thinking about the "here" on the tape from Monday night, the guy in the van whom Caitlin hadn't seen. If he made contact again, it could confirm the presence, possibly yield a name. Feet stomped above him; Alan could summon him at any moment; it was risky running a Q and A now. His tape recorder in hand, he located the darkest, quietest corner of the cinder-block-walled room.

Charles pressed the play and record buttons simultaneously, watching for a moment the tape on its Sisyphean journey from one reel to the other, before clearing his throat and leaning forward.

"It is Wednesday, April —. I am alone in the basement of the Hawthornes' home. Am I alone? Are you here?"

He was there, hunched on some old exercise equipment, the light from his phone casting a sickly glow on his face. He looked up at Charles. He smiled.

Caitlin slumped in one of the unused interview chairs in the dining room, looking at New Camera Guy, a Brooklyn beardo. She hadn't bothered to learn his name; she didn't expect him to be there come morning. The fact that people were not struck dumb, paralyzed over the oddness of the situation, was almost the oddest thing about the situation.

As always, Alan had his notepad with him and was reviewing it, though Caitlin couldn't believe that he didn't feel the very pulse of this house inside him. Caitlin herself couldn't step in the front door without losing her breath. She felt like she was accompanying the unwitting friend to a surprise party—aware of figures crouching behind the furniture, bracing herself in the half second before the lights went on and everyone screamed.

She tried not to stare at Mrs. Hawthorne, suspecting that everyone else was trying not to stare at her, either. Though she sat alone, a power swirled around her—all the energy in the house hinged on her. A silver disk someone had brought in to address a lighting issue narrowly missed her head; candle flames stretched their points to her face.

Charles came up the basement steps. Caitlin hadn't realized he'd been gone. He stood beside her, pretending to adjust something on his EMF detector.

"What's going on up here?" he asked. He seemed jumpy.

"You got an EVP in the basement?"

"Just now? How should I know?"

"No, Monday. Alan told me you captured one. Why were you in the basement just now?" Caitlin craned her neck to look at him. His lashes were long for a boy's, but they knew their place, standing clear of his dark brown eyes. "Are you okay?"

"Sure."

"So . . . what did it say?"

"The EVP from Monday? 'Here.'"

"'Here'?"

"I asked, 'Is anyone here?' and it said, 'Here.'"

"'Here,'" she repeated. During roll call, it stood up. Alan knew it was there, but she knew it needed to be asked.

She grasped Charles's hand without thinking about it and squeezed it, and he squeezed back, and both their faces reddened.

To move from skepticism to belief, from the "grudging" part of my title to the "ghost hunter" part, was not a matter of a single encounter that checked every box on a list of what a so-called supernatural event should be.

From across the living room Sandra watched Alan approach his team, captivated by his demeanor, which was somehow both tender and professional. He reached a cupped hand toward Caitlin's, not close enough to make contact but enough to adjust her handling of the device she was holding. She nodded to him gratefully and he smiled.

"We should get them miked," Ted said from behind her, and Sandra jumped.

"In a minute."

Her mind drifted back to the book she'd bought. *There are days even now, after decades of this work, when I look back on particular experiences, certain there must be some* other *explanation. But the balance sheet is irrefutable: I've seen and felt too much that I cannot explain, so much that I am now certain the invisible is much, much larger than the visible.*

"The psychic is ready to go."

"The Hawthornes and Alan are already miked?" Ted nodded. "Then it's just Charles and Caitlin who need it. That'll take two minutes." She wanted to preserve for a moment longer a space with no cameras running, the gentle hum of possibility before anyone had any obligation to the tape.

Ted fiddled with some dials. "Charles said they got something on their tapes Monday night."

"EVPs. Should we use them? Will they shed light on what's been going on here?" Sandra asked Ted. Ronnie hadn't followed the rest of the crew inside, and no one had commented on his return.

"You're asking me?" the boom operator replied.

No. Of course not. She was to Ted what Alan was to Caitlin.

I used to believe this thing we call "reality" was measurable, quantifiable, and that we could all more or less agree on what it looked like.

Sandra caught Alan's eye and he smiled at her, warmly. The smile flooded her. She had a vision of him above her in her hotel room, his stubble pressing into her neck, her hands on his hips as he slid into her. Two people who were not as thin as they used to be feeling younger and more alive than they had the right to be. Anti-ghosts.

I do not believe this anymore.

Alan released her gaze, and Sandra turned to Ted. "Okay, mike them. Let's get this thing started."

Regina called everyone to the table and an awkward, first-day-of-class moment ensued while PIP and the Hawthornes arranged themselves in the packed living room.

"Let us hold hands," Regina said. "For this is a safe space."

For a moment the room was perfectly quiet, perfectly warm; all sat within a circle of Nowhen and Nowhere that acted as a doorway. Regina resisted looking through the door to see how vast and crowded the space beyond truly was. This was trust, she told herself: to close one's eyes and let them in.

"We know you are with us," Madame Mandaya said. Her voice had slipped into a lower register, that of a perfect medium. Her heart began pounding, her body knowing before her brain caught up to it that something extraordinary might happen. "Please, give us a sign."

The psychic had placed herself next to Eve, so Ryan sat on his wife's right. Charles ended up on Ryan's other side, and Ryan winced as the boy took his hand, afraid not so much to hold hands with a boy as to appear on television holding hands with a boy. He was more aware in that moment than any other time that week of the presence of the cameras.

Madame Mandaya's voice guided them in how to direct their "energy," what to imagine that would allow the spirits in.

"Picture the door opening," she said, and Ryan, half listening, forgot where the door was supposed to be: Above them? Below? In the middle of the table? He was sensitive to the creaking floorboards, the brush of air as the TV crew circled the table.

"Focus on the door," the psychic instructed, but how could he, with the crew building up speed, jogging around the table faster and faster? The footage they captured must have been dizzying, unwatchable. This was some sort of joke to them—they couldn't even wait to get back to their offices to humiliate Ryan's family. His heart pounded as three or four sets of feet broke into an all-out run. Ryan opened his eyes and saw one cameraman standing a good five or six feet away, unmoving, the rest of the crew even farther behind, looking bored, barely paying attention at all.

———·—·———

Eve sat with one hand in Madame Mandaya's, one in her husband's. Their eyes had been closed for a while, though Eve wandered in and out of concentration on the directions Madame Mandaya gave the group. Ryan's hand was sweaty and kept lifting off his knee, hovering an inch or two in the air and bringing Eve's hand with it. And what did he have to be afraid of?

"There are other presences here with us tonight," Madame Mandaya said. Eve imagined wispy figures, cartoonish, emerging from behind each person in the room, circling them like musical chairs then dashing willy-nilly into whatever body happened to be nearest when the music stopped.

"Listen," Madame Mandaya said. Air swept the back of Eve's neck and Ryan stiffened, his hand now even farther off his knee, sending cramps up Eve's forearm. She tried to bring his hand back down, but he was frozen, trembling, his motions echoed moments later by the old china in the dining room cabinet, rattling in its display case.

"Listen," Madame Mandaya repeated, as if they could do anything else.

——— · ———

At some point Sandra, not entirely consciously, had closed her eyes along with everyone else. She felt the air just beside and behind her displaced to accommodate a weight. She didn't think anyone from her team would be so close, but she wouldn't be fooled again. The encounter with Ronnie had clearly been a dream. She had fallen asleep, right there on the porch. Her anger about his disappearance had turned to guilt and so she dreamed his return, was daydreaming now that he had climbed through the window, dusted with foliage but back for real. A floorboard creaked in confirmation. Sandra's eyes snapped open: she was in the Hawthornes' living room, the windows were closed, no one stood near her.

Madame Mandaya had been quiet for several minutes, and around the table everyone's heads were bent, as if in silent worship. Karl panned the camera back and forth. Sandra sought Alan's head in the circle. He had an intent look on his face, as if conjuring up some memory that was almost there. His head tilted; she saw his crow's feet a little more prominently, the small pouch under his chin.

Finally, Madame Mandaya sighed, a theatrical *hmmm* that seeded the room, and everyone dropped hands. Sandra, jumpy, reached for her purse, shlupped onto the floor beside her. She checked her phone: no email. But the gesture grounded her in who she was, what the hell she was doing there.

Caitlin and Charles still had their eyes closed, Charles's softly, Caitlin's face screwed tight in concentration, willing away all the squeaks and clatters that surrounded her. Even Madame Mandaya, though her head was down and eyes shut, was smoothing her hair, adjusting some bracelets on her wrist. Alan's eyes were open, though he looked restful, looked as if he could slip back into that other space at any moment. Ryan, on the other hand, was looking around, clearly waiting for a cue to stand up, his leg jiggling under the table, though Eve had tried to still it.

"It's late," Sandra said, the first thing anybody had said in what felt like a long time. In fact, it wasn't, particularly. But someone turned the lights back on, blew the remaining candles out.

"We can stick around," Alan said, nodding toward Charles and Caitlin. "Maybe there's too much . . ." He waved his hand at the crew and their accoutrements.

"I think my husband and I would like to go to bed," Eve said, and Alan nodded.

"Of course. I'll review the evidence first thing in the morning and let you know if we captured anything. No reason to think this was a complete failure."

Sandra started at the word. She turned to Karl, who shook his head, shrugged. Sandra reminded herself that it didn't matter. The script was written; the footage, combined with some spooky music and a well-crafted sentence out of Madame Mandaya, would make up for the past two ambiguous evenings. Her disappointment was silly, beneath her. To families, the crew brought with them an aura, an expectancy that once they arrived, something else would, too, to be worth filming in the first place. But as Patrick had reminded her, the magic happened in post. Those days spent on the couch, passively ingesting hours of television—how many of those little epiphanies were the product of a mild delirium, a desperation to justify her own behavior to herself? And now this, tonight—the show on the verge of cancellation, a run of unfortunate coincidences, Sandra sleep-deprived—how small a stimulus would engender the "meaningful" experience she craved?

It had been a long day. Earlier in the evening Sandra had been sure she would sleep with Alan that night. Every time he bumped into her or his hand brushed against hers he left a trail of heat, a tease for later, when there would be no clothes and no glancing away, no one around to keep them from saying to each other any number of things she wasn't even conscious now of wanting to say.

But she was exhausted, on edge, she didn't want to say anything that she'd regret later, closing any doors that had just barely cracked open. So she left, slipping out the front door and leaving in Patrick's car without saying goodbye to Alan or anyone else, preserving, as her mother had told her to so many years ago, some of her mystery.

——— · ———

The game was a disappointment. Patrick's team took a beating, Memphis maintaining their lead all through the second half and justifying to Patrick why he'd rarely gone to games in college. Servers came around, discreetly dropping bills on tables. His bill was low and this, too, disgusted him, as he tried not to think that a week from now he'd pay twice as much in Manhattan without even blinking. He left the sort of tip he would have left in a Manhattan gastropub, figuring he could make somebody's night.

He'd been drinking steadily throughout the game. Patrick knew he should suck it up and call Sandra to come and get him, enduring whatever she had to say to him now, so they could start fresh in the morning. But idling by the curb, mere feet from the door, sat a taxi. It was white and green, not yellow, but otherwise unmistakable, its phone number in block lettering scratched but legible across the doors. The lights in the cab were dim; Patrick knocked on the driver's-side window.

The cabbie rolled down the window. He looked straight out of Central Casting; all he was missing was the cigar stub. He appeared to have been reading a magazine.

"You for hire?" Patrick asked, certain someone must have called for it.

"All you," the cabbie said. *Maybe I* am *the luckiest bastard alive*, Patrick thought dubiously.

Patrick summoned from his phone the Hawthornes' address, then settled back into the seat. He called Sandra but her phone went straight to voice mail. "There in ten," he assured her.

"Nice night, huh?" the cabbie asked. He kept the dome light on, but low, giving the car's interior a mysterious quality, like those dreams in which Patrick turned on light after light but could never fully see anything, and grasped at objects in the dim. When he found the bar it seemed destined and right; this cab felt similarly delivered to him. He told himself to relax, let it happen.

"A beautiful night," Patrick confirmed, too late to matter, but he was keyed up, unable to quiet himself. "Extraordinary, really. I haven't seen one like this in a long time."

———•———

Alan was in the dining room, talking to Mrs. Hawthorne, and Charles was packing their gear. Caitlin walked around the table, dragging her fingertips across its surface, imagining she could still feel the warmth of the bodies that had been in each spot.

Caitlin had opened her eyes several times during the séance, because they never did Q and A's with their eyes closed. The TV crew looked bored, which didn't particularly bother her; Alan and Charles were focused.

Then she turned to the Hawthornes, wanting to channel, for them, the energy this ritual required. Ryan sat straight, clutching his wife's hand, his mouth pursed as if keeping himself from shouting out. But Eve: her eyes were also open and she looked as bored as the crew. This was her house—everyone was there to help her—and she looked like there was nothing that could happen that night that would surprise her, even given what had happened the two previous nights. She caught Caitlin's eye and held it, unashamed, unconcerned that the girl had noticed. Caitlin, suddenly scared, had squeezed Charles's hand and he turned his head to her, opened his eyes. She pointed her nose toward Mrs. Hawthorne, but Eve had already closed her eyes again. Charles scanned the circle for specters, hovering objects, a thundering to come from outside and enclose their circle in fear. All was still. After a moment Caitlin shook her head: *Nothing, never mind.* Her heart trembled.

Once the crew were in their vehicles, the Hawthornes preparing for bed, Caitlin said she had forgotten her sweatshirt and returned to the living room while the van idled. She walked the circle one last time, angrily holding back tears. There was a feeling she got when they stepped into a home and she knew they would get a reading that night—an EVP out of the darkness, a spike in magnetic fields. But now that zap of excitement was gone. Caitlin was pretty sure she was in love with Charles, and though she sensed he did not reciprocate, he had never said as much, and so, at sixteen, Caitlin had never had her heart broken. But this, tonight, was what devastation felt like: to be in a room that, hours before, was as dark and sparkly with possibility as a high-school gym set up for a dance. And how terrible it was to leave after the lights were turned on, revealing streamers hung limply from the rafters, burst balloons in wrinkled spots on the floor, and to have gotten from the evening nothing, nothing at all.

She opened the door at the same moment as someone from the outside was pushing it in, and Caitlin jumped, her heart already pounding with emotion. It was Patrick, the idiot director, carrying a couple of bags. The jerk had been *shopping*. If he worked for Caitlin, he'd be fired.

"Sandra here?" he asked, looking into a room that was obviously empty, a night that was obviously over.

"She left," Caitlin started to say, but she was interrupted by Sandra herself, pushing open the front door, a coat thrown on over sweatpants, her hair pulled back.

"I'm so fucking tired of covering for your ass," Sandra said, unconcerned that Caitlin was in the room. "I'm not doing this with you anymore, Patrick."

"How—how was the séance?"

"It was pointless, which you would know if you had been here."

"Because Cameron and Vince said—"

"Cameron and Vince don't know anything! They aren't here, week after week, while I do your job, and mine, and the writers', basically, and give this silly little show way more of my time and energy than it deserves. Why? Why do I continue to do this?"

She was really loud. Caitlin heard the Hawthornes in their bedroom, getting out of bed, crossing the floor.

"Meanwhile you don't give a shit about anyone in the world besides yourself. I could never count on you for the most basic—"

Caitlin watched as Ryan appeared at the top of the stairs, looking down in his T-shirt and boxers. Behind him, in the doorway to their bedroom, Eve stood, staring down at Sandra, her face glowing with fury.

"What the hell is going on?" Ryan asked, and before anyone could reply, a bomb of noise hit the side of the house, a boom that rattled the north wall, then the west, then the south. Then all the power went out.

COMING UP:

(Ryan stands on the campus of the college he attended and dropped out of, though he does not recognize it right away. It looks different, wild, like at the end of the semester; the pool [Ryan doesn't remember there being one] is filled with both trash and algae, though that doesn't stop any bikini-clad coeds from jumping in. Students sit on the lawn, tilting their faces to the sun. Moons dance in the sky above them, too many to count. Ryan watches the white disks hover and dip and pirouette around one another, and the students—kids—record it on their phones.)

RYAN: . . .

(Only Ryan seems to understand it isn't just the semester that is ending. Something much, much worse is coming. Ryan enters the library building in search of a place to hide, but finds himself back on the lawn again anyway. Shadowy figures approach from the edge of campus, getting closer, drawing in. Men in suits, businesslike, beamed down from one of the moons or up from the center of the earth, drag students to a place they'll never return from. On the fence posts that separate the campus lawn from neighboring farmland, birds line up, as organized in their approach as the dance of the moons as they perch, one to a post, settled, calm, watching.)

DAY 4

INTERVIEW—CAITLIN

CAITLIN: All week, I've felt there were things in this house that wanted to be heard. Some nights they're louder than others. Tonight was really loud.

Question

CAITLIN: I don't really *do* anything while it's happening. I just listen and observe. I don't want to, you know, scare it off. Ghosts are pretty shy. Or, at least, usually. *(grins)*

Question

CAITLIN: We get to know when something's going to happen because we always come back to the same place more than once. So the first time we just try everything, every room, see where there's activity. The second time we can run a more targeted investigation. I thought Alan would have told you all this stuff by now?

Question

CAITLIN: Tonight's banging did not sound like the banging from Monday. Monday there were a bunch of bangs in a row. Tonight it was like one huge bang on each side of the house. I totally thought the house was going to collapse.

Question

CAITLIN: I do think it's the same entity from Monday, because both came from outside the house, and both used banging to communicate. It just seems like tonight it had a little more power.

Question

CAITLIN: No idea. They don't usually get stronger, or anything like that.

Question

CAITLIN: I have no idea how the entity from Monday got stronger. If I had to guess, I'd say that whatever it had to tell us on Monday night, we didn't listen. So it returned, to make sure we knew.

———•—•———

Back at the hotel, Patrick paced the lobby. He had gotten back before they had even set out the free breakfast. One of the maids had been so bothered by his loitering that she'd slipped him a mini box of cornflakes and a look pregnant with *Go away*, but he wasn't waiting on the food. He didn't want to go back to his room, alone, the clunky noises of an old building all around him. When Patrick closed his eyes for more than a second he was back in the Hawthornes' living room, those sounds like the end of the world, then the plunge into darkness to await . . . he didn't want to know what. He wished, as he'd been wishing for a good twenty-four hours now, to be back in New York, where the hassles were predictable and hassle-obscuring drugs readily available. Patrick had never tried cocaine; he was too young to have caught the whole eighties Wayfarers-and-blow thing, and it was less common in TV than in film, he imagined, but in this moment he thought that he would like some cocaine. Something that made people feel good and sure of themselves and made them stride around hotel lobbies like they owned the place—not eliciting dirty looks from the cleaning staff who were vigilantly vacuuming over the tracks he was leaving in the carpet with his shoes.

He scrolled through his phone, looking for anyone who might have a hookup, and the first number that looked promising belonged to Melanie, the bartender he'd gone home with a couple nights ago. It was early to call someone who worked until two a.m., but even without drugs the prospect of being able to crawl into Melanie's bed, cup her firm, twenty-four-year-old breasts, and sleep a sleep untroubled by dreams of unseen horrors emerging from the dark was worth risking her temporary ire. They still had two days left. As director, he was expected to make decisions for the rest of them: their safety, their well-being. But he should not go down with the ship. Ronnie would probably tell him that. Wherever the fuck Ronnie was. Dodging the electrical cord of the vacuum and dirty look of the woman operating it one last time, Patrick plugged one finger in his ear and with the opposite thumb hit call.

———·—·———

Sandra lay on the bed in her hotel room, still wearing her coat and sneakers from when she had gone to pick up Patrick. She was not asleep, but she lay very still, with the curtains closed against the dawn.

Driving Patrick's car back to the hotel, Patrick nattering on beside her about candles, some cabbie, a basketball game, Sandra's first thought had been that she deserved this. She had skipped out on Monday; more than once over the past couple days, as those who were in the house recounted the banging, she had wished that she could have been there to experience it. So it felt right that she had. But it wasn't on tape—none of it was on tape. Sandra was starting to feel personally punished for doing a job she had been asked to do. At least this event had witnesses. Someone else who saw it, who could confirm she wasn't losing her mind.

Nothing of what she felt was fear, though. After the initial surprise—the jump scare—she hadn't been frightened. It had been awkward in the dark, listening to Ryan's cursing floating up the basement steps as he examined the fuse box. Once the power was restored she had left almost immediately, apologizing to Ryan and Eve for her outburst in a way she had never had to before. But she hadn't been eager to get away. She understood then Alan's compulsion to be in the homes, *just listening*. The banging was loud, it was shocking, it left no room for other thoughts or sensations, but it was over so quickly, and her first thought had been: *What next? What else might happen?*

As they left the Hawthornes', pulling away for the second time that evening in Patrick's car, she couldn't help but look back. The old white farmhouse seemed to have grown, swelled since she'd pulled up to it on Monday. It loomed, in the way of these buildings in lurid photos: the Shanley Hotel, Amityville. It contained something disproportionate to its physical size. The invisible—she had felt it, she had been there when it happened. She laughed out loud at the irony.

"What's with you?" Patrick had asked, his leg jiggling, thumb flicking a lighter she didn't know he carried.

"Nothing," Sandra had said, sorry she wasn't with Alan, someone who could appreciate her epiphany. Eve.

In the hotel room, on the edge of sleep, she wondered, would Eve give her another chance? What would that look like, in terms of the show, in terms of her job? In terms of the rest of her life?

——— · ———

Madame Mandaya's internet presence was limited to a dusty blog, begun with the intention of posting about her sessions, rarely updated. So rarely, in fact, that she needed to root around in a drawer for her password to log in to the site that hosted it for her. During a slow moment in the store she started a new entry, intending to write about the Hawthornes, the most inconsistent set of encounters she'd ever had. It was as if everyone in the house experienced their own personal haunting, with no overlaps. She envisioned a series, separate entries for each time she was in the home. It would build suspense, "go viral," though her readership was limited to clients and a few family members. A niece was the one who had set it up for her, recommending a free site and giving her advice on how to promote it, which Regina for the most part had never done.

Nonetheless, a few years ago she received a strange, unsigned email suggesting, based on her writings, that she might be interested in a secret project she could find more details on by Googling certain combinations of words. About ten words were listed, and she picked two that seemed likely. Almost right away she found a site describing a community forming out west: an off-the-grid, anti-government, self-sustaining group of like-minded individuals interested in pursuing spirituality and engagement with higher dimensions to a degree considered distasteful in mainstream society. The site promised extended spirit sessions in the desert, sweat lodges and such, in a place where those with astrological gifts could really see the stars. It was an opportunity to turn one's back on the vapid demands of "productive" society and explore the infinite space within. The website never mentioned sex specifically, but Regina thought she knew enough about these "like-minded individuals" to guess more precisely why they wanted to camp out in the desert, half naked and soaked in hallucinogens, with a handful of women miles from civilization. She could picture these men (for they had to be men; what woman would construct such a silly, easily

solvable puzzle to find the page?): unwashed trollish beings with
whom she'd be urged (or, worse, willing) to copulate, in order
to sustain the community past their inevitable deaths. (She was
on the cusp of menopause but no doubt someone would tell her,
Anything is possible out here, one filthy hand on her knee.) The
mating drama, the very reason this community was envisioned
in the first place by ones who couldn't compete in the standard
arena, would play itself out again, in a much sadder, grimier
way. It would be too hot, there would never be enough to eat,
eventually the life insurance money from the passing of someone's mother would run out, and they would have to trudge
back east and pretend that none of it had happened.

Regina had read the website, deleted the email, and moved
on, but she did from time to time wonder how, in the vastness of
the internet, these people had found her. If they contacted every
psychic they came across, or if there was something particular to
her blog that singled her out as a potential recruit.

The bell above the door rang and Alan entered her shop. He
was dressed for work, in a blue button-down tucked into trou-
sers, a sharp contrast to the black sweatshirt and jeans he wore
on most investigations, which she thought of as Alan's true self.

"Howdy," she said, a verbal affectation to match his sarto-
rial one.

"How's business?" he asked, looking around. An antique
bookcase in the front held bud vases from which sticks of incense
burst; under a glass jewelry case were crystals, some large and
worth several hundred dollars; much of the rest of the store was
books, though her bestselling item was candles. In the back, she
had an authentic voodoo altar and several sacred objects she had
sworn never to use. Some people keep a gun under the counter,
she'd told Alan when she'd shown it to him, then nodded to a
ritual bowl, ringed with dried blood.

"Same as ever. Can I interest you in a set of divining rods?"

"Never my thing, really."

"Alan the purist."

It hung between them, the letdown of the night before. Regina had scooted out of the Hawthornes' house as soon as she could, while Alan stuck around to debrief. She wanted to ask if his team had made any recordings, but she didn't want to know the answer.

"Last night—" he started to say, but she put up a hand to stop him.

"Alan, don't. Don't apologize for them. They're too weird."

He chuckled, but he knew what she meant.

"What do they want? What does Eve want? I was sure that she's psychokinetic and everything that was happening in the house was her doing, whether or not she was conscious of it. But I didn't feel anything last night. Not a single soul, despite what I said."

That, too. She had lied at one point during the séance, breaking a cardinal rule. She had said she felt many presences, but in fact she'd felt none. She'd hoped the gesture would bring a few forward. "If Eve had wanted something to happen last night, it would have. I'm sure of it."

"Something did happen last night."

"You captured EVPs?" Regina couldn't keep the skepticism out of her voice.

"No, after we left. Caitlin was in the house with someone from the show and the banging from Monday night recurred, and all the lights went out. The lights, at least, are classic psychokinesis, right?"

Regina shook her head. "There could be some other explanation for that."

Alan nodded at the books on the shelves and propped up by

the counter for impulse purchase, one of which was called *Detox with the Angels*. "There could be some other explanation for any of this. But this is the one we've chosen."

Where was the line between her shop and a sweat lodge in the desert, using peyote at her age and baring her breasts to the moon? Regina slightly feared the part of herself that might have relished the adventure. Once you'd chosen a thing, did you have to go all the way with it?

And maybe that was the answer—Eve, new to this world and skittish about her abilities, retreated under the glare of the lights. She had not yet committed. Perhaps Regina was to blame, for her overenthusiasm before the séance.

"We need to get back into that house with just her and her husband and no camera crews anywhere."

Alan smiled broadly. "It's like you read my mind."

———•—•———

Ryan was cleaning the basement, something he should have done ages ago. It didn't take long for him to build up a sweat, and for grime to stick to him as a result. He combined the contents of a few cardboard boxes, broke down the empties, and put them in a pile by the stairs. He swept and moved the stacks of Eve's old books from college and grad school onto the shelves they had put down there for that purpose.

Shifting old exercise equipment revealed an outlet that looked questionable, the NordicTrack plug utilizing it gone frayed and rusty. Ryan unplugged the machine and saw then a spreading stain around the outlet—a crusty black, like a thick mold or lichen, but in a starburst pattern, a charring left by sparks shooting out of the holes. He thought of the conversation he and Eve had had about her studio, her question—*Why me?* One time she had raised a concern about vibrating floorboards, energy from a power plant traveling through the ground into their home, scrambling their senses. Ryan didn't know if there was a power plant nearby, near enough to potentially shoot off excess energy through random outlets. If that was even how it worked. Reason said there must be some source: electricity coursed through their house, but he wasn't sure how it got there, what was at the end of those wires. He made his living off something he didn't understand the very foundations of.

His project sat in the crawl space, behind the wine. It was unplugged, as it had been for several days, a bland little box with two speakers facing the wall. He pulled it out of the crawlspace and set it on the floor in front of him, ripping one speaker out, then the other. He broke open the top of the amplifier and jammed a screwdriver inside, stabbing and prying the wires from the transistor, yanking it apart. Plastic and metal clattered to the floor around him.

He straightened, satisfied with his work. Whatever had happened last night—and really, Ryan couldn't be sure what had happened—his hands would be clean. And Eve would be pleased. Once all this was behind them, they could turn the basement into a rec room with a flat-screen TV and a video-game system, carpeting on the floor and concert posters on the walls. For the kids Eve would one day want, if he gave her a little more time. It had been a while since they'd had that conversation. He'd been fantasizing all week about the day the show left, how they'd look at each other and smile anew, this thing behind them once and for all.

He left the empty boxes in a stack to deal with later. On his way to the stairs he turned back to survey his work and that's when he saw the woman.

She wore a light summer dress that reminded him of one of

Eve's, and her hair was pulled back in a style Eve sometimes wore. She swung from her neck, gently from a wooden beam. Her feet did not touch the floor. Her figure was insubstantial—Ryan could see through her to the faint scoring of the cinder blocks that made up the walls.

He did not point, open-mouthed, as they did in the movies. He was learning about himself this week, learning about his own responses to things he couldn't explain. He had lain awake for hours last night, after that breeze on his neck during the séance, after the banging on the house, the power outage. He had slept briefly, dreamed strangely, and when Eve nudged him in the morning he told himself that whatever it was couldn't hurt them, or it would have done so already. This vision in the basement was more frightening than anything he'd felt with his eyes closed, but it, too, could not do much more than deprive him of sleep, or make him question his own mind, as it had been doing to Eve. Ryan would simply refuse to ask.

At the top of the steps he resisted turning around to see if the figure was still there before he turned the light off. She was and she wasn't. He carried every detail of her in his head. Even in his fear he had noticed the gold ring slipping down a limp finger of her paint-stained hands. He marched through the living room and took the stairs two at a time, straight into the upstairs bathroom.

———·———

Weird question. Has anyone ever died on the show?

Charles reread the words, scoffed, deleted them.

Hey, Ted, Charles from PIP here. You have a second? Couple questions for you, about the investigation.

But that, too, was stupid. Ted couldn't answer any questions about their investigation.

Charles had found Ted's number in his phone, stored from a previous filming, during which the two had had to be in contact about something, Charles couldn't remember what—giving a psychic a ride, maybe. Normally at the episode's conclusion, Charles would have deleted the contact info, the texts themselves, preferring to store as little on his phone as possible. But he'd kept the number. That meant something—Charles preferred not to ask himself what.

Charles didn't need everything tied up in a bow; for most encounters he was satisfied with just a little backstory on the property—some local tragedy that served up a name, a date of death, business unfinished enough to speculate about. He had his impressions, the house had its history, and Charles left room for whatever wanted to inhabit the space between. He was deeply skeptical of anyone who could claim a single explanation for a set of encounters.

The Hawthornes' case was different. The range of activity made Charles want something specific. Something he could point to—a former owner with a macabre hobby, a train derailment on the other side of those trees—and say, *This is bigger than you*. But he hadn't been able to locate it in city records or on microfiche.

Though if he was honest with himself, it was his private encounters he wanted to get to the bottom of. The show had been in production for only a few years. Long enough, statistically, for one of its employees to die, especially a young male, Charles thought sardonically, thinking of binge drinking at the wrap party, a fateful encounter with the third rail. But if it was the ghost of some departed production assistant, why show up at this investigation, to which it would have no connection—theoretically no idea, even, how to get there? Why specifically seek Charles out?

His research wandered into crisis apparitions: ghosts of the living in distress. There were plenty of accounts. Elizabeth I, while in a coma, was seen (according to multiple reports) walking the halls of her palace. In other cases ghost hunters, in the thick of an investigation, briefly lost contact with their own souls: one famous researcher's wife reported his return home, the clear sight of him hanging up his hat and coat in the entryway, hours before his body stepped through the door. The book Charles was reading assured him that one did not have to be on the brink of death to project one's spirit; "any strong emotion can produce such an effect." And any person with telepathic powers was capable of transmitting their pain to others, even over distances.

Was the guy from the crew his crisis apparition? It was atypical: it didn't look like him, and appeared only to him. A true crisis apparition would have resembled Charles and, as a cry for help, appeared to someone else. To Caitlin, most likely—Charles wasn't sure how he felt about that. His closest companion in the world had a learner's permit and a hammock of stuffed animals over her bed. But she was the one who would see him. The one who would understand.

He thought back to when he was in high school, the reason he'd saved for his first car: to drive to the edges of town, or two or three towns over as he grew more bold, and investigate. How many Friday nights did his parents think he was out raising hell, how many weeknights did they give him permission to go to a friend's and study? How would they have reacted if they knew instead of studying he was poking around the old hospital, the Quaker cemetery, any random barn that had been left empty and unlocked? Tape recorder, notepad. Never quite bold enough to close his eyes, to sit back and trust, as Caitlin did, that the spirits would take care of him. He had a small cache of recordings from those days, since digitized, his notes typed up as well, though he still listened to the original tapes from time to time. When listening, he'd strain to hear not EVPs, but the thing that was verifiably never there: another voice, human, accompanying his. *Did you hear that? That was awesome.*

He bookmarked the page about crisis apparitions to return to later. On the corner of his desk sat his tape recorder, which he hadn't rewound or listened to since last night.

CHARLES: It is Wednesday, April —. I am alone in the basement of the Hawthornes' home. Am I alone? Are you here?

And then, instead of the customary pause, he heard a clomping on the stairs followed by Caitlin's voice:

CAITLIN: What are you doing down here?

Charles stopped the tape. He looked at the date on the label, rewound the tape, listened again to his time stamp, looked at his digital watch. The tape was from yesterday. But he remembered last night: he had been alone in the basement. It had been just five or six minutes, enough for a dozen questions, before guilt and unease drew him back upstairs to participate in filming with everyone else. He hit play, his mouth tipped open.

CAITLIN: What are you doing down here?
CHARLES: Remember the EVP from Monday? I'm trying to get another. Now you're messing it up.
CAITLIN: Sorry. Everyone's upstairs.

CHARLES: I know. That's why I'm down here.
  (Stairs creak.)
CHARLES: Well, come down if you're going to be here. Maybe you can help.

But she didn't help. Instead of running a normal Q and A, they entered into a more philosophical discussion than they normally had.

CHARLES: I don't know why I'm even doing this.
CAITLIN: You got a recording on Monday. Why shouldn't you try again? It's what we always do.
CHARLES: And why do we do it?
CAITLIN *(softly)*: What do you mean?
CHARLES: Who are we doing this for? The families? Half the time, we know what they need, we're just afraid to tell them. "Get marriage counseling." "Get a divorce." "*Listen* to your kids once in a while. You don't have a ghost." But we never say it. And our stacks of tapes pile up. We're no better than the show.
CAITLIN: That's bullshit, Charles, and you know it. Lots of those tapes do have evidence on them. If they didn't, we wouldn't—
CHARLES: Wouldn't we? Are you sure?
CAITLIN: What are you saying?
CHARLES: That a hundred blank tapes wouldn't stop us from getting up the next night and going out and doing it again. That maybe we even prefer it that way, because we haven't thought about what it would mean to find an answer. What that answer would look like, and what we'd do with it. What we'd do next. What's our real reason for being here?
CAITLIN: You know what it is, Charles, we—

But he stopped the tape again, not wanting to hear the thing he never put words to, mangled in its translation into language. The voice was Caitlin's, but she was shy about cursing, wouldn't have let a "bullshit" roll off her tongue like that, when she used the term "f-bomb" instead of the actual f-bomb. Nor was this a conversation he'd had in his head, with other girls, about this very subject. But the voices sounded right; whatever questions he could remember asking the night before—the standard *Who are you, Why are you here, How can I help you cross over*—were entirely rewritten.

He rewound the tape, opening the word processing program on his computer to transcribe it. He could play it for Caitlin, see what she thought. But when the tape stopped and he played it again, he heard nothing. The wheels rotated, but no sound issued from the speaker. He stopped the tape, looked at the player. He adjusted the volume, opened and reclosed the cover so the tape was in its proper place in the well. He tried again: nothing. Fast-forwarded thirty seconds: nothing. Whatever that snippet of conversation had been, it was gone. He sat still, listening to the faint hiss that trickled from the speakers. He feared, irrationally, he knew, that Caitlin was a crisis apparition herself—that she had *never* been real. His mind created a montage, like in the movies: all the times he'd seen her interact with other people. Caitlin in the front passenger seat of Alan's car; Caitlin's report card on her family's fridge. He stopped the tape, rewound it a third time. He put his head in his hands and took a couple of deep breaths. *This is real*, he told himself, feeling the cool tips of his fingers against his warm forehead. You are real, you are sitting in a chair at home. The usual desk chair, the known home. He did a physical inventory, a technique for when he was feeling anxious, moving from awareness of the tips of his toes in their socks and sneakers, up along his entire body, inch by inch, ending with an awareness of an itch on his scalp. By the time he finished, his breathing and heart rate were regular. He hit play on the tape again.

CHARLES: It is Wednesday, April —. I am alone in the basement of the Hawthornes' home. Am I alone? Are you here?
(Pause)
CHARLES: Can you tell me your name?
(Pause)
CHARLES: Can you tell me why you are appearing only to me?

This was the recording he remembered making. Between his questions were pauses so regular he might as well have been a computer; he hardly needed to count in his head anymore to know what was long enough. He stopped the tape again, took it out of the player, and set it down separately on the desk without bothering to slow it down or listen for EVPs. He sat very still. The radio that his mother listened to as she made lunch wafted up the stairs; the cat padded nearly silently from room to room. He felt like he was floating a half inch outside of his body. He stayed in his desk chair, gazing out the window, perfectly situated to see a crow heading straight for the glass, slamming into it, tumbling down.

——— · ———

"Babe?" Eve rapped on the bathroom door.

There was a pause, followed by Ryan's strained *In a second*, followed by a flushing toilet and a lengthy period of handwashing. When he opened the door, the smell slipped out ahead of him, but Eve was a pro at not reacting, understanding that sometimes the body expresses what the mouth cannot.

"Want some tea?"

Ryan stepped out of the bathroom and shut the door protectively behind him. He didn't look Eve in the face. "Not right now. Thank you." He reached one hand for hers, limply, then dropped it. "I have to tell you something." He looked down the hall, to the stairs that would lead back to the living room, but Eve led him instead toward their bedroom. He was pale, his forehead damp. He lay down on top of their quilt with his clothes and sneakers on. He stared at the ceiling, falling easily into the role of weakened patient. She sat beside him, her hips and thighs flanking his with just the slightest amount of pressure. She took his hand, which was a little clammy, and squeezed it between both of hers.

"Tell me," she said, trying to keep her voice from sounding too excited. Eve had not wanted anything to happen, told herself nothing would happen, and now here was her husband, flat on his back, faintly sweating in fear, an experience she had had no hand in. Her mind unspooled, imagining a malevolent entity taking plates from the cupboards and hurling them across the room, or returning from work one day to a vortex spinning in the living room, blood dripping from the walls. She didn't *want* such things, but they would certainly defy whatever powers Madame Mandaya thought Eve had.

"I can't explain what happened last night." He was staring at the ceiling. Could *she* explain it to *him*? *I was furious at Sandra, furious at all of them for using us, instead of helping. I wanted to punish them, so I shorted the power with my mind.* While things she had said earlier to Ryan sounded ridiculous only when he repeated them back to her, this sounded ridiculous right now.

"Why should you? This is why we called the show, to figure it out."

"But the other banging, on Monday . . ."

"What about it?"

"I can maybe explain that."

Eve's heart became perceptible in her chest.

"I connected a couple of old speakers, at work. It wasn't supposed to be that loud. I put it in the basement. I just thought, if nothing happened while the crew was here . . ."

"They told me they didn't expect anything to happen. That's why they shoot re-enactments. They said in seventy percent of episodes they make nothing—" Eve stopped. Ryan was looking her in the eye. "You never saw anything, did you." She saw in his face the ten-year-old boy confessing to Mommy that it was he who broke the vase, he who lied. "You made up all of that stuff you said you experienced."

"I don't think you're crazy." The refrain, a common one, sounded less hesitant this time, more forceful. But Eve wasn't relieved.

"But you never thought this house was haunted, either. That's why you're like this today. You're scared shitless. Literally." She laughed once, a harsh bark she hated herself for being capable of making. It shouldn't have been easier for a stranger, an interloper in her home, to see the truth. Yet her husband, the one with whom she would enclose herself then shut the door, had never been concerned about any of it. He'd brought her internet printouts of other people's stories, discussing them at the kitchen table the way other couples discussed finances. Eve had been doing research as well, in medical journals, for diseases or environmental factors that could cause hallucinations. Ghosts seemed benign in comparison to brain tumors or contaminated soil. What a relief a simple haunting would be! And the whole time their discussions on the subject had been a pantomime. He had played along the way parents did when their children turned boxes into rocket ships or ran away under the dining room table. Eve had thought she'd been the one with the power in the relationship—stemming from her worldliness, her knowledge of life beyond Ninebark. But she hadn't understood the weight of Ryan's power, the power to confirm or deny her reality. As with her childhood experience in Oklahoma, he did not trust her interpretation of her own goddamn life.

"No, babe, listen—"

"Don't 'babe' me. This was your idea! The show, the disruption to our lives, all of it! And you were just going to stand back and watch as they brought in their little devices and didn't get a single blip on their radar screens. And then what were you going to say to me?"

"I don't like this, Eve." Ryan, who had been leaning up on one elbow, who had been gathering a bit of color in his face, paled again and fell back on the bed. His intestines burbled. But Eve sat heavily, leaning toward him, that much more blocking the way to the door. "The past two nights, today . . . Something bad is happening."

"What."

"I think we should leave this house. I don't know if it's safe for us here anymore. I'm sorry I—" But before he could finish the sentence, the myriad things he had to repent, he sat up, rushed past Eve and out of the room, escaping entirely. But then Eve heard the bathroom door shut, the toilet lid clank into place.

Eve remained on the bed, looking purposelessly around the room. They hadn't vacuumed in here in a while; if they had surely they would have noticed before now the way the paint was peeling off the baseboards, bubbling up in great islands of a dusty-rose color Eve had chosen so carefully less than two years ago, quarter-sized pieces of which now lay in broken chips on the floor. Her eyes fell on Ryan's bedside table, the cup of water he took to bed almost every night and rarely drank from. She stared at the glass until it began to wobble on its coaster, the surface rippling and bubbles that had formed along the sides of the glass loosening their grip and rising. A drop splashed over the side. Eve sucked in her breath. The glass righted itself and was still, the surface of the water lapping gently at the sides. The toilet flushed. Eve stood, her heart pounding through her whole body. With some hesitation she took the glass, brushed past Ryan coming out of the bathroom, and shut herself in. She tipped the water into the sink, then sat on the edge of the tub, trying to steady her breathing.

———·—·——

Alan paced his house, dictating into a tape recorder.

"The banging recalls the knocking of the nineteenth-century spiritualism movement, knocking which was easily fabricated—"

He paused. The word left him uneasy. He'd hoped that putting his thoughts together might help him connect the events at the Hawthornes', find a thread that would guide him toward the center of this maze.

"In the case of the Hawthornes', the knocking was much louder and more forceful than anything conjured up in one of Madame Blavatsky's drawing rooms, and happened outside the house entirely, surrounding those who were there. I wish I had been there."

He switched the tape off. This was probably a day to write by hand. Alan alternated between writing and dictating, and as a result his project was getting unwieldy, legal pads and tapes, all carefully labeled, nevertheless piling up in a way that filled him with dread when he thought about sitting down and putting it in order. Typing it up, which he would have to do at some point. His overall premise was that ghost stories and urban legends continued the American oral folklore tradition while pointing to the particular anxieties of the age from which they sprang. So even though he envisioned his project ultimately as an audiobook, he hated the sound of his own voice and he wouldn't be the one to read it.

The project had begun as notes from his cases, which Lauren had later typed up for their files. Alan was a slow typist, impatient with computers in general, and liked to pace, look things up, walk around outside while he reflected on the work they'd done. At some point he'd started noticing parallels between some of the experiences homeowners were reporting and the urban legends and stories Caitlin relayed from camp and school. Caitlin would readily describe herself as the first into a haunted house at Halloween, the one to suggest summoning Bloody Mary at sleepovers. She loudly repeated what had been whispered in locker rooms among the girls, and her parents tolerated the stories until she got to middle school and the content became markedly more sexual. But Alan was interested in adding her stories to his project and had Caitlin dictate them herself, which relieved him of saying words like "vulva" repeatedly. He felt there was a connection between the teenage horrors she gleefully described and the nineteenth century, the things women hid inside themselves to reveal mid-séance. That primal mystery, Alan mused, a dark place men feared, which for all they knew could be limitless, capable of discharging not only entire humans but any number of secreted objects, women larger on the inside than they were on the outside, the reverse of most men.

And what about Sandra, her body warm against his in his office, her face in his car open, curious in a way it never had been before? What was she pulling out of her vagina? The whole damn show, of course, the dream of the Hawthornes. She shaped the disparate incidents of a confused family into a salacious story, then resolved it in time to get her small army of assistants home by the end of the week.

Alan pictured Sandra in a long green velvet skirt, her hair shiny around her face, holding eye contact as she pulled from between her legs—her body veiled by the skirt, but her gestures unambiguous—sticks of incense; hard, glistening objects, like crystals; feathers, scarabs, and other small occult objects, which she set on the floor in front of her.

Alan stopped pacing, realizing that he was turned on. The tape player, too, was on, capturing his footsteps and the silences between, though he was sure he had switched it off. And how much of that fantasy made it onto the tape? Every paranormal experience is a psychic experience, he had learned early on. And though he didn't spend much time developing his own abilities, content to let the self-designated mediums and devices communicate to him, he found himself concerned about what he might have projected. The desires of the living, one would hope, could only be that much stronger than those of the dead. Even three words would be telling. Plus, no point in wasting tape. Alan sat at his desk, pressed rewind, then was startled by a knock at the door.

———•·•———

Alan's house was small but charming, soft gray with navy shutters and trim, a cottage set back from the road and framed by blooming dogwood. There was something tragic about it: it was the least haunted-looking house Sandra had visited for the show.

But she realized that despite mailing him checks, Sandra had never considered the fact that Alan lived somewhere. She had imagined him perpetually roaming the country in the PIP van, eating in diners and trying to make contact with all the restless spirits in America. She'd never pictured him gardening on weekends, watching TV in his socks.

He was wearing shoes when he answered the door, and the TV was off.

"Sandra! I wasn't expecting you."

"Am I interrupting? You look like you've seen a . . . well, you know." Sandra tried to laugh.

"Oh, no, ha." Alan turned a bit pink. "Do you want to come in?"

"Thank you. I wanted to talk to you alone, and this seemed like the best way."

Alan stepped aside to let Sandra into an open-plan space with leather couches, a glass coffee table, flat-screen TV and kitchen in back. It was aesthetically pleasing in a broad way; nothing indicated Alan's particular tastes. Sandra recalled the divorce, could imagine him, stripped of belongings, indifferently pointing to a random page in a catalog and buying everything at once.

He was standing close behind her, so close he could have reached out and wrapped an arm around her waist, pulled her to him.

"What's going on?"

She turned to face him, took a half step back. "I don't want to put too much pressure on you, but it's really important we get something useful out of the Hawthornes."

"Useful?"

"You know about the banging last night?"

"Caitlin told me. I wish I had been there."

"I wish you had been there, too." They held eye contact a long moment. "But it wasn't on tape. Nothing's made it onto tape, this whole crazy week." She shook her head. The words came out in a rush. "The first night of investigation the Hawthornes were MIA. The second night the only thing that happened happened to a cameraman. And last night we got nothing we can use."

"I have to be honest with you, Sandra, I'm a little surprised. You said yourself you thought the episode was 'cursed.' I don't know if I would go that far, but there has been plenty of activity in that house this week. More than on a lot of the other cases we've tagged along for."

"I told you, we can't show the stuff with Macon and Ronnie, it's not—"

"The nature of the show. I know. You like to pretend you're all impartial observers, but the truth is your presence *does* impact the activity. You're a part of this."

"We just need to get Eve on board. If she feels heard . . ."

"So listen to her."

Sandra snorted; easier said than done.

"What is this actually about, Sandra?"

She sat on his couch, put her head in her hands. "The show is probably going to be canceled. This is the week the network orders new episodes. *Searching for . . .* has never pulled much in the way of ratings, and it doesn't fit the network's overall brand identity. I haven't heard from my team in New York, which is a bad sign."

"So try something different. Show what's actually happening. It sounds to me like you have nothing to lose." He sat down, angled his body to make eye contact. "What is happening? Talk to me, Sandra, I want to help."

She lifted her head. "Can I ask you something?"

INTERVIEW—ALAN

Question

ALAN: I would say about five, six years old. I saw my uncle
standing in the doorway to my room. He didn't say
anything, but I felt very strongly that he wanted to.

Question

ALAN: I think what people who have never had an encounter
don't realize is the experiences are very dense. They last just
a second or two, but they manage to communicate in that
time a tremendous amount of information.

Question

ALAN: Emotional information, history . . . there's a collapsing
of time. I think this is how some psychics believe they can
see the future. You receive, in those moments, a wall of
information, some of which doesn't make sense, and it's
not a stretch to assume the unfamiliar images are ones that
haven't happened yet. It can be pretty frightening.

Question

ALAN: That was it, really. He stood in the doorway to my
room, looking at me. But he wasn't in the house at the time.
Later I found out he'd died that day. Quite possibly at the
moment I'd seen him.

Question

ALAN: I don't know if he did choose me specifically. One thing
I've always wondered is if they can appear in multiple places
at once, because they know not everyone can see them. I
wasn't the favorite nephew or anything. But I was open to
the experience.

Question

ALAN: It's not quite that simple. When you do this work
you hear a lot of stories. People have told me about their

experiences in great detail, then concluded with, "But I don't believe in ghosts." It's a lifelong process, figuring out what you believe. Part of my role may be helping people decide if this is an explanation that satisfies them.

Question

ALAN: I can't just give you a list of events, paranormal in column A and not paranormal in column B. Is there something specific you want to ask me about? Did something happen to you this week?

"This isn't about me."

"I think it is."

What could she tell him? First Ronnie, her encounter in the yard. But wouldn't Alan chide her for not working harder to track him down—failing that, going to the police? He said himself, he always tried to rule out more plausible explanations first. Then there was the banging, a moment so all-encompassing it denied analysis, categorization.

"My turn to ask you a question now?"

Sandra smiled faintly, nodded. All her walls had crumbled over the course of the week, a once-mighty castle felled by an otherwise average snowstorm.

"What would you lose if the show was canceled?" He said it so casually, but Sandra's throat closed at the thought. "You've got plenty of talent. I've seen it. You can work on some other show. Probably make more money, too." He smiled, a gentle callback to her comment in the car.

For the wedding couples, she'd known what they wanted, and why, and was almost instantly bored. But the ghost couples' unconscious agenda was more elusive. She'd thought their experiences, at heart, had nothing to do with ghosts at all. But what if they did? Could she leave now, on the verge of learning one way or the other? Of seeing for herself what it was like inside this particular fear, a place that defied the rules even of storytelling?

"I want to get it right. I'm starting to feel like I simplify things that aren't that simple." Everyone got what they wanted at the end, and nobody had to change. So what, then, of her own life, which still felt like a rehearsal, with no premiere date on the schedule?

"So let it be complicated," Alan replied. "The Hawthornes *are* kind of a mess. Regina can't for the life of her figure out what's going on over there, and I've seen this woman go to some dark places in her work. This could be your opportunity to tell the story you really want to tell, and actually help a family out."

That stung, though Sandra didn't think Alan meant it to. Her job wasn't to help the families, it was true, though she didn't think that was so obvious.

Alan leaned forward. "What do *you* want? Not your network, just you. Do you want to lead the Hawthornes through the same dance as everyone else? Or do you want to challenge yourself, maybe for the last time on this show?"

"I don't know," Sandra said, resting her head in her hands again, but this time leaning into Alan a bit on the couch beside her, aching for some of his warmth. "I just don't know."

"Hey," he said, and she looked up. He lifted a hand to her hair to comfort her and she kissed him. He wrapped both hands around her waist and kissed her back. Her lips caught his stubble; it was how she knew he was there—not a spook, not a product of her imagination.

"I do," he whispered, kissing her neck, while she unbuttoned his shirt. "I've known for a while," meaningless words he murmured while he lay down, pulling Sandra on top of him, wrapping his arms around her waist, she her legs around his. She let go of that part of herself that said it was wrong, and concentrated on the feel of his hands, moving from her back to her breasts, her hips, her ass. She smiled at him as she sat up to remove her jeans, then crawled back on top of him and hovered a moment on her knees, his legs between hers, looking into his eyes.

"Hey," she said, but it wasn't the preamble to any further talk. She guided herself onto him and put her hands on his chest, grinding against him, utterly unselfconscious of her body or noises she made. He pulled her to him; his hands roamed her body as if trying to grasp all of her at once. Sandra leaned into him, wanting total skin-to-skin contact, her body awakened by his touch. Approaching orgasm, with all of her blood concentrated in a few inches below the waist, Sandra opened her eyes and found herself alone, fully clothed, in a large open area. It was hard to tell if it was inside or out—the floor beneath her was hard, packed dirt, and she did not have the sensation of freely moving air, as outside, but at the same time, if she was indoors the space was so large she would have had to walk a long time to find its walls. The only light came from candles stuck directly into the ground, illuminating a sort of mandala that had been painted there. Symbols, or words in a language she didn't recognize, were barely discernible, and the candles fluttered, seeming to burn too rapidly. She wasn't sure how long until she'd be in complete darkness, or how she would get out. She was crouching over the circle, trying to determine its message, when she became aware of a presence behind her. She stood, turning to face a tall figure in a hooded cloak, ink on wrists peeking out from the cuffs. Sandra searched for a face within the hood, in vain. The figure tilted toward her, intentions obscure, and she gasped and came back to the couch, where Alan's hands were on her hips and she tipped forward woozily, with him still inside her.

"Sandra," he said again, or maybe for the first time. "Are you okay? I lost you there for a second."

She slid off him, felt the firmness of the couch under her arm, grabbed his kneecap with her other hand to steady herself. She was wet between the legs.

"That hasn't happened to me since high school," she said, sliding into a seated position and touching her forehead. It had been during one of her first orgasms, while messing around with a boyfriend whose parents were out, when she slipped into darkness and came to a moment later, afraid for years afterward to let herself get too close. The French did refer to it as "the little death," after all.

"Do you want a glass of water?" Alan was up, attentive, though she would have liked to lie against him for a moment, her head on his chest, safe in his arms. He went to the sink, naked but for his socks, running the tap with a finger in the stream. He brought a glass back to her and she sipped it, though she did not register the feel of it entering her mouth.

He sat beside her and kissed her shoulder. "It's Thursday," he whispered. Sandra smiled. In the ensuing silence an old wall clock she hadn't noticed before became audible, ticking resolutely. She listened to it, each beat evenly spaced from the last.

She turned to Alan. "A couple more questions?"

"It's been a long time since Psych 101, but if I had to put a name to it, I'd say you use your job as a defense mechanism."

She didn't reply to that, and Alan gestured for her to go ahead.

INTERVIEW—ALAN

Question

ALAN: I don't need a definitive, once-and-for-all encounter because the . . . *mushiness* of ambiguity feels better. I hope I'm still doing this when I'm seventy.

Question

ALAN: Because it'll mean there are still dimensions of the world that remain unexplored for me, right on top of this one.

Question

ALAN: Look, I can only speak for myself. But ever since I was young I've felt what I can only describe as a disappointment with the world as it appears. I know this may surprise you, coming from a small-town real estate agent, but this (gestures) was never enough for me. And I'm not the type to go skydiving or cross Antarctica on foot. We have the option to go outward, right, to seek thrills or new experiences. Or we can go very deeply into one thing. It comes with its own dangers, though.

Question

ALAN: I know the stories that go around about me, how I destroyed my marriage to chase ghosts. On one level, that's not what happened. But on another level it is. I was never going to "settle down" the way she wanted me to, and we both knew it.

Question

ALAN: No, it's all right. I'm glad you asked.

Question

ALAN: I can't promise to ever show you something that will feel definitive. I like to think some of the pleasure is in the search. But consider it this way. Think about optical illusions: when you go from not seeing to that click when you suddenly see. You know the video ones, where you're so busy with a counting task that you don't see the person in the gorilla costume walk right across the screen? Studies have been done in which participants are shown a particular image or series of images, and because of how the image is presented, ninety-nine percent of the time they don't see it. The image is one hundred percent there. But the brain can't sort it, so the eye effectively ignores it. I imagine that these things are there all the time, but most of the time we filter them out. Otherwise we might go crazy.

———•———

They were perched on the roof, a neat line of them, and wherever Eve noticed a gap between two birds, soon enough another came and slotted itself in. It was hard to tell from where she crouched in the backyard, but they all appeared to be looking toward her. And would she have wanted it any other way? Without standing up, Eve did an awkward shuffle until she was facing away from the house, her knees still bent, arms wrapped around her shins. She stared out at the fields, the big empty nothing that faced her in the mornings when she woke. Occasionally a crow would swoop down, on the hunt, reminding Eve of their existence, then curve back up and over her head, resuming its place on the roof.

Eve had a joint, half smoked. It was a little old, but it got the job done. When she went back to New York she could usually cop some from friends who felt sorry for her. Ryan knew local dealers, but Eve turned her nose up, said this stuff came from Vermont, when in fact that was one root she didn't want to put down quite yet.

Eve didn't sense Sandra coming up from behind until she sat down next to her, right in the dirt. She was wearing jeans and one of those sleeveless sweaters that always baffled Eve: what were the precise meteorological conditions that made it ideal to cover one's torso in a sweater while leaving the arms bare? Her shoes were worn-looking ballet flats, her hair was pulled back in a ponytail. Casual. Eve wondered if the outfit was some kind of trick, designed to encourage her to let her guard down. Sandra didn't immediately launch into any agenda, either, deepening

Eve's suspicion. Eve extended the remains of the joint in Sandra's direction. Sandra demurred, but after looking at it for a good moment, as if honestly considering it.

"Are we . . . do you need me for an interview or something?" Eve turned to Sandra, who was looking out over the fields as Eve had been doing.

"Not at the moment."

"Are you guys on a break?"

Sandra gave her a look that said, *Come on.* "Eve, what are we doing here?" It was one of those perfect questions that worked on so many levels: What are you and I doing in the backyard? What are any of us doing on this planet? But Eve knew what Sandra was asking was somewhere in between.

Eve splayed out on her back, arms and legs wide, poised to make angels in the patchy grass under the tree. "Did you know the French word 'séance' also means 'film screening'?" she asked the underside of the leaves.

"I didn't, actually."

"It's perfect, though, right? Like, if you fuck this life up, you can always leave an image of yourself behind. No one can touch it, but it'll look like you, and talk like you, and if you play your cards right, maybe capture you at the moment you were at your very best. And when people miss you, they can conjure it up and hear you speak. And if the soul persists after death, hopefully it knows you aren't completely forgotten."

"You're very, very young to think you've fucked this life up. What are you, twenty-seven, twenty-eight? You have plenty of time. It's not even getting started for you."

Eve snorted. "You can't believe that."

"Why not?"

"Think about it. Forget the big decisions—leaving the world center of culture and moving out to the sticks to teach finger

painting. I mean think about all the minute, forgettable decisions you've made to bring you to this moment right here. Could
you trace back a tenth of them? And did you have any inkling
at the time what you were setting yourself up for? Don't tell me
the die hasn't already been cast." Eve was aware of how high she
was; her hands felt buzzy, her mouth dry. She was sure her eyes
were red, and Ryan would notice, and chastise her for smoking
without him.

"Why don't you leave here? Go back to the city, or a different
city? Focus on your art, Eve, it'll be so much more satisfying. A
reality show won't ensure your legacy."

Storm clouds formed in Eve's throat. "If I never paint again,
what will it matter? I was never going to have the career I
wanted." Never going to be seen the way she intended, which,
for an artist, was everything. "It was only a tiny percentage of
my days, compared with working, sleeping, preparing and con-
suming meals. Dicking around on the internet, waiting for the
subway, standing in lines. Small talk at parties with people you
never want to see again. Putting on makeup, taking it off. At
some point, that's all of it, that was your life. Why fight it?"

Sandra reached over and took the joint out from between
Eve's fingers. Eve raised her eyebrows. Sandra took a long drag,
held it, blew out with the smoke the last couple decades, revealing the lingering college student within, who wanted to get high
and debate art in a dorm room. "You are fighting it, that's why
we're here. You must have some ego to want to be on TV at all.
And whether or not it makes up a big part of your days, one
single work of art can open a, a *rift* for those who come into
contact with it. Great works—even not-great works, good ones,
ones that won't last twenty years—can still stop time for a few
minutes. Pull us out of our drudgery."

Eve remembered one of the last concerts she had been to in

Brooklyn before moving to Pennsylvania. It was rumored to be the band's last show, so tickets had gone quickly. Eve loved their entire first album, but especially this one song, as did most everybody, so of course the band had played it near the end. The song took her back to the first time she'd heard it, in a coffee shop not long after moving to the city for college. Eighteen, pretending to be a grownup with her latte, tilting an ear toward the ceiling, asking, *What is this?* Her friend said, *It's good, I'll burn it for you.* Then cut to years later, Eve and that same friend dancing in the balcony, cheering and clapping. The audience made so much noise when the song ended that the band had to wait to start their next. It might have been, for all they knew, the last time anybody would hear it live. It was the perfect bookend to her time in the city, singing along with a room full of strangers trying to relive their own first encounters: in a car, tearing through the Valley with his hand on her knee; at an outdoor music festival at the height of summer; or just sitting on the floor of a friend's apartment. *Hey, listen to this, I think you'll like it.* The important thing is no time has passed, you haven't changed, the world is as rich with possibility as it was back then, those irrevocable decisions Eve referred to have not yet been made.

Except the world kept churning, spitting out relationships, sending friends to other states, pursuing other goals. The goal became not to give in, but to seek those moments outside of time, outside of language. And for those who were capable— which Eve had believed, at one point, she herself was—the responsibility was to create them, to keep in mind all the people who were dying, literally dying, to find one.

"I can't just stroll back to New York and start again. I've lost those connections I made in grad school. I wouldn't even know where to start."

"That sounds like an excuse. It'll take work, sure, but what you want is difficult, not impossible."

"How are we supposed to know what's possible and what isn't?" Eve's voice rose to a pitch she was uncomfortable with. She sat up and looked directly at Sandra for the first time since Sandra had joined her under the tree. "Does anyone know for sure? Where's the list? What good is your bullshit show if you can't even determine the, the *nature* of what you observe?"

Sandra didn't look upset; the cannabis had not stripped her of her professional neutrality, which made Eve resent her even more.

"The show is storytelling, which people need. An organizing principle, not unlike a list. Without one . . ." Sandra took one more drag on the joint, held it a long time without exhaling. Eve watched the cloud of smoke lift and dissipate, wondering if that was the end of Sandra's sentence. That the panicked soul, with nothing to anchor it, floats free. "If you can't get resolution in life—which you won't—at least you can see it on the screen." Sandra nodded, as if having come to a decision. "The last show I worked on was called *Get Her in the Gown*."

"Ryan's mom watches that show."

Sandra smiled, in a way Eve couldn't read. "The premise is reluctant brides." She rolled the joint between her fingers, considering its smoldering tip. "One episode I worked on was a second marriage for both, and she—Angela—had a kid. We don't talk about divorce on the show. She might be described as 'single-mom Angela' or 'mother of Jason, Angela' but the d-word doesn't come up."

"The show is Christian?"

"It avoids hot-button topics. It's a show I've seen playing in my dentist's waiting room." Eve waited for her to go on. "So Angela, one of the last days of filming, wants to talk about her

ex in the interview. Again, it's not in the script. I didn't ask.
But she brings him up, because he's at the root of her hesitancy.
Turns out he was abusive, the ex. To both her and Jason. I won't
go into details. Halfway through we were both crying, but she
kept going, because there was that much more to say. Early on
I gestured to turn the cameras off. But she, Angela, gestures for
them to stay on. I couldn't tell her, in the middle of this absolutely heartbreaking story, that there was no way this stuff was
going to make it into the final cut. I just let her keep talking."

"Did it make it in?"

Sandra looked out over the fields behind the house. "The con-
flict was centered on her shoes."

"Her *shoes*?"

"She wanted to wear these heels that would have made her
taller than the new guy, and he didn't like the idea of that in
the photos—her being taller. But they were her quote-unquote
dream shoes."

"My god."

"Again: dentist's waiting room." Sandra took another hit,
then stubbed the joint out, though Eve might have been able to
get one last hit in herself. "A lot of weird stuff has happened this
week. I've felt . . . things I've never felt before. But what *I* feel,
what *I* experience when the cameras are off won't do anything
to help you."

"It sounds like you can't even help me when the cameras
are on."

Sandra leaned in. "Please, Eve. I want to tell your story the
way you want it to be told. I'm ready to do that. But you have to
meet me halfway."

"What does that mean?"

Sandra looked at her: *Don't you know?* She stood and brushed
the dirt off the back of her pants.

Eve's blood crackled. She didn't know. She wanted answers, didn't want the show to depart until she understood her house better, and right now she understood less than when they'd arrived on Monday. Sandra walked back toward the house without saying anything further about interviews or reenactments or anything, sinking the fear in Eve an inch deeper. As Sandra approached the house, all the birds along the roof lifted themselves in concert and flew off, scattering in a hundred directions. Sandra appeared not to notice, and the screen door banged behind her, leaving Eve once again alone.

——— · ———

Caitlin lay on her bed, a pillow smashed over her face to block the daylight. Every time she closed her eyes she was back in the Hawthornes' living room, in that moment between despair and vindication, when the banging had returned and all the lights had gone out. She must have felt it before it happened: why had she left her sweatshirt in the first place, unless she sensed she would need to go back? She never forgot things. Something wanted her there, wanted another chance to communicate. Two people from the show, true skeptics, had heard—*everyone* had heard—and were as freaked out as she was. It was tremendous.

Caitlin's life ran along two distinct sets of tracks: to keep up with her schoolwork, which could be a struggle, and all the regular responsibilities of her life—being a good sister, a good friend—and at the same time to seek out experiences on the boundary of what was safe, and known, and regular, as well as others who were, if not exactly like her, capable of reassuring her that these experiences were true, and good. They felt good. She hated not being able to talk about them. At first her parents had tolerated her "hobby," exchanging raised eyebrows over her head as she recounted experiences in the cemetery at Halloween, occasionally buying the equipment she put on her Christmas list every year. But in middle school Caitlin returned from a class trip to Gettysburg with a new companion, a boy who'd starved during the war. He followed her off the battlefield and all the way home but barely made it in the front door before her parents said *enough*. Since then, she'd fantasized about a community, six or eight people who lived together and hunted ghosts and counseled people who'd had encounters but ordered pizza and played video games and were able to have "normal" lives as well. Sometimes she wandered the hippie store at the mall, touching the batiks and picturing them hanging above her future bed, a giant four-poster in this big old house they'd all live in together, she and Charles and the others whose faces hadn't taken shape yet in her mind but who were out there, surely, waiting for her as intently as she waited for them. Maybe they'd even see her on the show, these future housemates, and get in touch.

She rolled over to face the window. At some point Charles's car had pulled up to the house, though Charles hadn't gotten out yet. He sat gesturing in the driver's seat. Caitlin looked at the time. Whenever she wasn't sure about something, she looked at the time. She feared the impending confession—something bound to hurt her, or else why practice in the car?

Finally Charles stepped out and walked his slightly juddering walk to the front door. *No one could ever love your walk the way I do*, she projected. *No one else will ever see you cross the boardwalk at the shore in the summer, holding a plate of funnel cake perfectly horizontally, like a robot who is trying so hard to be human, and feel her heart expand to swallow everything in the world.*

He knocked on the door and Caitlin thumped down the stairs to let him in.

"Hey," he said. He looked morose. His eyes scanned the living room, where her sister was plunked on the couch, blaring cartoons. "Can we talk?"

"Sure." Her voice was just a little too high. "Come up to my room." She pretended she hadn't just seen him in the car, rehearsing. Pretended she hadn't, in the moments before he reached the front door, hastily made up her bed, kicked a few things under it. Her room was in that transitional stage of stuffed animals jammed in a mini-hammock hung high in a corner over posters of scary movies. Christmas lights hung year-round, purple sparkly garlands surrounded her mirror and photos of herself with friends from camp were taped up around it. It wasn't a room a boy would want to have sex in. She wasn't sure if that bothered her.

Charles sat on the edge of the bed. Caitlin moved to sit down at her desk chair and then, taking a chance, sat beside him. The mattress bent them toward each other a few degrees.

"Caitlin, I am so sorry," he said, staring at the carpet. He didn't gesture the way she'd seen him practicing. She felt like she couldn't speak or swallow.

"Charles—"

"The show is probably going to be canceled. *Searching for . . .* , it's done."

Caitlin felt like she might float away into the air. Charles was looking right at her. His words didn't quite register. It would take so little motion for the two of them to move toward each other, just six teeny inches for the kissing to begin.

"Are they going to finish the episode?" She tried to keep herself together.

"They don't have enough material. Monday night doesn't count, because the Hawthornes weren't there." He tipped his head forward into his hands. "I feel like an idiot."

"You didn't do anything wrong." She placed a hand on his arm.

"What about the other stuff: the shelf, everything last night? The EVP?" What more could they want? An abundance of evidence and the show a brat in the face of it, refusing the forty-two flavors offered and demanding something not on the menu.

"None of that stuff made their tapes. Last night was after they had left and packed up."

"Alan told you this?"

"The producer told him," Charles said. "I think he wants to fuck her." Charles never used language like that: so crude, to describe something that was supposed to be beautiful. He flopped back on the bed, his T-shirt riding up to reveal an inch of pale skin, a surprisingly dark line of hair between his navel and the top of his pants.

"We never should have gone into that house Monday night."

"But we did. And it was incredible." Caitlin got up on her knees, leaned over him. He looked—dare she think it?—scared. "I can't believe they're walking away from this. That house is so powerful."

"What if it isn't?" He stared at the ceiling. "What if we've been . . . ? What if they've all been . . . ?" He threw an arm over his eyes, shielding himself from an honest response.

"They haven't," Caitlin said firmly. She felt the night before flash across her skin, the tingling before the lights went out. Her knee was in Charles's side, his waist if he'd had one. She shifted her weight to move away, but his hand lifted ever so slightly from his leg, gesturing ever so subtly for her to stay.

"How do you know?" His voice plaintive, his eyes still in the crook of his elbow. "How can you tell when something isn't just in your head, it's in the world, when other people don't see it?"

Caitlin remembered the boy from Gettysburg, that *zzzt* in her blood whenever she stepped into a space she knew was haunted. She occasionally imagined her life without these things in it: her time spent playing field hockey, or taking pictures for yearbook. Those were worlds she could visit—to help her college applications, to maybe make a friend. But she didn't belong there.

"I don't," she replied. "But I don't know anything else, either." Charles opened an eye, peered at her. "I don't know what other people experience. That's their problem. And if we're wrong, we still have lots of time to figure out what else to do instead."

This got him to remove his arm fully from his face.

"You don't believe that."

"Not a chance." She smiled. "The week's not over yet. We can still go back and convince them about the house. Do they have another investigation scheduled?"

"I don't know."

Caitlin jumped off the bed, jostling Charles in the process, and knelt in front of her open closet door. She rifled through plaid skirts, sparkly boots, a T-shirt with her name airbrushed in a bubble font purchased on the boardwalk last summer, and pulled out a red and black cylinder with an antenna sticking up from the center and lights around the top.

"Oh, no," Charles said, waving his hands as if to ward something off. "Where did you get the money for it? Aren't they like two hundred dollars?"

"Babysitting," Caitlin said simply, then sat cross-legged in front of the REM POD and turned it on. It beeped, somewhat unpleasantly, the lights blinked once, and then it sat, waiting for a signal.

"Alan won't allow it."

"I don't need Alan's permission. Look, if they want something that's going to look good on TV, this'll look good on TV." She turned the device in her hands, admiring it. It had five different-colored lights on the top that responded to ambient temperature changes, and the antenna picked up electromagnetic-field readings. "REM-POD-EMF" was written across the black label in red capital letters. It looked both scientific and spooky.

"It looks like a disco ball," Charles said derisively.

"This is what they use on the other shows." She could imagine it so clearly: PIP and the Hawthornes standing in a circle outside the house where the banging had been, the REM-POD on the ground at the center. Without physical contact it would light up and make noises, providing the kind of instant-gratification evidence the show needed, that no one could deny.

"I wish you wouldn't watch those other shows."

"Charles," Caitlin said, clapping her hands on each word, "You. Don't. Have. To. Believe. Its. Results." She stopped clapping. "Do it for the show. Do it for Alan. For Sandra, even, what do I care." She looked at him. "Maybe you have a crush on her, too."

"I *don't* have a crush on her."

"We've had tons of contact, you and I. Tons," she repeated. "We don't need them to prove our work." She believed this, but it made her sad to hear herself say it. "But they need us to do theirs. This will help. And . . . *fuck* 'em if they can't take a joke, right?" The word sounded funny in her mouth, but it got a reaction out of Charles, who looked at her in surprise. "Okay?"

He nodded, smiled, looked down at his chest. "Okay," he conceded. The tips of his ears were red.

Caitlin could have kissed him, but at that moment the REM-POD screeched, and they both jumped, then dissolved into giggles.

———·—·———

Ryan had gone out for a drive. When he came back, Eve was waiting for him in the kitchen, a mostly untouched cup of coffee on the table in front of her. She hadn't been reading, or sketching, just sitting, in a house that suddenly felt alarming in its emptiness.

"Where is everybody?" he asked, throwing his keys on the counter.

"They've gone."

"For good?" But the presence of tripods in the dining room, wires still taped to the floor, answered the question for him.

"I don't know if they're going to finish the episode or not."

"Why not? Shit keeps getting crazier."

"The psychic thinks it's me," she said, watching her husband. Ryan raised an eyebrow. "She told me about this thing called 'PK.' She thinks my mind is causing whatever's happening in this house."

"If anyone has the power to take picture frames off the wall with their mind, it's you." Ryan patted her shoulder, then pretended to look through the mail.

"So you don't believe that, either." She wanted to feel relief, wanted to join her husband in whatever reality he inhabited, but did he even know where he currently was?

"We never called any of those inspectors we talked about. Maybe there's still a rational explanation for all of this."

His dismissal sounded forced, given his earlier state, the reaching of a man desperate for a conversation with a definitive end. And Eve wanted the opposite. This wasn't another ordinary house in an ordinary neighborhood where ordinary people lived. She would never move to a house like that. She would never live a life like that, despite what she had said to Sandra. But she couldn't seem to say these things to Ryan, either. How could he understand that she wanted things too complicated to articulate? It couldn't be framed as a simple request—*Honey would you, Honey do you mind*. Though neither could she fathom that she'd created this swirl of activity out of perverse boredom, a reluctance to engage with the life she actually lived. How had she done it, if she didn't even know such things were possible?

Alan had told her the question was not *Do they exist?* but *Who can see them?* Invisible, immeasurable things, damaged upon entry to this world, nevertheless hovered nearby, ready to be intuited. She'd assumed that after the show aired their lives would change accordingly, as a couple who had been affected by forces larger than themselves, the very energies of life and death. But Ryan didn't want his life to change. He was content, and she was restless. That was what it came down to.

Tears rose behind her eyes without warning, but she contained them. "Do you think I have control over what's happening? Do you think this is what I wanted for us?"

Ryan looked startled, dropped the mail. He crouched in front of her, put one hand on each knee. He looked up at her and his concern made space for a few tears to spill down her face. "No," he said. "I have never thought that."

"But you do believe there's something going on in this house?"

He ran his hand over his ultra-short hair. "Before, I thought most of that stuff could be explained some other way. Now I'm not sure."

"Because of the shelf? The things that happened last night? What convinced you?" She leaned toward him, her hands on the back of his elbows, wanting to pull him into her circle of presumed insanity, to no longer feel so dreadfully alone.

"I don't know how to . . ." He looked around the kitchen and it occurred to Eve that Ryan hadn't taken a drive to get away from the show, or from her, even, but to get out of the house altogether. And if Ryan did come around to believing the activity was in some way due to her, then the simplest solution would be to leave her.

She imagined the house without him in it, if he went back

to Allison or just got in his car and took off. Eve pictured herself alone in their house the night after everyone—the crew, the ghost hunters, her husband—left, the clamorousness of her anxiety bending the walls. *Don't leave me until I know,* she silently pleaded. *I cannot bear another day not knowing.*

"I'm sorry." She started to cry in earnest, surprising herself. For some couples things like children or career would be the issue they couldn't agree on, the crack that would split them up. For her and Ryan, it was a stupid ghost. "I am. I don't know how to move forward, and I'm terrified."

"Hey." He was sitting beside her now, pulling her body to his, rubbing her back in a tight embrace. "You didn't do anything wrong," he assured her. "We're going to figure this out, okay? Together. Always." She nodded, wiped her eyes. She slipped her arms around his waist, kissed him once on the mouth, then again, and then again.

———•———

The house, in preparation for what was coming, quietly tightened its screws.

———•———

Ryan looked at his wife, who was breathing heavily, a shimmer on her upper lip, her hair a mess. They had started to talk about the show, the house, and then they had ended up here, just like in the beginning, when they couldn't keep their hands off each other. Ryan nudged Eve with one socked toe. He could smell her on him, the places she'd kissed and licked and bit. He could smell himself on her, too, traces of his sweat on her chest.

She rolled onto her side to face him, ran a finger down the

center of his torso, poked it gently into his navel. He was softening a bit around the middle, had started to do sit-ups in the back of the store during his lunch break, without making a big deal out of it. Eve had a couple gray hairs—four, at the most— that she discussed with him but refused to dye or remove. Ryan had more, and noticed them, but said nothing. Occasionally he glanced at Eve's tweezers on the shelf under the mirror, but resisted, unsure if removing them would be out of vanity, or fear. She was watching her fingers trace the contours of his body, not looking him in the eye. "Could it be psychokinesis?" she asked, shattering the serenity that had flooded his body after he came. Why couldn't they stay like this awhile longer? But Eve always had to have everything put away again. She was always first into the shower.

Ryan rubbed his eyes, resisted turning to the clock, which would only encourage Eve to do the same. "It doesn't square with anything else I know about the world." One of Ryan's employees read science magazines, and sometimes Ryan asked him about what he was reading. Tyler would try to explain to him the latest developments in physics—the Higgs boson, gravitational waves—using simple drawings, sugar packets, whatever was lying around. Ryan couldn't follow much of it except that there was complicated equipment running experiments that generated thousands of pages of results. Numbers. He might have been more open to the idea of paranormal research if the people doing it looked professional and had quantified data to throw around, even if Ryan didn't understand it. What they looked like were a couple of kids following a man with a twenty-year-old tape recorder. But maybe he was fooling himself—he probably wouldn't have trusted them even if they'd shown up in lab coats with stethoscopes dangling from their necks. Not that that made much sense, either.

Ryan put his arms behind his head. He thought again of the woman in the basement. Maybe there were spirits hanging around him, sticking out their tongues and calling him names in a thousand dead languages, and he had been too blocked off to see. Why complain about it, though? If the alternative was every time he turned a corner he risked bumping into a suicide, no thank you. He'd stick to blissful ignorance.

"But you don't know everything," Eve said, sitting up. "There are thousands of things—" Her lecture, which had clearly taken shape before she'd opened her mouth, was interrupted by a single authoritative bang from downstairs, followed by a succession of crashes.

Patrick woke up for the second time at Melanie's, sprawled out on her futon on the floor, searching her dirty kitchen for a mug that wasn't ridiculously child sized into which to pour some coffee that Melanie, adding one check in the "pro" column, took blissfully strong. She liked her coffee thick as mud but only little thimblefuls of it, her antique teacups all stained brown on the inside and in the hairline cracks. After his night he'd crawled in her bed and almost instantly passed out. But this morning (really, afternoon), when they woke she'd asked him point-blank what kind of TV show he was making, because there were people in her bar, and they were talking. And Patrick, with all the shame he could muster about a job he had disassociated himself from within weeks of starting, had told her the truth: it was one of those ghost-hunting shows. They were here to look for some ghosts, in one of those old houses on the edge of town. Not that he believed in ghosts himself, but you have no idea how hard it is these days to get a job—

"Fuck you," she interrupted him, hurling one of her dirty socks at his face. It was so small, and even after a full day on the job barely smelled at all. It turned Patrick on a little. "I believe in ghosts. I've had conversations with them."

"What?" Patrick sat up on her couch. "With who?" It came out sounding jealous.

Melanie sat down on the edge of the couch and clasped her hands with their many rings and bracelets. She had a nose ring and a line of studs cascading down each earlobe, plus one or two more under her clothes. Patrick estimated she was 15 percent metal.

"One time, I was staying at my girlfriend's while her husband was out of town. Her grandfather had just died and she didn't want to be alone. But she took all these sleeping pills so she could go to bed, so she was out at like nine o'clock. Meanwhile I was up, brushing my teeth, and I saw this figure, sort of glowing, standing outside the bathroom. I said, 'What do you want?'"

"What did it say?" Patrick had no idea what to make of this story. Without being too obvious about it, he scanned her apartment for dreamcatchers.

"It didn't say anything. It just sort of floated down the stairs. I didn't see it again."

Patrick considered this. "I wouldn't call that a conversation."

"That wasn't the only time. Just the most recent."

"Were you on drugs?"

"I took a couple of the sleeping pills. I wasn't going to sit up by myself at her house."

"Well." He patted her knee. "It sounds genuinely scary."

"Fuck you," she said again, and hit him with a throw pillow. "Can I come on the set with you today? It's my day off."

"I don't know—there might be liability issues."

Melanie nodded; being in the business of dealing with drunk people, she understood liability.

But Patrick had never inquired into bringing a friend to a shoot. He assumed any rational person who was not being paid to be there would not want to go. He had also become adept at discussing many aspects of his work without using words like "ghost" or "paranormal" at all. Patrick had never paid close attention to anyone on location who believed such things might be real, and he wondered what it would be like to see Melanie there. The risk for him was limited: he was heading back to New York tomorrow either way. "I can ask."

"I could come by for like an hour."

"Say hi to some old friends."

She reached to swat him again but he grabbed her wrist to hold her off, so she kissed him, and soon enough they were making out.

But Melanie hadn't forgotten, and when his phone had buzzed one too many times to ignore and Patrick started to gather his clothing, she looked at him with her bright green eyes and he nonverbally relented.

They parked on the street, the Hawthornes' driveway already at capacity. They stepped inside a maelstrom of voices and activity in the dining room. Patrick, seeking Sandra, was startled by his own crew admonishing him to watch where he stepped.

"What?" He looked down.

"Oh, wow." Melanie was already in a deep-knee bend, waving her hands a centimeter or two above broken plates and glass that lay scattered around her feet. "Can you feel that? They're still hot."

"They're hot?"

"Not literally. But whatever force compelled them to the floor, you can feel its presence. It's intense." She lifted, from between the shards, a long black feather.

"Excuse me, who are you?" The gawky kid Patrick tried to ignore was standing over them.

"I'm a friend of Patrick's. Melanie. I have some gifts." Patrick groaned inwardly. He had a feeling she didn't mean wine. He stood up and tried not to listen to Melanie tell Charles about the signs of fate. "I mean, what are the odds that you come into my bar, of all the places in the world?" She slipped an arm around Patrick's waist, displaying more affection toward him than she'd shown all week.

"I guess it was meant to be." He kissed the top of her head, finally placing that scent: patchouli. Initially her perfume had reminded him of college, good-natured stoners playing hacky sack on the grass, and he thought he'd be in for a laid-back time. But he should have known. It was a bat signal for wack jobs. He dropped his arm from her waist and craned his neck. "I should check in with my team. Don't, uh, touch anything."

"I wouldn't dream of it, babe," she said, flashing him a hundred white teeth gorgeously aligned, then turning to Charles. "So what about you? Are you clairvoyant, clairaudient, what?"

Patrick got away before he heard Charles's response.

He found Sandra in the living room, in a circle of the crew. Patrick broke right into the middle of it. "What's going on?"

Sandra looked at him, her eyes and brain taking a minute to register who he was.

"I don't know," she said. She did not sound tired and impatient, or like she did know but didn't want to tell him in front of everyone else. She sounded like she truly had no idea.

"What are all those plates and shit on the floor?"

"I don't know, Patrick, where have you been?"

"I've been . . . working."

The crew had fallen silent, watching what looked like a lovers' spat, one that was long overdue. But Sandra didn't escalate. She pressed her hands to her face and when she removed them said she was going to make a call, walking out of the house and leaving the front door open. Everyone turned to Patrick briefly, then dispersed, confident they wouldn't be needed for a while longer. And Patrick did nothing to keep them.

———·———

"Psst."

Eve sat on the interview chair in the dining room while the TV crew that had entered her home ostensibly to film paranormal activity conferred in the living room, their backs turned to the latest example of said activity. Eve swiveled her neck to see who had signaled to her and saw the girl ghost hunter sticking her face through the living room door.

"Want to talk for a sec?" She smiled, a gleam in her eye, and motioned for Eve to follow her to the back porch, where the girl and boy had set up a camera, tripod, and chair of their own.

Footage courtesy Paranormal Investigators of Pennsylvania

INTERVIEW—EVE

Question

EVE: When I was ten my family drove across the country in two cars, and the car I was in fell into some sort of time slip and came out four days later, though it only felt like we'd slept for a single night. I didn't sleep, and so I saw everything that happened. Crows circled the car. They

showed me things—visions of myself and my family, wild
landscapes I'd never seen before or since, places I'm still
not entirely sure were on earth. It was like being forced to
watch a graphic movie, unable to close your eyes because the
images are already inside your brain. I was so young. I was
paralyzed by the images.

Question

EVE: After we moved, I had a hard time at school. I didn't
make many new friends. They thought I was weird. Because
I could see things—people in the classroom no one else saw.
I got made fun of a lot. The art room was the only place I
felt safe. It was where my "imagination" was an asset, rather
than a liability. I could sit in that room and draw by the
light of the enormous windows. And if I saw anyone else in
there with me, who nobody else saw, it didn't bother me.

Question

EVE: I had one friend, though, for a little while, and she would
sometimes sleep over. Every time she did, weird things would
happen. The TV would turn itself off and on. One night we
took a frozen pizza out but forgot to turn the oven on. An
hour later it was still on the counter, still in its box, burnt
to char. One morning when we woke up all the stuff in
her bag was covered with this weird goo. I pretended I had
accidentally spilled lotion, but we both knew that wasn't true.
She might be the only one who ever saw stuff at the same
time as me. She never made fun of me, but she eventually
stopped coming over. We'd go to her house, or go to the mall.

Question

EVE: In high school I had a Wicca phase, which didn't exactly
make me popular with the other girls, though once I got
to art school I learned plenty of people there did, too. The
girls in my high school were more into bullying over Instant

Messenger. I was a target just once, after one of them caught me in the library reading about astral projection. They started calling me "Devilyn." That night, or really the next morning, coming out of a dream, I felt my soul pulled back into my body, as if attached at the end by a long string. I have no idea where I had been, though.

Question

EVE: Around that same time I took a babysitting job for a family friend. After the first time, I didn't let him drive me home, but I needed the money, so I kept taking jobs. The kids were small and would go to bed early and then I'd do my homework on the couch, or watch TV or whatever, in, like, an oversized flannel, anything that would cover my body, in all seasons. They had these two doors—one between the kitchen and back porch, the other between the kitchen and dining room—and they'd always slam in succession: *SLAM SLAM!* No one touched them, they closed on their own, no matter the weather or any other conditions of the house. It got so I could predict when it was going to happen. I'd get this feeling, a quivering behind my ears, almost nausea, and then they'd shut, one after the other. The kids slept through it, every time.

Question

EVE: I took a year off between college and grad school. I didn't work very much. I didn't know what I wanted to do—I was too precious to take just any job, so I didn't apply for many. I had pretty bad insomnia. There was this radio show every night, about ghosts, conspiracy theories, alien abductions, the end of the world. I would listen to it on this old clock radio. People would call in with their stories—one woman claimed she had a psychic connection to Bigfoot, and that her sister had a psychic connection to one of

Bigfoot's siblings. She would call in to tell the host how sad
Bigfoot was about climate change. How do these people
live? I mean practically—what jobs can they bear to hold
while maintaining these visions of the world? How do they
reconcile the mundane requirements of taxes and laundry
with their beliefs?

Question

EVE: The day we moved into this house I felt something. At
the time I was excited. I saw it as an opportunity to dig
into this part of myself I had been suppressing. I thought if
Ryan started to experience things as well, we could have an
open conversation about my past. Everything was coming
together perfectly. A culmination. But it hasn't been like
that. You think someone else is going to join you, share your
vision, but really they just want to align the tangible stuff—
the bank accounts and weekly routines. The bodies. Your
vision of the world—that remains yours alone. And you are
alone in it. That was something I got wrong.

Question

EVE: On my fortieth birthday I went to bed early. Ryan
organized a really nice surprise party for me, but I didn't
take it well, getting older. My father died suddenly when I
was thirty-seven, and the night of my birthday he appeared
to me, and beamed into my head messages of pure love and
warmth and support. The next morning I got up and started
to paint in a way I never had before.

Question

EVE: I saw Ryan's soul depart his body. I wasn't there, I saw
it with my third eye. Death is thought of as a great leveler,
but the journey of Ryan's soul was uniquely beautiful.
Though I was far away at the time I knew that he had
achieved total peace. I was not quite beyond jealousy at

that point, so I allowed myself to feel some envy for the completion of his path. Mine still stretched, long and inscrutable, in front of me.

Question

EVE: When I was two hundred and twenty-two I finally found the entrance to the Temple of Mystics, at the base of the *(indecipherable)* Mountain. The initiation process takes eleven seasons and can only conclude during a very particular alignment of the planets. But in that time the door remains open for one entire moon cycle, during which crossing between the worlds is so simple it's laughable. From the base of my throat I was able to expel kobolds into our world, three of them. They danced down my tongue. It's not encouraged, but it was not, ultimately, what prevented me from being ordained. Still, I saw a lot in that time. Many, many things. Answers to questions I wouldn't form for another three hundred years. Sometimes it works backward, that way.

———————

Sitting in Patrick's car outside the house, Sandra took a deep breath. She told herself to stay open, to try to listen to Eve. She had, after all, wanted a challenge.

She'd arrived at the Hawthornes' to find the couple standing still, making a show of waiting for her before they touched anything. Like a tableau. Or a crime scene.

"What happened?"

Eve and Ryan were staring at the dining room floor. In the corner, opposite the black curtain and interview setup, a built-in cabinet had had its glass doors blown off, and shards of glass lay everywhere, mixed in with ceramic wedges from a broken dinnerware set the cabinet had contained.

"We don't know." Eve dropped her hands, the desired effect having been achieved. "We came downstairs and found it like this."

Sandra stepped over some of the broken glass to examine the cabinet. Bits of glass still wobbled in the wooden frame of the door, and a few split teacups remained on the shelves within. Rocks, maybe, hurled through the glass with tremendous force, could have done damage like this, though Sandra didn't see any rocks around. In the midst of the mess, Sandra noticed a black stain, a nasty-looking mold, spreading around an electrical outlet near the floor.

"These are antique pieces." Eve's voice wavered. "They belonged to my grandmother."

Irritation blossomed in Sandra, fed by an assumption that Eve and Ryan had schemed some blowout while Sandra had been on the phone with her editors, bargaining for one more night shoot. She didn't have a script, just a kernel of hope that she could both help Eve and generate good TV. As Alan had reassured her, she had done it many times before. But the crew couldn't shoot in the dining room as it looked now: all the furniture was pushed to the side to make room for the interview setup. The "event," whatever it was, couldn't have happened in a more inconvenient spot.

Ted, ever punctual, stepped in the front door.

"Ted, grab a broom or something," Sandra gestured. "Let's help the Hawthornes clean this up."

"Wait," Eve held out her hands, "don't you think we should capture this on film? This *just happened*."

"And how did it happen?" Sandra pushed her. Opening up to Eve in the yard had clearly backfired. All week Eve had been resisting the show, resisting Sandra, disappearing when things didn't go the way she wanted. And now here was one more exciting event in a week of them, and Sandra hadn't been here to see it, and the cameras were all still stowed.

"I don't know, we were upstairs. We were fucking," Eve added, as if daring Sandra to check the sheets. Ted glanced up the steps, then gave Ryan and Eve a once-over.

"She's not crazy," Ryan said, and Eve shot him a look. Sandra had a vision of Eve and Ryan in thirty years, Ryan stooped and put-upon, dutifully nodding his head and packing groceries into a bag while Eve barked orders, little trace of the composed beauty she was now.

"No one said anyone was crazy," Sandra said. She looked to Ted, her only ally at the moment—behind Eve and Ryan, he mouthed at her, *I did.* Sandra bit her lip to keep from smiling. She also wanted to cry. Nothing had even started yet: she could hear a car pull up to the house, but from where she was standing she couldn't see if it was Alan or the rest of her crew. No matter who it was, they were going to ask her what to do, then what to do after that, then what to do after that. She had wanted an hour with Alan and her team to make an itinerary for the evening and plan some setups. But Eve had her own plan, and it was in motion. The rest of them would have to catch up.

It was Patrick who had arrived, with the jailbait who had presumably been putting him up. Sandra excused herself, and from outside the house watched Alan pull up in his car and cross the yard to the front door, followed not long after by Madame Mandaya, all scarves and clanking gold jewelry. It was seven p.m. and for once everyone was exactly where they needed to be at the time they were told to arrive and Sandra had no fucking clue what to do with any of them.

She thought she might sit in Patrick's car for a few minutes, reminding herself who she was, putting a distance between her and Eve, between her and the house, that would allow her to move forward. To just finish the week. She closed her eyes, but was startled by a knock on the window.

"Alan?" She rolled down the window.

"I'm sorry, were you asleep?"

"No, god, no, how embarrassing. I just . . . needed a minute. Is everything okay? I know there's a situation in there . . ."

"I was looking for you. Do you have another minute? Do you need to go right in?"

"What's going on?"

"Take a walk with me?"

They walked to the side of the house, the side where the banging began, right underneath the living room windows where her crew and Alan's were inside, waiting.

"I've never done this outside before. Sort of an experiment." His eyes were shining.

"Done what?"

"Let's sit. That way, we won't be seen. Caitlin would never let me hear the end of it if she knew."

They sat crossed-legged in the grass under the window, at a ninety-degree angle to each other, Sandra's left knee not quite touching Alan's right. From within the kangaroo pocket of his sweatshirt, Alan produced a small black box, a kind of handheld radio with an extendable metal antenna and a digital screen. Then he removed a set of headphones, bulky noise-canceling ones.

"Someone's shopping at SkyMall," Sandra joked.

"This is a spirit box," Alan said, indicating the device. "It scans radio frequencies the way the scanner in your car does, but instead of looking for signals, it looks for static. It produces a sort of white noise, and, ideally, spirits send messages through that, in the spaces between frequencies."

Sandra became nervous.

"The idea is, I'll ask the questions, and you'll wear the head-phones and hopefully get some answers. But you won't be able to hear the questions. So no false positives."

"*Me* as in a hypothetical me, right?" Sandra asked.

"No, you as in the actual you, right now. I thought we could try it for a few minutes. It's not a form of communication I can do alone."

He looked shy, tentative, as if they hadn't seen each other naked just a few hours before.

"Alan, I . . ."

"Five minutes. That's all I ask."

Sandra glanced toward the window, feigning concern for the shoot, her crew.

"Five minutes," she said, and held her hand out for the head-phones. Alan couldn't hide the pure pleasure on his face as he connected the headphones to the spirit box.

"What are you going to ask?"

"Tsk, tsk, Sandra," he said, flirtatious now. "That undermines the whole thing." He pushed a button on the device, static filled her head, and she saw Alan mouth: *I'll see you on the other side.*

The white noise swelled and receded, pulsating as the scanner rolled through the airwaves. It was a lulling, predictable sound, and Sandra relaxed into it, leaning back against the house, clos-ing her eyes and letting it wash over her and back, like an oscil-lating fan.

She had no idea how long she'd been listening when the first word came through. She was beginning to believe that this static was the point—a sort of aural sensory deprivation bath that would reset and restore her, when a word popped through.

Yes.

Sandra whipped the headphones off.

"What did you hear?" Alan looked excited.

"*Yes*, the word *yes*. What am I supposed to do?"

"Just repeat whenever you hear something, that's it. Was it a man, a woman, a child?"

"A man, I think. I'm not sure. It was so brief."

"Good," he touched her knee. "You're doing great. Try not to panic. Just repeat whatever is said. I'm recording this"—he held up a digital voice recorder—"so later, we can listen to the questions and answers together. But for right now, just tell me what you hear."

Sandra nodded, took a breath, put the headphones back on. She closed her eyes, leaned back against the house, listened to the static, a gentle lapping at her ears.

Visitor.

"Visitor, it sounded like, I don't know, it was hard to tell." Sandra couldn't hear if Alan replied. He didn't touch her; she didn't open her eyes.

The next one didn't take long to come; the spirit was getting chatty.

Circle.

"Circle," she repeated. She didn't feel so nervous this time. She could tell the voice was definitively a male's, possibly one around her own age.

Home.

"Home," Sandra repeated, but she wished she could hear it again: there was something about the 'o' in 'home' that stood out to her, a regional pronunciation she couldn't quite put her finger on.

Sandra.

Sandra did not repeat it. Her throat had closed.

Sandra, the voice said again, clearly, unambiguously. A male voice, someone trying to go *home*. Someone she'd seen around a *circle*, reaching for her. It all either added up to the same thing, or it was meaningless, each little scrap so tattered that it could be made to fit any number of bigger pictures.

"Sandra," Alan was touching her knee now, and she removed the headphones. "What are you hearing? Forgive me, the headphones aren't perfect, I thought I could hear a word or two coming through."

"That's good," Sandra said, standing up shakily, brushing the dirt off her butt. "Thank you for this." She handed the headphones back to him.

"What did you hear? Just tell me for the recording, I'm happy to go through any of it with you later, talk you through any—"

"Alan, what do you want from me? Why did you bring me here?"

"I thought you wanted an experience. You asked me so many questions about mine. I thought if I could get you away from"—he gestured beyond the window to everything that Sandra was now desperate to be in the midst of, all those bodies in a too-small house, clattering even when trying to be quiet—"I could maybe show you something. I sense that it worked?"

"And what am I supposed to do with it?" Sandra asked him, aware that she wasn't being fair, unable to stop herself. "I need to stay on this side of the lens. It's the only thing I know." She knew it was true as soon as she said it, though she'd never articulated it to herself before. Sandra walked away from Alan, sure she was burning a bridge but leaving several others, bigger ones, standing. Her knees were wobbly but stable enough to carry her to the front door.

The screen door made a terrible screech when she opened it, calling attention to her return. She wanted to curse the Hawthornes, but couldn't believe what awaited her inside: the living room had arranged itself in her absence. The candles were lit, the overhead lights already dimmed. The Hawthornes, PIP, and the psychic had sat, without her prompting, around the table as they had the night before and her crew stood in an outer circle, gear trained inward. It was as supernatural as anything else that had happened so far, and Sandra tried not to impose on the scene the ring in her vision, symbols burned into the floor, everyone's impassive expressions melting into no expressions, no features at all. Alan came in the door behind her, touched her on the elbow, and mouthed, "Are you okay?" She nodded, and he took his seat at the table, a spot that had been saved for him. Sandra, of course, was meant to stand. They were waiting for her cue. The party, and whatever was going to happen at it, had begun.

NIGHT 4

(ALL FOOTAGE courtesy Roving Eye Productions, (c) 20—)

*(Alan, Caitlin, Charles, Eve, Ryan, and Melanie the bar-
tender sit around the table. In the center of the table are several candles, a tape recorder, and a smoking bunch of dried
herbs in a small stone chalice. Madame Mandaya walks the
circumference of the circle, sprinkling salt.)*

MME. MANDAYA: Our ritual tonight will follow the traditional
process, honed and refined through the centuries.

Step One: Open a passage to the Other Side

MME. MANDAYA: When the circle is complete, we will be
protected. *(sits)* Please join hands. Close your eyes. Imagine
your bodies bathed in blue light. This light is warm, and it
protects you. It covers you completely, from your head to
your toes. Focus on this light. See it all around you, and
around the bodies of your companions. Squeeze the hand of
the person next to you. This will charge the energy. Imagine
that with every squeeze, the light grows stronger on you and
on the persons on either side of you.
(Pause)

MME. MANDAYA: It's strong now. Imagine this light slipping off
of you like water, and all the light from all the bodies sliding
into a puddle. You can feel the warmth of it moving away
from you, and your body gets cooler, but the center of the
circle is very hot, with all the warmth of the light gathered
there. The light is rising into a column, a spiral of pure blue
warmth. The column stands at the center of the circle. It is

only an inch or two wide. We must make it bigger. Focus
on the column of light. Squeeze the hand of the person next
to you, and the column expands a few inches. It is growing.
Feel it get bigger, and spin, a spinning blue tunnel of light.
We must charge it a little more. Keep squeezing. Imagine
the column now eight inches wide . . . now ten . . . spinning
and expanding, up through the ceiling, down through the
floor, a pure blue tunnel of heat and light. It is brilliant, full
of energy at the center. Squeeze the hands of the persons on
either side of you. Keep your eyes closed and see the column
spinning and growing. Can you feel it? It is a door. It is
opening.

Step Two: Speak to the spirits

MME. MANDAYA: If there are any spirits with us tonight, please
make your presence known. We wish you no harm. We only
want to see you cross over and find peace.
(Pause)

MME. MANDAYA: I sense someone with us. You may ask.

CAITLIN: Is there—

CHARLES *(simultaneously)*: Are you—

CAITLIN: Oh. Did you want to . . . ?

ALAN: Go ahead, Charles.

CHARLES: Are you here?
(Twenty-second pause)

CHARLES: Why are you here?
(Pause)

CHARLES: If you can make such dramatic appearances, for
Christ's sake give us something. A sound, a word, something
with a little goddamn meaning.

ALAN: Ask a question like we always do.
(Pause)

CHARLES: Sorry. Go ahead, Caitlin.

CAITLIN: Can you tell us anything about yourself? Is there a reason you chose to visit us?

ALAN: Slow down, Caitlin.

(Pause)

CAITLIN: Was this your home while you were alive?

(Twenty-second pause)

CAITLIN: If you are here, please give us a sign.

(Brief pause)

ALAN: Let's let Eve ask a question.

EVE: I wouldn't know what to say.

ALAN: You do. Trust your instincts.

EVE *(clears her throat)*: Are you here?

(Pause)

EVE: Are you here for me?

(Pause)

EVE: Why me? Did you choose me?

(Pause)

EVE: Were you there in Oklahoma, when I was ten, and we were driving?

(Pause)

EVE: Were you in the classroom, in Texas, when no one would believe me?

(Pause)

EVE: What do you want from me?

RYAN: If you do anything to—

EVE: It's okay.

(Pause)

EVE: Did I invite you in? Did I have a choice?

MME. MANDAYA: *(emits a slight cough)*

EVE: Why is this happening to me? What have I done to . . . to welcome this?

MME. MANDAYA: Iscum.

EVE: Am I trying to sabotage my whole . . .

MME. MANDAYA: Nahpul. Brahkesh.

EVE: Did I just want some kind of weird assurance that I'm special, in a way that nobody could disprove?

MME. MANDAYA: NNNNNNNNNNNNNNN.

EVE: Can I function without . . . you? What are you? Are you me?

MME. MANDAYA: Annnngggghhh. Kkkkkkkkkkkk.

SANDRA (*off-screen*): Ease up a bit, she's struggling.

EVE: Who's "she"?

SANDRA: Madame Mandaya. Eve, look at the psychic.

EVE: Who are you people, to come into my house and tell me what to do?

SANDRA: Eve, please—

MME. MANDAYA: KUHKUHKUHKUHKUHKUHKUH. NNNNNGGGGG.

(*The TV makes a popping sound, the screen whitening then returning to black. Above the TV, a terrarium rattles on its shelf. A casement window in the living room opens, the top half dropping down to the sill, the glass breaking on impact. Ryan shouts, jumping in his seat.*)

SANDRA (*off-screen*): Let's stay calm.

(*Eve sits still with her eyes closed. Madame Mandaya's eyes are also closed, her head thrown back, glottal sounds emerging from her throat. Everyone else is looking around them. Shadows press on the outside of the windows, beating against the screens. Footsteps cross the floor above them, heavy, methodical: Thump. Thump.*)

MME. MANDAYA: UUUNNNNGGGG. TCH TCH TCH UNNNNGGGG.

(Caitlin's head briefly dips under the table, and when she sits up again, she is holding the REM-POD in her hands. She switches it on and places it in the center of the table.)

CHARLES: Oh god.

ALAN: Caitlin, I wish you hadn't—

RYAN: What the hell is that?

(Lights flash on the top of the REM-POD, red and green and yellow and blue. It screeches in the dying-battery wail of an old musical toy.)

REM-POD: *BEEEEEEEP.*

CAITLIN: Spirits, move toward the blinking lights. If you are here, move toward the lights.

REM-POD: *BEEP. Beepbeepbeepbeep BEEEEEEEP.*

RYAN: Does that thing have a volume button?

CAITLIN: Spirits, thank you for being willing to communicate with us.

ALAN: Caitlin, I really don't—

CAITLIN: What are your names?

REM-POD: *Beepbeepbeep BEEEEEEEEEEEEEEEEP.*

ALAN: Okay, enough.

(He reaches across the table toward the REM-POD.)

CAITLIN: But it'll look good for the show! The other shows use it!

ALAN: We don't make decisions based on what other shows do.

(As Alan's hand touches the REM-POD, it emits a white light, as bright as a star exploding. Everyone shields their eyes, and the cameras dip down to the floor as Karl and Macon look away. The light is intense enough to damage some of the cameras' mechanisms, however, and the remainder of the Night 4 footage is grainy, low-contrast, as if shot in a dim room on old gear. There is a moment of stunned silence.)

CAITLIN: Whoa.

ALAN: I need to talk to you.

CAITLIN: I was just trying to help. They can edit it out. So much has happened this week, and you know it. But they won't use any of it.

ALAN: Everyone, Sandra, I am so sorry.

(Alan stands and gestures for Caitlin to leave the circle. He is holding the REM-POD under one arm.)

ALAN: Mrs. Hawthorne, please don't let this disrupt the work that's already happening. You should continue.

(Alan leaves, followed by Caitlin.)

CHARLES: Regina, are you with us?

(Madame Mandaya remains in her chair, head thrown back, mouth open.)

CHARLES: Let's join hands again. Close your eyes, everybody.

(The thumping upstairs continues; footsteps draw nearer to the top of the stairs.)

CHARLES: Let's guide what presences are here toward the light, all right? Let them go in peace.

EVE: Please, stay. Don't leave me. Please, please stay.

(All the windows in the room rattle in their sills, like the beginning of a hurricane.)

CHARLES: We need to close the portal, right now.

EVE: Sandra, wait.

SANDRA *(off-screen)*: Just pretend we're not here.

EVE: But you were there, just now, in the flash. I saw you. Don't lie to me, Sandra, please, I saw you there.

CHARLES: What is she talking about?

(Macon's camera, which has been focused on Charles, registers a thud. The circle breaks up as Charles and Sandra go to Madame Mandaya, who has fallen to the floor, unconscious. Ryan and Melanie the bartender stand. Eve remains sitting,

hands extended though no one holds them, eyes on Sandra.
The camera swings down onto Sandra, kneeling over Madame
Mandaya's body. Sandra turns her head to the camera.)

SANDRA: Turn that off.

(Tape ends.)

COMING UP:

(Sandra is back in the circle drawn in the dirt and carved with symbols. Instead of candles, a fire burns at the center, contained in a small metal cauldron. The vastness of the space is greater, feels more definitively outside—a light breeze blows the fire, gently ruffles her hair. She is wearing a long green velvet dress, very Ren Faire, unlike her, and her hands are heavy with stone-encrusted rings. The hooded figure that was present last time is gone, but she is not alone—Eve is there, and Caitlin as well. The fire in the center of the circle begins to sputter and pop. Sandra perceives movement, the circle beginning to turn. She thought it was drawn in the dirt but it is actually a wheel. It rotates counterclockwise, then separates itself from the area around it: it is not a wheel, either, but a door, swinging inward, revealing a staircase into the ground. At the bottom of that staircase is a darkness so powerful it eats light. Caitlin descends the staircase without looking at anyone else, moving slowly and steadily. Eve reaches out a hand to Sandra. Though warm, her hand feels insubstantial in the face of what's coming. Eve steps forward, leading Sandra toward the stairs. Sandra opens her mouth to protest, but is pulled into

DAY 5

Transcript: SIW-221a-34/CAMERA A, 12:42:19

INTERVIEW—ALAN

ALAN: It's not uncommon for mediums to become exhausted by such a ritual. Not only is everyone in the circle giving energy, but the medium herself is giving a tremendous amount of energy throughout the evening.

Transcript: SIW-221a-35/CAMERA A, 1:37:21

INTERVIEW—RYAN

RYAN: And then at the end it was like, where the fuck did those birds come from?
Question
RYAN: I know I'm not supposed to curse. I'm genuinely asking.
Question
RYAN: Like a hundred of them, right outside the windows. I thought they were going to bust through the screen. Did Eve mention them?

Transcript: SIW-221a-36/CAMERA A, 02:29:40

INTERVIEW—EVE

EVE: I feel very positive about the ritual. I feel like I can finally share my experiences and have them be seen for what they are. I really want to thank you all for coming out here. It's just been exactly what I hoped it would be.

Question

EVE: No, I couldn't *identify* whatever presences we all felt last night.

Question

EVE: Hey, my word is all you need to wrap this up, right? It's not like you literally capture what's invisible.

Question

EVE: I didn't, no.

Question

EVE: Ryan said that?

Question

EVE: How many?

Transcript: SIW-221a-37/CAMERA A, 03:10:09

INTERVIEW—CHARLES

CHARLES: Sometimes in cases like these, it's enough to just listen, and to let them know we're listening. We leave a door open, a tape recorder running—or, god help us, a REM-POD—and hope for the best.

Question

CHARLES: No, it was completely *abnormal*. Like many of our other devices, the REM-POD is supposed to respond to ambient temperature changes or electromagnetic field fluctuations with lights and that horrible beeping. I never thought it capable of doing . . . whatever it actually did.

Question

CHARLES: I think last night definitely proved *something* is going on in this house. For anything to happen at a séance,

both parties have to want it. The spirits have to want to be
here, because it takes so much effort for them to appear.
And we have to be open to making contact with them,
which for people takes a lot of effort, too. A lot of biases to
overcome.

Question

CHARLES: I can't comment on that. The taxonomy of the spirit
world is fairly difficult to pin down. *(grins)* It would not
be unusual even for those of us in the same room to have
different experiences.

Question

CHARLES: You really don't give up, do you?

Question

CHARLES: "I did not hear any footsteps from upstairs last
night, but with everything else going on, I can't say
with any certainty that that *didn't* happen." Is that
sufficient?

Transcript: SIW-221a-39/CAMERA A, 04:02:38

INTERVIEW—RYAN

RYAN: No, I feel *less* safe than when we started. Did you ever
think about that, about the effect you have, coming into
people's houses and stirring up shit? You probably don't
show that on TV.

Question

RYAN: Sure, this one's on me. It's all on me. I take full
responsibility. Happy now? Where's my wife?

(Ryan stands and removes his microphone.)

———·———

Patrick flipped through Sandra's clipboard, trying to find a question that would compel Ryan to stay and finish the interview. He had only broad notes about the beats each interview should hit, the script outline not having anticipated the events of the night before. And Sandra's notes did not provide any response to Ryan's claim that the show had created more problems than it solved.

But Ryan was gone, out of his chair, his microphone left on the seat. Patrick craned his neck to make eye contact with Karl, or Ted, make it seem like the next step should be a group decision, and not just him fishing for help. But they too had slipped away, as the night weighed heavier and heavier. Or maybe they were never there to begin with. Maybe it had been only Patrick across from the subjects, Patrick solo who set up the camera on the tripod, clinging to some semblance of routine while the house rattled and shook. Melanie had left abruptly after the psychic fainted and surely was under the influence of some sedative now, curled up prettily in her messy bed. Patrick had stayed behind to run interviews, which had taken hours longer than he'd anticipated until, one by one, yawning deeply, the subjects excused themselves to go to bed, leaving Patrick alone. He scrolled through his phone, saw an email he'd missed from yesterday. A producer friend was alerting him to an open position on a new show: a scripted comedy, hardly innovative but with some decent names attached. Did he want in? He wanted in. He could start, he replied, on Monday. With less reluctance than he should have felt, Patrick sent the email into space, then thumbed back to the home screen and called Sandra.

——— · ———

But Sandra was already on the phone with her editors when Patrick called, and bumped him to voice mail. She was sitting in

Patrick's car outside the hospital, where she had taken Madame Mandaya to the ER. When the psychic had come to, she said she was fine, but Sandra wanted to be sure. And, indeed, once in the car Madame Mandaya had admitted to feeling a little stunned by the evening and her role in it.

"I'm not generally a trance medium," she'd said. "I tried, when I was younger. It's not for the weak, believe me. I never thought I could . . ." She shook her head, gazing out the window in silence the rest of the ride and for the several hours they sat in the ER before a doctor could see her. Madame Mandaya sipped water from a paper cup, and Sandra coffee.

At nine, Sandra excused herself from the curtained-off area where Madame Mandaya rested, awaiting a few test results, though the doctor hadn't seemed too concerned, seemed to think she'd be okay to leave in a bit. The call to her editors was mostly a pretext to leave the hospital, breathe some other air, though she had sent footage ahead of her, while they'd been waiting. She sat with her laptop in the car, and was scrolling through what Macon had captured the night before. She felt jittery, her body overcompensating for pulling an all-nighter, and wondered how much nervous energy leaked through the call.

As Caitlin had predicted, they loved the appearance of the REM-POD, its explosion and aftereffects.

"First the windows, then we have this . . . light," Cameron summarized. "And then the psychic faints. Intense stuff, Sandra."

"We have Charles's webcam footage as well. I'll have them send that ASAP."

"Patrick's doing follow-up interviews?"

"Yeah, he's still at the house."

"Where are you?" Vince spat.

"I'm at the hospital. Outside it, waiting for the psychic to be released."

She could picture Cameron gently silencing Vince.

"So where do we take this?" Cameron asked.

Sandra inhaled. She had had the whole night to think about it. She admitted to herself that she hadn't given these families enough credit over the years—they were cannier than she'd realized. They may very well have understood their desires couldn't be tied up so neatly in life, but what a gift to see it that way on-screen. Sandra could give Eve an ending that accounted for a lot, even if it wasn't what she would be hoping for. It didn't explain all the activity, but Sandra didn't think it was wrong, either. She surprised herself with what suddenly seemed plausible. In time, she hoped Eve would forgive her.

"Eve and Ryan married quickly, in the heat of passion, without knowing each other well or thinking it through. Eve gave up the chance to be a successful artist in New York to move to Ninebark. Madame Mandaya thinks her repressed artistic ambitions are generating the activity."

"What about the first night?"

"She wasn't there, so we strike it. The psychic wasn't there, either. Start with the second night, when everyone was in the house."

"That first night was pretty dramatic. If the Hawthornes are upset that we didn't include it, I wouldn't blame them."

"I don't know what you want, Cam. There's no backstory. Whatever's going on, the calls are coming from inside the house."

"And last night, this . . . ritual?"

Sandra considered it, tweaked her own story: "Eve's energy is so strong, it literally knocked out an experienced medium. Everyone left in fear."

There was silence on the other end of the line. Vince spoke first.

"I like it."

"It works," Cameron confirmed. "A kind of dueling medium-ship."

" 'Crystal Ball Cat-fight,' " Vince laughed.

Sandra winced, glancing at the hospital entrance.

"We can cut that together from what we have. That works great, actually. It would be awesome if you could get a couple more lines out of Mrs. Hawthorne, about how she's skeptical of the psychic's abilities. Something we can show at the beginning, to establish that tension."

Sandra confirmed, made some notes, and they ran through final details. The last day was almost always a half day, so they could get on the road and be in the city by dark. Normally Sandra would be running on autopilot by now, but when she thought about leaving she felt a tugging, a reluctance she'd never experienced before: too many loose ends.

"Anything else we should know?" Cameron asked. She hadn't told them about Ronnie. She was vaguely aware of a window of time before you could report an adult missing, knew she would have to make a decision about that pretty soon. In another town, under other circumstances, she might have worried that Ronnie's disappearance had a cause that was rational, a return possible only with the aid of detectives. Out here, though, the explanations seemed to be paranormal, or nothing at all. Something about what he'd said to her about where he'd been— *You've been there . . . You will be*—made her feel, irrationally she knew, that he was safe. After all, she *had* been there, twice now, and lived to tell the tale. Or maybe, this time, she really had lost her mind.

"I think that's everything," she said, a false uptick in her voice.

"Glad to hear it. Then let me just follow up about the net-work. I know this isn't the news anyone was hoping for."

"Oh, I hadn't—" Sandra scrolled back through her email. She'd been so caught up in Eve and Ryan, the feeling of Alan's body against hers, that she had barely glanced at her phone the past couple of days.

"But a six-episode quote-unquote mini-season is not a death sentence," Cameron said, with his usual optimism. "I think it's a great opportunity for us to really dig into those applications and root out the families with the most compelling stories. Focus on what's going to be most impactful."

"Generate buzz," Sandra said, mechanically.

"Buzz, exactly." Cameron sounded relieved. "And for what it's worth, Vince and I both have complete confidence in you—in everyone. We'll give them six tight episodes, wow them with some big stories, and then at midseason they'll re-evaluate and hopefully order more. There's no need for your crew to start handing in their resignations."

"Too late for that," Vince's voice came through the line.

"Just please, Sandra," Cameron's voice was suddenly louder and she could picture him bent over the speakerphone, trying to block Vince's cynicism with his body, "communicate that there's no need to panic. We still have a couple of episodes left in this season, plus six more to go. We can't start hiring everybody over from scratch now. We'll really be fucked."

Sandra said something reassuring, and they signed off. She put her phone on silent mode, staring at the hospital without seeing it, imagining her life on some other show. She thought about a Monday becoming just a Monday again, regret shadowing her, and the rest of her days spent vacillating between the small and self-preserving decisions she had made and the vastness of the ones she hadn't. She wondered what she owed Alan, especially if the show was canceled. While sitting next to the psychic in the hospital, she'd had a realization: Eve wasn't the fuel for the reality TV machine, *Alan* was. He'd brought them together. Sandra could manipulate the story, but Alan was the true producer, whether or not he realized it. She knew if she told Alan about her vision, he would understand. Would anybody else?

At some point she fell asleep and dreamed she was on a date with Alan. They were at a movie theater. The film had started, but there were few in the theater with them, so they spoke quietly, Alan gently kissing the tips of her fingers. On-screen, a boy wore a football jersey, and Alan confessed to Sandra that in high school he'd been a huge Ravens fan. He watched all the games, had a jersey of his own, the whole bit. Sandra giggled. When the movie was over, Alan told her, they'd have to leave through a different door.

"It's a different time," he explained. She couldn't go out the way she went in, he elaborated, and although it made sense, it scared her, and she woke with a start in the driver's seat of Patrick's car, the sun beaming down, six missed calls on her phone, the last from Ronnie.

———•·•———

In Midtown Manhattan, Cameron stared at the ritual footage, watching Madame Mandaya in her trance, before the REM-POD had been brought out. At one point the windows crashed and the participants jumped at the sound, some turning to look, others hunkering in fear. Cameron slowed the video down to just a frame or two per second, then paused it. He and Vince leaned in, peering at the video, Cameron extending one finger toward the screen. Over Ryan's left shoulder, a black shape against the window, silhouette of wings blocking the light from outside, there and then gone.

"Do you see that? What was it?"

———————

While Charles put the last of their stuff in the van, Caitlin strolled through the Hawthornes' house one more time, sad as always to leave, to see the TV crew pack up, to return to her bedroom and wait for a sign of what to do next. Her life between cases was colorless, but there were many cases, far weirder, still to come. Thanks to the show, Alan gets a call from a pub several counties away where they spend the night listening to bottles clink on their shelves, actually see—and photograph—a ghostly figure in the mirror behind the bar. Then there is the apartment of a single woman tormented by the sound of toddler feet running back and forth across her ceiling all night; she lives on the top floor. One of the last cases for PIP as Caitlin knows it is unexceptional, except that the night after their investigation she is woken up in her bed by invisible hands grasping her ankles, yanking her under her sheets. She goes to college not with Charles, but Charles knows her schedule and invites her to visit him during her spring break. He takes her on a drive to the woods about an hour from campus and tells her his new theories re outdoor hauntings, and why they don't get the same attention as ones that take place indoors. He talks rapidly the entire drive. He assures her he hasn't become one of those Sasquatch hunters, but he looks unwell, too skinny, with dark circles under his eyes, and at night she says, *The hell with it* and crawls into his sleeping bag and holds him, his face against her collarbone, his teeth chattering, her savage heart beating away. She loses some of her ardor for the paranormal after that, and the rest of her college career is more or less like anyone else's, except for Charles showing up on campus at least once a month, or calling her to talk late into the night, giving everyone the impression that he's her boyfriend. Caitlin says nothing to convince her friends otherwise. Besides, maybe he is.

It was early for them to wrap on the case, and there was still evidence to review, but neither particularly wanted, upon driving away from the Hawthornes', to rush back to the office. With the afternoon ahead of them, Charles turned to Caitlin in the passenger seat.

"You okay?" he asked. He did not have to elaborate.

"Yeah," Caitlin said, and she meant it. She didn't tell Charles about the encounter she'd had. That after the REM-POD flashed, for a few seconds she was plunged into darkness—what she'd thought was her eyes needing to readjust. They were all in the circle around the table, but after a second Caitlin realized that some of them weren't there, and the table wasn't there, either. It was just her, Eve, and Sandra, and they were someplace else, a place that felt like outside, a place with a weird vibe—the habitat of some creature who wanted to be alone forever. Before she had time to think about anything else, a disembodied hand grabbed her out of the darkness and plunged her back into the Hawthornes' living room. It was Alan, telling her she needed to step away, the REM-POD under his arm. Caitlin had looked to Eve, then Sandra, but neither was looking at her. She'd let Alan lead her out of the room, sat quietly while he told her why what she'd done was wrong. She didn't protest. Didn't tell him, either, what she'd seen in the flash, and that not telling made her sadder than anything else. He wasn't there with her, and, cognizant of it or not, Sandra and Eve, two people she barely knew, were.

She wondered if the secret interview she'd conducted with Eve had made the moment possible. But then why would Sandra be there and not Charles?

But Charles hadn't been there, so she didn't tell him about it. They'd have plenty of shared encounters in the future, ones that would be easier to describe. The REM-POD was in her backpack, wrapped safely in a towel. Alan had said he would reimburse her for it, but Caitlin still had both the receipt and the desire to take it to her favorite cemetery, alone, the night of the next full moon. Well—she met Charles's gaze—maybe not totally alone.

"Are you hungry?" Charles asked.

"I could go for a bite," Caitlin said, and turned the radio up.

——— · ———

"Where are we going, the diner?"

"I can't go to that diner anymore. My arteries are organizing a coup."

The last afternoon was the same as the first morning, but in reverse: cords were untaped from the floor, wound around arms into coils. The big blackout curtain came down, flooding the dining room with afternoon light, revealing the damage done by all the rearranging of furniture, weird stains on the walls and the floors that they hadn't noticed on Monday. Though maybe the damage had always been there, the show's displacement had only revealed it.

"You don't have to order mozzarella sticks every time we sit down, you know."

"I beg to differ."

Van doors opened, shut, opened again as phone chargers were remembered, last bathroom visits required.

"Let's just drive for a little while. We'll find something on the road."

"That okay with everybody?" Ronnie, driving one van, looked into the rearview mirror at the rest of the crew.

There was no answer among the crew, and the silence stood in for assent. The thought of leaving Ninebark as quickly as possible was appealing, though none wanted to express that and risk having to say why.

It was a small town, and soon enough it was behind them. On the highway, the return to civilization was signaled by familiar signs: red and white for fast food, gleaming silver car dealerships. As they drove, a sort of light amnesia slipped over the group, and whether willed or the result of a glamour, it hit them all the same, so that within an hour the pungent oddity of the episode was as concretely behind them as the town itself. A few looked askance at Ronnie with that tip-of-the-tongue feeling, sure there was something they were going to tell him, or ask him, maybe, but none could remember what. Ronnie, for his part, may have been a bit quieter than usual, but then he was usually pretty quiet. He may have just been tired of telling the same stories over and over again, and, when pressed, would state he didn't have any new ones.

On the turnpike, signs indicated restaurants at every exit, but no one wanted to stop. They preferred to stick to the road, a wide-open stretch of nothing as blank as the arrow overlaying it on the GPS, which kept moving them forward, urging them home.

NIGHT 5

CHARLES: Ready?

Regina arrived at the Hawthornes' shortly before sundown. Alan was already at the house and had helped Eve and Ryan clean after the crew departed. In the kitchen, the dishwasher made a rhythmic, lulling noise, the churning water a perfect synchrony of nature and mechanics. The dining room table had been restored to its proper place, and on it Regina set her incense, some salt, a bowl for water, and three candles from her store: a black one, to hold the negative energy Eve would release; a blue one, to heal and protect; and the one Eve had chosen that afternoon, vermillion, to represent herself.

"Do you want to leave for a bit?" Eve asked Ryan, and in response he reached for her arm and squeezed it.

———·—·———

Upstairs, Caitlin and Charles sat in the guest room, as they had the first night, with a tape recorder and a flashlight on the floor. Caitlin had been banished from taking part in the cleansing ritual. Even hot tears, fruitlessly fought back, couldn't change Alan's mind. He wasn't mean about it, but he was firm. Charles had volunteered to do a Q and A with her, a follow-up to the first night that they'd never had a chance to do.

"Before we get started," Charles said, fiddling with a pen cap, "I need to tell you something."

———·—·———

Alan dimmed the lights, and Regina called them to the table.

"We're not here to confront any forces this evening," she said, before they sat down. "My purpose is never to stir up what lies still. Quite the opposite. Let's approach tonight with the intention to still what's been stirred, on both sides of the veil."

Eve stayed focused on the ritual the best she could; she tried to summon gratitude for Alan and Regina coming back to work with her after a considerable amount of brattiness on her part. Eve tried to dislodge from her brain the connotations she had around the word "cleanse": the charcoal smoothies and cayenne-pepper-and-lemon-juice diet her old roommate in New York had tried. She imagined instead her entire inside a pale and glowing pink, crystalline like the salt sauna she'd visited with that same roommate, lying on a bamboo mat feeling sweat trickle out of her body and away. But she couldn't help but see their dining room through the lens of the show. It was the room in their house where it had started, a room one camera had never left, even if it had always pointed at the wrong things. Eve imagined the way she would have been framed: holding hands with her husband and Alan while Regina, across the table, bathed the candles in salt water before lighting them.

Regina occasionally had to tap the incense burner back into place as it floated up and wobbled a few millimeters above the table, though no one but her seemed to notice.

———·———

"Is he here now?" Caitlin asked, equally thrilled by the story of Charles's contact and miffed she hadn't sensed it herself.

"I don't know," Charles replied, his voice and face near tears. "I don't know if he was ever here."

Caitlin shrugged that off. "Maybe he was and maybe he

wasn't. As in, maybe we'd get some evidence that matched your perception, and maybe we wouldn't. What difference does that make for you?"

"*All* the difference," he said, calmer now, but a bit baffled. He thought of the ghost Caitlin on the tape, another thing he hadn't told her about.

Caitlin leaned in: "Did it feel real while you were experiencing it?"

"Well, yeah." Charles sniffed. "I wouldn't have told you about it if it didn't."

"And did it feel good?"

He considered this. "It felt like something I wanted so badly to happen that I made it happen."

She nodded at this. "Maybe it was," Caitlin said, suddenly equanimous. "That doesn't mean they all have been. You're not the only one freaked out here, Charles, or freaked out at any of our other cases. I think you forget that sometimes, when you're sneaking off to make EVPs by yourself. Instead of trying to prove everything on your own, give the rest of us a little credit for our work. Our intuitions."

Charles snorted, looked at Caitlin, shook his head. He smiled a bit.

"You know?"

——— · · ———

The show was gone, and Ryan wasn't entirely sure why these people weren't as well. He hadn't, of course, said this to Eve, had assumed that her emotions had been running as high as they were all week because of the cameras. Once the pressure of performing had passed, he'd expected the two of them to laugh it off. But Eve hadn't laughed, and now the psychic was back, and the kids were upstairs making tapes, and Ryan was, for the third night in a row, sitting at his dining room table, which had been accumulating polka-dots of dripped wax over the course of the week, little coins he dug at with a fingernail while waiting to be asked to do things.

He listened now to Madame Mandaya, trying to hear in what she said some difference from the past couple of nights, trying, as Eve had begged him to, to "give it a chance." But it all sounded the same to him, sounded like horoscopes—vague statements that could mean anything, depending on how you looked at them.

Then something shifted. Ryan couldn't have pinpointed what, or when, the tone of Madame Mandaya's voice changed, but suddenly she wasn't speaking to all of them anymore. She was speaking only to Eve, and Eve was speaking back. Ryan opened an eye to see that Eve and Madame Mandaya had their eyes open and were looking right at each other. The dining room had dimmed around them. And then Ryan realized it wasn't the dining room anymore—they were in some other space, enormous and black. The candles on the table sputtered, and Ryan worried they would be extinguished by the gentlest of winds, leaving them all in a darkness unlike any he'd known.

Madame Mandaya continued to ask questions, and Eve responded.

"Are you there now?"

"I'm there."

"What does it look like?"

"It's dark."

"Can you see?"

"Yes, I can see."

"What do you see?"

"Figures."

"Are the figures human?"

"Yes."

And then Madame Mandaya's voice shifted, became more firm. "You brought us here."

"No."

"Release us, Eve."

"It's not my fault. I didn't do it on purpose."

"You can return to this place anytime. You created it. It waits for you. But you can't live here."

"I can't live there."

"Return, Eve. Bring it with you. Find wholeness."

"I don't know how."

"You will. One day, you will."

Tears emerged from between Eve's closed lids. "I don't want to be alone." In his fear Ryan squeezed his wife's hand, but hers was limp, unresponsive.

"You are far from alone. You are surrounded by a circle of love and light. We see you. I see you, Eve."

Ryan saw then in Eve's face a slackening, a gratefulness, as if she were finally, after years abroad, speaking her native tongue. It flooded her body with color, despite the smallness of her voice, which sounded like it came to them from the other side of this dark expanse. As the psychic continued to talk to his wife, coaching her, the space around them began to dissolve, melting away to reveal the usual walls with art prints Eve had selected, the dining room window framing a darkness that was soft, laughable in comparison to the darkness they had just been in. It was then that Ryan noticed they were all—the psychic, his wife, himself and Alan, the dining room table and dining room chairs—levitating, an inch or two above the ground, not quite enough for their feet, otherwise flat on the floor, to fully dangle. It lasted just a moment, and a half second after the room had fully returned they dropped, no more than the involuntary jerk of muscle spasms that sometimes hiccup the sleep. The candles didn't fall over and the salt water only splashed a little out of its bowl, its stain a small trace on the tabletop that would last long after everyone had finally left for good.

———— · ————

Caitlin opened the front door as quietly as possible. Eve, Ryan, Alan, and Regina were still in the circle, and didn't seem to notice, though Caitlin looked back and saw Alan's eye open in her direction, saw him wink as she eased the door shut behind herself and Charles.

"Thanks," she said to Charles once they were outside. "It was getting stuffy in there."

They didn't have anywhere to go, so they headed down the empty road, figuring they'd walk a few minutes, clear their heads, and come back. It was quiet, and although most houses in the area were dark, across a field they could see the orange glow of windows in one home whose occupants were still awake. They were out of sight of the Hawthornes' house when they were stopped in their path by a deer, one so majestic that the word "deer" seemed unworthy: a tall buck, great candelabra of antlers atop his head, came out of the empty field across the street and stopped in front of them not ten feet away. Caitlin sucked in her breath, daring to look at Charles. He was staring at it. The three of them stood a moment, watching one another, and then the deer resumed its journey, cantering up a driveway, slipping into the backyard of a house whose unwitting owners slept within.

All the things that could have been said didn't need to be: that had they left the Hawthornes' a minute earlier, or a minute later, they would have missed it. Too, that Pennsylvania had many deer, a busy hunting season. They were everywhere if you knew where to look. But Caitlin and Charles felt special in their encounter, and, without having to say anything, went back to the Hawthornes', crept up the stairs while the ritual was winding down, and sprawled out in the guest room side by side, falling into a sleep of remarkable depth and warmth.

"Everyone came in here wanting to tell the story their way. Nobody ever asked us how we wanted to tell it." Eve leaned across the couch toward Alan, stretching one arm along the back. She didn't mean we, though. She meant herself. "It's our life."

Ryan sat beside his wife, a hand on her knee. Alan thought that in five days Ryan looked five years older. Maybe it was lack of sleep. Or maybe not. Alan thought the man had, in some ways more than Eve, a difficult road ahead of him, the need to accept a reality he didn't have words for.

"What about tonight—do you feel like we saw things your way?"

Eve looked at him with a knowingness, almost smug. She could see, around them, the space she had created, the dark sanctuary for her most private self. She could deliver anyone to it—or drape it over the known world—anytime she wished. If she was brave enough to believe she could, or angry enough to believe others deserved it. The last time Alan had had such significant contact it had been a vision he'd never care to see again, the image of an afterlife he was terrified to meet. But this evening the encounter was different, not so much evil as plaintive, imploring—a darkness everyone present in was asked to find the dimensions of. Eve had a power, and he didn't blame her for being cautious around it. The world as it stood wouldn't give her much space to use it, at least not wisely. He sensed a similar power in Caitlin, but she had, he felt, better coping mechanisms. The urban legends she was drawn to, the stories her parents silenced at the dinner table, midtelling . . . while Eve dipped a toe into the abyss, Caitlin had been staring at it directly for as long as Alan had known her.

Alan tried a different approach. "When the ritual ended, you were crying. Do you mind if I ask why?"

Eve shook her head. She looked out the window behind them. Her eyes watered a bit.

"Could it be both?" she asked, turning back to Alan, blinking a few times.

"Both what?"

"Something . . . *of* me, and something else here *for* me? That's possible, right?"

Alan nodded. "I don't see why not."

"Because I'm not . . . if I am, this is not all I am."

"No one said that." But she and Alan both knew that was, in one sense, the easiest explanation: Eve as the source of the disturbances, the key to resolving them. Eve had wanted the show to confirm for her the multitudes she contained, and she—perhaps willingly—forgot the way reality shows reduced everyone to two dimensions, lacquered and thin. Sandra, given total freedom, might have told it differently, let Eve's story unfold over weeks, diving deep into her art and childhood and all of it, leaving viewers unsettled, unsure. But that decision was certainly beyond Sandra's control, beyond the control of those above her, and the ones above them, a ladder of responsibility climbing all the way up to some mysterious force, indiscernible, but nevertheless calling the shots.

"How does the house feel to you both now? That's usually the best indicator that we've identified the source of the activity, and perhaps cleansed it. You know your house the best. Does the energy feel different?"

"It feels lighter," Eve said. Ryan nodded.

"And that may be all you need. The belief that the manifestation is gone may be enough."

"A placebo."

"Not exactly. Listen, Mrs. Hawthorne, I'm not a therapist. But some of these issues may not be strictly paranormal. Though they may very well be intertwined." Eve looked unsurprised by his assessment, looked like she'd been hearing this line all week. "That being said, if you continue to experience anything unusual"—he reached into his pocket—"here's my card." He left it on the coffee table.

Eve thanked him; Alan roused his team and left a few minutes later. He didn't think he would hear from Eve again. Going forward, she and Ryan would speak honestly with each other about their fears and frustrations, their hopes and desires, and go to bed at night secure that their marriage was stronger than it had ever been. The house would settle around them, typical house noises, exacerbated at times by repair work Ryan would do without having to be reminded, aided by Eve in old jeans and a freshly paint-spattered shirt. (In Eve's studio, a portrait was taking shape, layer by layer: Madame Mandaya, her face soft, lit by candles, the darkness around her all-engulfing.) And they'd joke, and in the basement getting his toolbox Ryan would bang on the pipes or knock on the walls to scare her and walk up the steps with a devilish look in his eye, and Eve would mock scowl at him, though on the inside, she'd be genuinely annoyed, feeling as if he was picking at a wound that was still raw. But overall, they would be content. Then someday she'd get home from work and the sconce that Ryan had hung in the hallway would be shattered on the floor. Some night Ryan would go out drinking with his buddies and get too wasted to drive home, at which point he'd crash on someone's couch, and Eve, alone in the house, would tiptoe around, following the noises and squeaks, poking her head into the attic, looking for mice or raccoons, finding none. There might be brief flashes of something in the corner of her eye, too quick and shapeless to describe, shadows dissolving as soon as she turned her head. The cup might wobble in its bathroom holder under the mirror, the cabinet doors in the kitchen might rattle a bit when all the windows were closed. She might lie awake at night for hours after Ryan dropped off, resenting his steady breathing while she listened to creaks and groans, acorns hitting the roof of the house—though that wasn't an oak tree above them, was it? One night, desperate for sleep, she'd decide to change locations, because the bed had become a source of angst. She'd traipse down to the living room, which, after all that had happened, was now where the dining room used to be. She'd stretch out on the sofa with a blanket and her pillow as the sky lightened behind her and stare at the picture frames, willing them to move, to lift off their hooks and fly above her, hovering for a moment, then crashing down.

SIX MONTHS LATER

Alan pulls into a parking spot in front of the old mental hospital. He turns the car off, but he doesn't open the door. The stone building spreads its enormous wings on either side, looming and crumbly. The sun has not yet fully set and scattered clouds are gray on top, orange and pink on the bottom. It couldn't be a more perfect evening if it had been ordered up.

"Is this weird for you?" he asks.

"Of course it's weird for me," Sandra replies.

Alan squeezes her knee. "You didn't have to come. It being Halloween and all, the place is going to be a circus. I don't even really expect to get anything tonight. I'm just doing it because it's good promotion."

Sandra puts her hand on top of Alan's, still on her knee, laces her fingers between his. They lean toward each other and kiss.

"Shall we?" Alan asks.

"Just need one more thing." Sandra reaches behind the passenger seat to a plastic bag she's snuck into Alan's car. She tears it open, removing a PIP sweatshirt. She pulls it on over her head.

"Where'd you get that?" He's beaming.

"I found it in a box in your office. I hope it's okay."

"It's more than okay. I love it."

They step out of the car. Sandra's traveling light—a voice recorder, flashlight, water bottle. Alan's got a bit more gear on him—electromagnetic field detectors and cameras in hard cases—though Sandra knows he's mainly brought this stuff in for the show. At the thought of said show she is suddenly very, very nervous. She counts the number of cars in the parking lot, tries to gauge who might already be here. There's no telltale van, but maybe the crew of *Historic and Haunted* doesn't arrive in vans.

No, wait, there it is, lumbering over the speed bumps into the parking lot. Sandra doesn't have to be a psychic to know the nature of the conversation happening inside, to picture the motley bunch the van will disgorge. She follows Alan up the steps, into the lobby of the hospital building.

A producer is already inside, in pencil skirt, chunky heels the concrete floor will make her regret an hour in. She's got forms for them to sign—a waiver the hospital's foundation requires, a waiver for the show. Sandra signs them without reading them. She gives the producer a curt smile, hoping not to be recognized. She's safe. The woman is bustling about, meeting her crew at the door, coordinating via walkie-talkie with another producer already upstairs with another crew. The team on the first floor is easily twice the size of the *Searching for . . .* crew; Sandra can't imagine how many more people are upstairs. But as Alan said, it's Halloween, so maybe they went a little overboard. Plus, *Historic and Haunted* is in its fifth season. *Searching for . . .* fizzled after two and a half.

Sandra received a middling severance package from Roving Eye; combined with her savings it's enough for her to explore for a bit before looking for a new job. She misses television less than she expected, though she knows at some point she'll need a real salary again and isn't sure what else she'd be good at. She occasionally gets texts from Patrick, questions about how to do things he should have known how to do all along. She sometimes pretends, because he's on a scripted show, that she has no idea what he's talking about. Other than that, she doesn't really hear from anyone, and she's relieved, side-eyeing *Historic*'s crew, that she doesn't know any of them.

The last people through the door are Caitlin and Charles, arguing in their usual way, with no heat behind it, no real irritation. They both give Alan big hugs, then look at Sandra cautiously. She's the beloved uncle's new girlfriend they aren't sure about. She isn't offended, accepts Charles's high five.

The mental hospital squats four floors above them. Beyond the first floor there's no electricity. The rooms are small, the windows painted shut. In its 150-plus years in operation it served thousands of patients, each in their own kind of pain. Previous investigators have reported so much activity in so many different rooms that Alan has a map, with little red stars penned all over its wings. He's going over the map with the producer, and she's relaying it all to her colleague upstairs, letting them know the path Alan's team plans to take through the building. Sandra becomes nervous again, in a new way. She's been on a few investigations with Alan, but small ones, houses. What activity there was, while exciting, was limited to one or two events per evening. Despite what he said in the car, Sandra knows Alan is anticipating a lot of activity tonight. He told her they can stay together the entire time. Caitlin and Charles like to go off on their own, run their own sessions, but he won't leave her side. Nor will, she suspects, the cameras, and she doesn't know how she feels about that aspect of the evening—her television debut. But Alan has assured her that despite their constant presence, she'll soon be immersed in the history of this building and her interactions with its residents. At some point she won't be aware of the cameras anymore.

Caitlin is eating a bag of M&M's, tipping five or six into her hand then slamming them into her mouth all at once. She sees Sandra looking, proffers the bag. Sandra holds her hand out for the candy. She, too, tosses them all in her mouth at once, then catches Alan looking at her, smiling, and she laughs, covering her mouth with her hand.

"It's going to be so dark up there," Caitlin says, excited. "Are you ready?"

"Ready," Sandra says, and follows her team up the stairs.

ACKNOWLEDGMENTS

This is my first book, and from conception to publication, fourteen years have passed. Thus, I have a lot of people to thank.

To begin at the beginning: Thank you, Mullica Hill Friends School. Thank you, Friends Select. Thank you, thank you, thank you, Sarah Lawrence. Thank you, Brooklyn College, particularly Meera Nair and Ernesto Mestre, for running novel workshops with so much care, attentiveness, and generosity.

Thank you to Aimee Ashcraft, my incredible agent (and sometimes therapist), who never wavered in her belief in my weird little book. Thank you to Ellie Pritchett, who even after I thought the book was done-done had the wisdom to see it could be better. Thank you to Maddie Partner, for the perfect visual representation of PA-Turnpike-as-gateway-to-another-dimension. Thank you to Thomas Mar Wee for excellent notes, and the entire team at Vintage Books, my dream publisher.

I did a lot of research for the book, but the most impactful was experiential. Thank you to Dan Sturges, who gave a lecture at the Merchant's House Museum in 2014 that shaped my thinking around Alan's philosophy of ghost hunting. Thank you to Kathy Kelly of Paranormal Books and Oddities of Asbury Park, New Jersey. I acquired a lot of my research books from the bookshop and attended a powerful séance there in 2015. The bookstore/museum is worth a trip, as is a ghost tour at the Trans-Allegheny Lunatic Asylum in Weston, West Virginia. Thank you to the entire hardworking staff of the asylum for hosting overnight explorations, and especially to our guide Ryan for stories, advice, use of his spirit box and dowsing rods, and deep knowledge. I gained a lot of ideas from these experiences; any errors, embellishments, and/or creative liberties in the book are entirely my own.

Thank you to Guy Maddin for "The Forbidden Room," and for sharing at a Q and A that "séance" also means "film screening." Thank you to Mast Brothers for your Almond Butter Chocolate, numerous bars of which were consumed during the revision process. Thank you to Jothan Cashero for always being down to do something spooky.

Thank you, Brian Hall and all novel workshop participants in the Summer 2018 Colgate Writers Conference: Jennifer Savran Kelly, Scott Ondercin, Martha Rand, and Fred Schneider.

Huge thank-yous to my generous early readers Colin Asher, Ivy Blackman, Becky Fine-Firesheets, Matt Matros, Gene Slepov, Maria Slusarev, and Dave Wingrave. Thank you to Craig Shilowich, who read multiple drafts and told me when it was ready to be sent out (even though I then revised it again). Thank you to David Wiggin, who has been reading my work for twenty years, and in that time has pulled exactly zero punches. Same thanks to Alex Templeton (though thank you for softening the blows).

Thank you, Brian Morton, for truly being a model writing instructor; for getting me into my first NYC apartment; for lunches in Bronxville; for a conversation about fiction writing (and now teaching) that has unfolded over the past twenty years.

Thank you to my family: Helen, Andy, Chris, Kate, Emily, Ian, for endless support. Thank you to my dog Karly, with whom I brainstormed the book on long walks around Brooklyn, listening to paranormal podcasts.

And finally, thank you to Kole. When I started this book in 2009, I could not have imagined I would actually finish it in western Pennsylvania. I wouldn't have moved for anyone but you, and I don't think I could have finished it this way without your support, your partnership, your unconditional love. Not to mention your willingness to take me on a ghost hunt in an old mental hospital in West Virginia in the middle of the night. Thank you for all the life-changing trips so far, and all the ones still to come.